REVENGE AT CHARLOTTE LAKE

By D.L. Reavis

ii

Chapter One

---•●•---

Ethan sat silently in the overgrowth next to the broken concrete sidewalk. He knew his enemy and knew him well. As a trained special force operative, he studied his targets. Now it was a waiting game. Just before two in the morning a car pulled into the drive, its lights illuminating the unkempt lawn. As the car door opened the dome light revealed his target. His adrenaline raced.

As the target walked by his position, the stench of alcohol made Ethan's nose twitch. He silently stood moving in behind the unsuspected target. Unexpectedly the target stopped to relieve himself in the bushes and at that instant, Ethan relieved him of committing any future crimes. Fishing through the now deceased criminal's pockets he found the house keys. Dragging the heavy body up the broken wooden steps caused Ethan to question his plan.

Shining his flashlight around the room, Ethan could see the inside mirrored the deteriorated exterior. The aged velvet wallpaper was peeling off the walls and the dusty antique furniture told the story of neglect. Walking down the hallway he found a filthy bathroom. He gagged. *How can anyone live in this environment?* Shining the light in the bedroom, as expected, he found an unmade bed and clothes littered the floor. He had seen enough, it was time to get out of there.

Making his way back through the living room, he froze. It was one of those moments where you see it but can't believe it. A number of pictures sat on the mantel, but the one of his wife was what stopped him in his tracks. It was the picture he had taken of Kendra on their honeymoon in Hawaii. He felt a chill of anxiety as he looked down the row of pictures. It helped Ethan feel justified in his actions to know that no more trophies would be added to this criminal's mantel. He grabbed the picture of his wife and locked the door behind him. Walking away from the house he had mixed feelings as he had done often overseas during the war. It was never easy to dispatch the enemy. It was so permanent.

In the predawn hours Ethan navigated the moving van thorough the empty streets of suburban New York City. He needed a place to rest and hide out for the day. He rented a room at a small run-down hotel. The room, while clean, had the distinctive odor of deterioration. Plopping on the bed he soon drifted off to sleep.

The noise outside the door woke Ethan long before his alarm. The sound of domestic squabble was always difficult to take. He got up and took a shower before going over his plan. As the sun started to set, he slipped a backpack over his shoulder and started the long walk to his next target.

Darkness hid his presence as he surveyed the front porch through his night vision goggles. The man sitting in the chair was not his target. Repositioning for a better angle his NVG focused in on the occupant. *What's he doing here?* Looking up the street Ethan identified the congressman's car. *Where's his henchman?* The glow of a cigarette answered Ethan's question as he found the man leaned up against a tree. Moving away from the target, Ethan crossed the street undetected and quietly made his way up to the far side of the porch. Out of sight, he could hear the rhythmic clicking of the rocking chair competing with the small pebbles under its rocker.

A car pulling up in front of the house caused Ethan to move a little deeper into the shadows. The driver got out of the car, and Ethan was able to identify him as his target. Through his NVG, Ethan could see the henchman moving closer to the porch. In his right hand, close to his side, he was carrying a handgun with a silencer attached. *Is this a hit job?* Ethan couldn't believe what he was seeing. He tapped the button turning on the integrated video recorder. *This is not going to go well.*

Ethan's target was halfway up the porch steps when he noticed he had company. "What are you doing here?

"You know why I'm here. Did you get them?"

"Maybe. We'll discuss them, when I see the money."

"Don't get smart. Where are they?"

"Relax. They're here in my pack. All seven of them."

"The deal was for eight. Where's the other one?"

"How would I know? I just do what I'm told. There were only seven. The cops must have taken it. Where's my money?"

The congressmen stood and walked to the steps and motioned for his henchman. "Jeff handles my financial dealing. He'll discuss your pay." With that the congressman walked down the steps and headed for his car.

It did not appear as if the target had even seen the henchman or the gun as the muffled flash did its job. Ethan's target dropped to the ground, and the henchman picked up the backpack and walked to the car.

Ethan hit the stop button on the camera and moved away from the scene. All the way back to the hotel, he tried to process what he had heard. He would have to review the tape for some sort of clue.

The morning news channels carried the homicide. Someone had made the connection that the victims of these back-to-back homicides were from the famous trial that had ended in their exoneration.

Ethan groaned. This only makes the third leg of the mission all the harder. He would have to go to plan B and take his third target out in public. An operation he hated to do. He hastily loaded his equipment into the back of the moving truck and drove to the designated location. There he waited. He knew it was only time before his final target lost his nerve and came running to the protection of the other gang members.

Three hours for some may be an eternity, but for Ethan, he had waited longer for the enemy. It gave him time to process his thoughts as he peered out through the slit in the side of the truck. Many patrons had come and gone from the rundown bar, but no target. He knew his next step all depended on timing and he had a tendency to let his mind drift only to snap it back to the here and now. *Stay focused.*

Ethan maintained his vigilance as dusk turned into darkness. Once he could no longer identify the individuals he donned his night vision goggles. He had used these many times in the war and found it eerie to see the enemy when they had no way of seeing you. His patience paid off when two cars pulled into the parking lot. He was certain the white Pontiac would be carrying his target. He quickly switched to his sniper rifle and turned on the night vision scope. Having already calculated the distance and with a no wind condition felt confident in his chances.

Four men got out of the first car and looked around. Once they seemed satisfied, they motioned to the Pontiac. *Great, he has a whole posse riding with him. This is going to get interesting. It's time to execute.*

As the target stepped out of the car and started standing up, Ethan confirmed identification and gently squeezed the trigger. The silencer muffled the sound as the target disappeared below the car. Ethan quickly refocused on the right rear tire of the first car, which he deflated with a three-inch projectile. Within seconds of taking the first shot, the enemy had been taken down and both vehicles disabled. Knowing full well the impact of his first shot, Ethan quickly moved through the hatch into the driver's seat and pulled into the flowing traffic.

Chapter Two

A handful of stoplights later, Ethan took the on-ramp for the one-hundred-and-fifty-mile drive to Albany. His original plans were to leave out of Penn Station, but the thought of spending another fifteen hours in the city didn't settle with his anxiety. It would only be a matter of time before he became the primary suspect, and he didn't want to be anywhere near the scene of the crimes.

It was two-thirty in the morning when he slowly drove down Summit Street. Just two blocks from the Albany train station he found the address. As expected, there were no vehicles in the driveway, and the house was dark. The realtor's sign in the yard declared it was priced for a quick sale. He had done his homework and knew the foreclosure would be vacant for a long time. Carefully he backed into the driveway and turned off the key. Sliding open the hatch between the cab and cargo area he suddenly was overcome with exhaustion.

It was after noon before the sound of a garbage truck

broke Ethan's sleep. He slid out of his sleeping bag and rolled it up. His stomach growled reminding him that he had not eaten for over twenty-four hours. Sliding back the hatch he peered out through the windshield surveying the surrounding area. Other than a trash truck, nothing else was moving. He decided it was time to head over to the café.

The streets were quiet, but toys scattered in the yard told Ethan that it would be different once school let out. He glanced at his watch and made a mental note to be back in the truck before that happened. Two short blocks later, he crossed East Street and walked into the old converted firehouse. The garage doors were up, and the late spring breeze was pleasant. Choosing a small table off to the side, gave him a view of the exit and somewhat isolated him from nosy diners.

The grilled chicken Panini took care of the growling. Not in a hurry, he scanned the news looking for any sign that he was a wanted man. So far, only the general information was being broadcast. "Investigation underway" was all the news blogs displayed. His email box was begging for his attention, and he wondered why he didn't just delete it like he had his voicemail.

Back in the truck, he changed into his old military uniform. He knew most people, including law enforcement, respected the active military and would leave him alone. With his weapons safely secured in his duffel bag, he finished packing his backpack. Fortunately, he didn't have to take either through metal detectors. Precisely at six p.m. he locked the moving truck and walked the two blocks to the train station. It wasn't as quiet as earlier. Children were playing on the sidewalks, and the sound of lawnmowers could be heard scattered throughout the neighborhood.

Walking past the cafe it was obvious that a lot of folks patronized this place in the evening. The tables were filled, and several patrons sat at the bar. It reminded Ethan of the dates he and Kendra used to enjoy. How he missed her. He walked into a half-filled train station and found a place along the wall to wait. Checking the status of the Lake Shore Limited, he looked at his watch. *Only fifteen minutes.*

The sun was slipping below the trees as the train left the station. Two minutes later they crossed a trestle bridge over the Hudson River and slowly started picking up speed. Settled comfortably in the sleeper car, Ethan dimmed the lights and pulled back the shade just enough to give him a view of the outside world. Streetlights, house lights, barnyard lights, and the car lights at the road crossings all mesmerized him to sleep.

A knock on the door brought Ethan's dinner. Rubbing the sleep from his eyes he thanked the kind, elderly gentleman. It was obvious the porter enjoyed his occupation. The aroma of the grilled chicken drifted out from under the silver food cloche. All of a sudden Ethan was hungry. He thanked the porter and took the lid off his dinner revealing not only the chicken but steamed vegetables and a baked potato. It had been a long day, and a healthy meal would be a step in bringing his life back into focus.

After dinner, Ethan left his room and went downstairs for a shower. Returning, he was surprised to see the porter had prepared his bed. Crawling into bed he instantly fell asleep. It was a fitful sleep. Between the nightmares of the last few days and visions of his wife and daughters telling him, "Everything is going to be okay." The sway of the train was like rocking in a cradle, while the periodical stops along the way interrupted his sleep.

Morning brought with it the cornfields of Indiana and the occasional spotting of a horse and buggy as the Amish were busily going about their day. While Ethan enjoyed breakfast, he turned on his phone to catch up on the news. He knew this was dangerous. If they were looking for him, only a couple of pings would give away his general location. He was pretty sure it was still early for that to be happening. Even though no one would care about three gang members being terminated, he knew it would not go unnoticed by the Department of Justice.

The headlines were full of information about a world gone seriously crazy. *Where's the sanity?* As he continued to read down through the articles, a blurb on page three caught his eye. *Man wanted for questioning in murder investigation,* stood out in bold. Ethan quickly read down through the two paragraphs. Sure enough, his name was mentioned, and he had not been seen or heard from in three days. *This sure changes the game. It's time to disappear.* For one last time, he checked his email. He ignored the scores of inquiries from associates in New York City, only opening one from an old friend.

Steven had served with Ethan in Afghanistan. The two of them had been through a lot together. Many nights were spent lying silently in hiding just waiting to dispatch the enemy with a single shot. After the service, Steven had insisted Ethan come to the Big Sky Country. "You'll love the wide-open spaces," he had insisted. "Get away from the concrete jungle." That was years before he had met Kendra and had a family. Just the thought of his family caused emotional upheaval. Now here he was, unbeknown to Steven, on his way to meet his old friend. The message was brief, only telling him that he had received a call from the authorities in New York, and they were looking for him. It ended with Steven requesting Ethan call if he needed help. Ethan switched the phone to airline mode and set about devising his next move.

It only took a few minutes to know a change in direction was necessary. He still had to go through Chicago but instead of heading towards Montana, he would go further south. He only had a few minutes to make his next move.

He pulled on a pair of pants and grabbed his phone. Switching it on, he headed towards the front of the train. Once he was in the coach car, he descended the stairs to the luggage racks. Acting as if he was hunting for his luggage, he read the tags until he found one with an Elkhart, Indiana address. Sliding the zipper back on the side pocket he slipped his phone inside. Back upstairs he took an empty seat beside the window and waited. Ten minutes later he watched an elderly couple get off the train with the suitcase in tow. With an uneasy feeling, Ethan slowly got up and made his way back to his room. He may have waited too long.

Twenty minutes later as the train was slowing into South Bend, Ethan's uneasy feeling intensified. He pulled the curtains closed leaving only a small slit to give him an unobstructed view of the northern Indiana city. He was thankful he had made his reservations under an assumed name.

As the bright blue building with its white strip came into view, the first thing he saw was the uniformed police officers on the platform. Sweat beaded on his forehead as he started to panic. *Calm down,* there could be other reasons for their presence. Once the train had come to a stop, he watched as the conductor stepped off the train and spoke to the officers. The conductor nodded and led them back to the train. Now Ethan was in full panic and hurriedly made his way to the shower room. Locking the door, he sat down on the commode and tried to get his breathing under control.

What seemed like an eternity went by before Ethan heard the voices outside the door.

"As I told you, we don't have anyone with that name on board," the conductor was telling the officers. "But if you insist, you can search the rooms."

Ethan held his breath as the officer explained. "We have reasons to believe the suspect may be on this train. If you don't mind, we would like to clear the train before you proceed."

"Well, please hurry. We are on a timeline and would like to get to Chicago on time."

Ethan heard the tapping on doors and apologies being offered as the officers made their way down the train. "It's all over," he thought as he resigned himself to a life behind bars. The quick rap on the door shook him. "Just a minute," he blurted out, "I'm not dressed." His raised eyebrows told that his response even surprised him.

"Hurry up, sir," the officer firmly spoke through the door. "We need to inspect the shower."

Ethan just sat there not moving a muscle. All at once, he heard the officer's radio come to life, "Calling all officers. It appears as if the target is moving south out of Elkhart. Please stand-by for further instructions." Ethan heard the officers quickly thank the conductor and hurry off the train. He laid his head down on the sink and shook. The crisis was over for now but not for long. It wouldn't take them long to find the phone and come back looking for him. He needed to get off this train. Checking the schedule, he found the best place to do that was Chicago. He needed to be ready.

Packing up his bags, Ethan moved out of his room and headed up the train. Three cars later he found what he was looking for. A very tired mother trying to contain three very active children. He sat down across the aisle and looked out the window. It didn't take long before he felt a tap on his arm. Looking down into the wide eyes of a toddler, he smiled.

"Where you going, mister?" the child asked.

"Wherever the train tracks lead," Ethan answered. "Where are you going?"

"We're going to see grandma. She lives a long way away."

The child's mother apologized and asked her son to leave Ethan alone. This was the opening Ethan used to start a conversation with the mother. Before long, he had extracted the needed information. He pulled out his tablet and within a couple of minutes had made his new reservations west. The two-hour layover in Chicago may be a problem, but now he had some help.

Ten minutes from the station as the passengers were starting to restlessly prepare for arrival, Ethan made his move. "I am heading west on the same train," Ethan told the mother. "How about, if you let me help you make the transfer."

The tired mother didn't even hesitate. "I appreciate your willingness to help, but I promised the children we would get something to eat at McDonald's."

"Not a problem, we have time. By the way, my name is Ethan." He was quickly assuming what would be the appearance of the father. Just in time, as the train made its way into the underground structure and clanked to a stop.

"Thank you so much. I'm Krystal. This is Cathryn, Christiana, and your little friend there is Jonah."

They waited until the initial crowd made their way downstairs to the exit and Ethan picked up Krystal's suitcase and followed her out of the train. Tugging at his pant leg was Jonah, the little boy who had initiated their meeting. Ethan was relieved to see the platform was void of law enforcement but did not let his guard down. Arriving at the station they headed for the food court where they found the McDonald's. Ethan led them to a table somewhat hidden, yet where he could observe what was going on in the Mezzanine. Getting the family seated he told Krystal to stay seated, he would get their lunch.

She half smiled as her shoulders sagged. "Thank you so much. You are my new hero." She picked up her diaper bag and pulled out a couple of bills. Ethan ignored her offer and headed for the counter, returning shortly with a handful of happy meals and a sandwich for each of them.

They were halfway through their meal when Ethan noticed six officers walking through the Mezzanine. A couple would not have been a concern, but six could only mean one thing. They were looking for him. He made sure not to make eye contact but to become actively involved in a conversation with his assumed family. Much to Ethan's relief, after looking around, the officers continued on their way.

It was time to make it to their train. Leaving the restaurant, they headed downstairs to the tracks. Ethan knew the children would qualify to pre-board and stopped by the desk, for approval. The smell of burning diesel filled the air as they made their way onto the platform. Ethan tensed as he noticed the undercover police officer coming at them. He was looking way too intensely at them. Ethan reached down and picked up his assumed son just as they passed the officer.

"Excuse me, sir!"

Ethan froze in his step. Slowly turning around, he found the officer staring him down. "Yes."

"Just want to thank you for your service. It must be hard with a family."

Ethan was happy the children's mother was getting on the train and did not hear the comment.

"Yes, sometimes it is hard. We do what we must when called." He turned back around and stepped up onto the train. After getting the family situated, he excused himself and headed back to the sleeper car where he found his room. He was pleased to see the porter was his old friend from the earlier train. He looked around the Superliner Bedroom Suite. He didn't need all this room, but it was all that was available. He stored his packs and headed back towards the coach car. Finding the porter, he made the necessary arrangements and slipped the elderly gentleman a hundred-dollar bill. That should keep him in his good graces for a while.

Finding the mother already struggling, he questioned his decision, but knew it was the right thing to do. *Fifty hours with this chaos? It will be interesting.* Sitting down next to Krystal he picked up Jonah and set him on his knee. "I have acquired a room in the sleeper car. It is big enough for all of us if you're interested in sequestering the children."

"Why would you do that for us?" Krystal asked.

"The room is big, and I'm all alone. And I like your children."

"I don't really know you."

Ethan looked around the coach car. "Do you know all these people?"

"You make your point. Let's see how the children like the sleeper car."

Ten minutes later they were all settled into the room, and the children were happily stretched out on the beds. Ethan and Krystal sat across the table drinking a cup of coffee as the train made its way out of the tunnel on its way to Sacramento.

Leaving the city behind the train picked up speed. Ethan was again relaxed as the sparsely populated farmlands of Illinois sped by. Eventually, the rocking of the train lulled the youngsters off to sleep. Silently they rode along staring out the window. Ethan periodically noticed tears in the corner of Krystal's eyes. He was trying to figure out this strong mother when she looked up and caught him looking at her. A small smile formed on her lips, and she reached across and took his hand.

Ethan gently squeezed her hand. "Tell me about

yourself," he prompted.

"What do you want to know?"

"Who are you? Tell me about the children's father. Where are you from? Where are you going?"

———•●•———

Krystal wasn't sure how much she wanted to share but felt she had already judged the character of the man sitting across from her. "I was born and raised in Colorado. I met my husband in college. After college, we got married and moved to Syracuse, New York, where he was employed by Lockheed Martin. Soon after we married, we started a family and were quite happy in our suburban home. We were very active in our church and had our whole life ahead of us. Then one day our lives were shattered." Krystal pulled a Kleenex from the holder and wiped her eyes. Ethan squeezed her hand as she continued. "Six months ago, I lost my husband to a freak accident at work. Four months we spent at the hospital waiting for him to come out of a coma. We had hope. We prayed, the church prayed, and all of our family and friends prayed. It did not help. God took him from us."

———•●•———

It was one of those things Ethan never thought about with his loss. "So, you blame God for taking your husband?"

"I did, but not anymore. I have found much comfort in God's word. As you can see, my time is limited, but I try each day to spend time alone with God. He is my strength. I could not survive without Him."

Ethan looked into the eyes of this struggling mother who was now telling him about her faith. He had tried to blame God. But how do you blame someone you don't even know exists? It had been much easier to blame the criminals that had brutally murdered his family. He knew they existed and could be found.

"Are you on your way home to your parents?" he asked.

"Yes, Mom has asked us to consider moving back to Colorado where they can help with the children. What about you? Who are you?"

Ethan knew that he could tell her the truth without revealing the last week. For the next fifteen minutes, he shared with Krystal about his life in the city, his time in the service, his job, and the loss of his family. Krystal sat there wide-eyed as he explained the tragedy he had gone through.

When he had finished, she took both of his hands in hers and asked, "Do you mind if I pray now?"

Caught by surprise Ethan didn't know what to say, so he just nodded in approval. Just like that Krystal bowed her head and talked to God. She asked for healing for Ethan and thanked God for sending him to them as they traveled home. When she finished, her countenance had changed. Ethan could feel a peace fill the room as he had never felt.

He shook it off as emotions. "Thank you, Krystal. I appreciated your company. Maybe you should consider taking a nap before the children wake."

Krystal agreed and lay down next to Jonah and soon was fast asleep. Ethan laid his seat back and drifted off to sleep.

The train came to a stop in Burlington, Iowa, bringing Ethan wide awake. Opening his eyes, he caught Krystal studying him from across the room. She was sitting with her children around her looking at a children's book.

"You guys ready for some dinner?" he asked.

"We can't afford to order dinner," Krystal answered. "We did bring some things to eat."

Ethan felt foolish. He hadn't even considered the financial situation of this young family. It was time to put them at ease. "Meals are included here in the sleeper car. You can order anything on the menu. Do you want to go to the dining car or eat here?

They decided on the dining car, and Ethan advised the porter. It was six p.m., and the train was speeding across southern Iowa as they sat down at their table. The children did their best to work through their excitement to be eating a fancy dinner on the train. Ethan studied the little ones and briefly wondered what it would be like to be their father. It made him miss his daughters. Looking at Krystal he felt for her, struggling to raise her family alone.

After dinner, they returned to the room where Ethan watched as the children played a card game with their mother. What a peaceful time. As darkness closed in outside Krystal dressed her children for bed and gathered them around her. The children were all attentive as she read from a Bible storybook about Jesus feeding the five thousand. The periodical questions from the children were always answered with gentle understanding. It intrigued Ethan. Why had this not been explained to him as he was growing up? Maybe he would have believed.

As Krystal was putting the children to bed, Jonah ran over and gave Ethan a big hug. With choked emotions, he smiled at the little boy. Cathryn and Christiana not only hugged Ethan, but also thanked him for letting them sleep in his room.

Ethan sat at the table staring out into the darkness as Krystal took a shower. Seeing her come out of the restroom, clean and refreshed, brought back memories of his wife. How he missed her. He told Krystal he would be back and left the room. His heart ached for Kendra and seeing Krystal in this vulnerable situation was more than he wanted to experience.

Ethan stopped by the snack bar and picked up a cup of coffee. Sitting back in the observation car, he propped his feet up on the ledge and stared out at the lights passing by. Like the moon moving in and out of the clouds, his emotions moved in and out of his past. Words from the Bible story Krystal had read were permeating his thoughts. If what she was reading was true, he really was messed up. If it was just a bedtime story, Krystal was leading her children down a road of deception. He was certain that Krystal believed what she was teaching her children.

He had been quite content with his spiritual belief and did not want to upset that apple cart. As soon as he would dismiss it, the words would return. For the next few hours, he sat there drinking his coffee, trying to understand his uneasiness. It wasn't until the train pulled into Omaha before he got up and returned to his room.

Everyone was sound asleep when he quietly made his way into the room. He took a quick shower and crawled into bed. Restlessly he tossed and turned for what seemed like hours before drifting off to sleep.

Ethan was stirred to wake by three young children attempting to whisper. It brought back memories of his daughters when they were this age. He sat up and stretched just as Krystal came out of the washroom. He was battling with his emotions over her. She was beautiful on the inside and out. But he was not looking for a relationship. He only wanted them around for protection during this trip. He had plans, and it didn't involve a family. He stepped into the washroom to wash up and brush his teeth.

They were busy eating breakfast as the train rolled into Denver. For the last half hour, they had been catching views of the eastern wall of the Rocky Mountains. The ever-growing snow-capped peaks were a change from the flatland they had just crossed.

As they rolled into the station, Krystal asked Ethan if he minded watching the children for a few minutes. He watched as she walked down the platform towards the terminal. *From stranger to babysitter in two days.*

Fifteen minutes later she returned with a couple of packages and a newspaper. Sitting down next to her children, she had a scared angry look in her eyes. Ethan had seen that look with his wife many times, just before they would get into an argument. What had he done wrong? The kids were well-behaved while she was gone and were busy looking at books when she returned. He shrugged his shoulders and went back to reading.

All morning long as they were climbing over the

Rockies, he tried to get her to open up and carry on a conversation. They took lunch in their room and soon afterward the children were down for their nap. Krystal came over and sat down next to Ethan. Her disappointing anger was evident as she opened up the paper and threw it down on his lap. There on the bottom of the front page was a picture of Ethan. It was fairly recent. Most likely it was taken during the trial.

"Why didn't you tell me about this?" Krystal asked.

Ethan didn't say a word. Picking up the paper he started to read. Krystal grabbed his arm, laying her head on his shoulder. "I trusted you with my children. I was really getting to like you.

Ethan saw that he had more trouble than an angry mother on his hands. The FBI had gotten involved and had the whole nation looking for him. So far it was only for questioning, but he knew what it meant.

"It says you are suspected of murdering the men that were acquitted for killing your family. Is that true?"

Ethan laid the paper down and looked out the window. They were winding their way down along the Colorado River into Glenwood Springs before he spoke up. "I'm not a murderer. I am a soldier and am trained in finding and eliminating the enemy. Those three thugs killed my family and by doing so became my enemy. I only did what was necessary. I am sorry you had to find this out. I mean no harm to you or your children. I only wanted to use you as a diversion in Chicago, but then something happened."

"Exactly what might that be?" Krystal asked.

"I enjoyed spending time with you and your children. It dulled the loneliness I have experienced since I lost my wife and girls."

"To tell you the truth," Krystal whispered as she squeezed his arm. "I have enjoyed the company as well. You have been so good to my children. For a fleeting moment, I imagined them having you as their father. So much for that. What are you going to do? They're looking for you everywhere."

"I'm sorry but for your protection I can't tell you where I'm going. I will tell you, it is off the grid and far away from civilization. I have lost all faith in humanity and wish to go into isolation."

"Does that mean that we will never meet again?" Krystal asked.

"I suppose it does. I don't see any other way."

They sat in silence as they continued their ride along the Colorado River. It would only be a couple of hours before Krystal and her children arrived at their destination. Had he known he could have these feelings for someone again he would not have done such an irreversible action. Now, it would be impossible to settle down in civilization and keep his freedom. Choking back his emotions, he put his arm around Krystal, giving her a false sense of comfort.

As the train approached Grand Junction, Ethan helped the family get their things together. He could see the sadness on Krystal's face. They made their way down the steps trying to keep the excited children under control.

Stepping out onto the platform the children ran into the arms of their grandparents. Ethan carried their suitcases over and set them down. Introducing himself to Krystal's parents, he quickly excused himself returning to the train.

He had just started up the stairs when Krystal stopped

him. "Ethan, thank you for being so kind to my children. I pray that you find peace wherever life takes you." She squeezed his hand and just like that, she was gone.

Chapter Three

The train continued towards Salt Lake where Ethan was certain the law would be waiting. Krystal had to know from the tag on the door that Sacramento was his destination. He had never told her he was leaving the train in Reno. Still, he couldn't trust that. It was apparent she was very conscientious, which could lead to doing the right thing and notifying the authorities. Looking over the schedule he decided to cut his train ride short.

It was dark when Ethan stepped off the train in Provo. Earlier in the evening he had moved his bags forward away from his room. The 'Do not disturb' note on the door should prolong the discovery of his absence. Walking away from the train station, he hiked the mile south to the Hampton Inn. A good night's sleep would give him time to think.

After a healthy continental breakfast, Ethan took a reinvigorating swim in the indoor pool. Back in the room, he switched on his tablet and went to work. His mission was to find a way to get to Independence, California. He looked at rental cars, but where do you return the car? If he took the bus, he had a good chance of getting caught. If he just had an airplane. *That's the answer.*

It didn't take him long to find an airport four miles away that prided itself on its ability to teach anyone to fly. After checking out of the hotel, it took an hour and a half to make it to the airport. Arriving at the flight school, he asked the attendant if there were any pilots around wanting to build time. It didn't take long before a pimpled-faced kid in his late teens showed up.

"Where is it you would like to go?" he asked.

"Independence, California. Any chance you can do that?"

"That's about a three-and-a-half-hour flight in the Archer. That would be like a thousand bucks. That okay?"

"Good for me as long as you get me there in one piece."

Twenty minutes later the red, white, and blue Piper took off from Runway One Three and made a right turn out, climbing over Utah Lake. They climbed to 8500 feet as the wastelands slowly passed beneath them. Ethan watched as his youthful pilot went through his routine. It was obvious he was trained by a professional instructor. Just over an hour into the trip, they climbed to 12,500 feet and maneuvered around Wheeler Peak. The snow on the 13,000-foot peak made Ethan question his plans for the days ahead.

They crossed a few more ridges and deviated around a couple of higher peaks before starting a slow descent into the Owens Valley. Walking across the tarmac, Ethan took in the seventy-degree sunshine. He knew that where he was headed, it would be just a bit cooler. He thanked his pilot and handed him twelve hundred dollars in hundred-dollar bills.

"I added a couple extra for you forgetting about even bringing me here," Ethan added with a smile.

He rested on a park bench long enough to watch Junior depart. It didn't take long for the small plane to disappear heading northeast. Hoisting his backpack, Ethan picked up his duffel bag and headed for town. He was hungry. A brisk ten-minute hike brought him to an older hotel where he was happy to find a room. Asking about a place to eat he found out he had a choice between tacos and a café.

Arriving at the café, an elderly, grizzly-looking mountain man opened the door for Ethan and walked in behind him. Ethan didn't know which one of them was concerned more about the other. They were the only two in the dimly lit restaurant. Pans and dishes could be heard banging around in the back and shortly a middle-aged woman stuck her head around the corner.

"Never heard you come in," she said as she handed them each a menu and took their drink order.

Ethan was minding his own business consuming his dinner when the old fellow started up a conversation.

"You're not from around these parts?"

Ethan finished chewing his mouth full of cubed steak, giving him time to think. *Why would this guy care anyhow?* Swallowing his food he gave a simple answer, "Nope!"

"So, where do you call home?"

Ethan pointed to the American flag on his arm. "I'm on a mission and can't discuss it." He looked back down at his plate and continued eating. Inside he was laughing. He knew that this grizzly old fellow was most likely a patriot and would not question a soldier on a mission. By the time he finished, the place was starting to fill up. As he walked back to the hotel, the evening sky highlighted the eastern wall of the Sierra Mountains.

Logging into the wifi he did more research on his destination. It was time to repack his backpack and prepare the remainder of his possessions for storage. He started by pulling everything out of his bags and throwing them on the bed. One item at a time he weighed their necessity and put them in the appropriate pile. A small black book caught his eye. Knowing that he had not put it in his pack caused his pulse to quicken.

Picking it up Ethan recognized the Bible as the one that Krystal had been reading on the train. Opening it he pulled out an envelope. It was sealed with a simple "Ethan" written in beautiful handwriting. This did not slow down his heartbeat as that alone revealed the author. He pulled out his knife and sliced open the envelope pulling out a single sheet of paper.

Dear Ethan, by the time you read this you will be far away. My heart will still be aching as I deal with the fifty hours you spent with us. Setting aside the dark secret that lives within you, I found the love you showed us revealed your true character. When my husband died, I tried to find someone to blame. Unlike with you, it just wasn't there. It is hard for me to understand what you did. Still, I feel you are a good man, who wants to find your way. I have figured out that your destination requires you to carry everything on your back. Please take this Bible with you and read it with an open mind, starting with the Gospel of John. If you ever return to civilization, try and find us. Krystal signed it and added a little heart. Under her signature, she had written her email address.

Ethan had sat down on the bed to read the letter. In one hand, he held the Bible and in the other the letter. His head was spinning as he tried to decipher the information. He had to carry on. He would send Krystal an email before taking off in the morning. It was close to midnight before he finished packing his bags. On the floor, a cardboard box was ready to tape up for storage.

Chapter Four

Shadows still darkened the valley as the sun glowed off the peaks of the Sierra Nevada Mountain range. After connecting to the Wi-Fi, Ethan's first order of business was to download a Virtual Private Network and soon had it set for maximum security. He then created a new email account using a fictitious name and typed out a message to Krystal.

Thank you for the Bible. And even though I am not a religious man, I will attempt to read it. There's nothing I can do about my past. You deserve a good man that loves God as you do. I will be going off the grid for the unforeseeable future. Give my love to the children. Ethan read back over his email before clicking the send button. Switching off the tablet he slid it into the box. He walked down to the gas station and soon found someone heading south that was willing to give him a ride.

Fifteen miles later his ride dropped him off at the self-storage units on the north side of town. The solitary box looked lonely in the otherwise empty space. All his years of collecting came down to what he carried on his back and this one little box. Beside his tablet, the other items in the box were his military uniforms, a two-way radio/scanner, and three hundred thousand in twenty-dollar bills. He would not need the cash where he was headed. He had thought about leaving his sniper rifle and other weapons in storage but felt he might need them.

One last look at the lonely box, Ethan closed the door and headed into town. At the recommendation of the self-storage manager, Ethan found the Alabama Hills Café. Off the main street, the café was filled with locals sharing every form of gossip possible. Sitting in the corner watching the interaction amongst the patrons, he learned a lot about this part of the world.

Returning to Independence using the same method of transportation, Ethan checked out of his hotel and headed up Onion Valley Road. It was thirteen miles to the Onion Valley Campground where he would spend the night. It wasn't so much the miles but the almost six thousand feet of vertical climb that would kill him. Between his backpack and duffel bag, he was carrying almost eighty pounds. It didn't take long before he questioned not leaving some of this stuff in storage.

Three hours later, and almost halfway to the trailhead, he stumbled into the Upper Grays Meadow campground to rest. Sitting under the shade of a scrub oak he took off his shoes and soaked his feet in Independence Creek. The ice-cold water was coming directly off the snowpack just a few miles away and felt refreshing on this hot day here at the lower altitudes. That would change as he made his way up the mountain.

"Are you planning on camping here tonight?"

Startled, Ethan turned around to find an elderly gentleman walking a small dog. A tag hung from the pocket of his shirt declaring him the official camp host. Turning back around Ethan continued tying his shoes.

"No sir, I'm hoping to make it up to Onion Valley before calling it a day. It's hard to say if I'll make it. I still have over three thousand feet to climb, and I think it's about seven miles. I probably should get going."

"If you wait until I finish my rounds, and I'll drive you up there. I'm the host there as well and need to do my daily drive-through."

"Thank you, you're a godsend. I'll wait at the exit."

What would have taken almost three hours and expended a load of energy was over in fifteen minutes. Arriving at the trailhead, he was surprised at the number of campers already occupying the campground. He had expected to have it to himself. Looking at his watch, he decided to move on. He could put in at least a couple of miles before dark. Hoisting the eighty pounds on this back, he headed up Kearsarge Pass trail.

From the very start, the trail had a constant climb back and forth up the switchbacks. After about a mile the switchbacks shortened and got steeper. The sound of the water tumbling down the valley to his left gave him a break from the monotonous painful climb. Cresting a rise, he came upon Little Pothole Lake tucked away in a basin. He was tempted to camp here for the night, but the tents scattered about drove him on. A dozen switchbacks and five hundred feet of climb later, he crossed over a large gravel slide and passed along Gilbert Lake. Once again, the scattered tents urged him to keep going. It was only a quarter mile to the smaller Flower Lake, and even though it had hikers scattered about, he found a somewhat secluded spot and set up camp.

It felt good to get the weight off his back. Sometime earlier the sun had dropped below the peaks, and the temperature was dropping rapidly. Ethan boiled some water and fixed his dinner. Sitting there in the chilly evening air he watched the sky change from yellow to orange to red. As the sun's influence dissipated, the sky turned to the darkest blue he had ever seen, before revealing a night sky full of millions of stars. The Milky Way stretching across the sky washed out the constellations. With his back leaned up against a rock, he was in awe at the vastness he was witnessing.

Ethan crawled into his sleeping bag. Laying there on the hard ground he struggled with his past. He tossed and turned throughout the night, just trying to get some answers. Finally, fatigue overcame his unrest, and he slept.

Ethan was startled awake as the sun popped over the mountains flooding his campsite in its morning brilliance. The freezing temperature outside made it difficult to crawl out of his warm cocoon. Finally, the desire to get to his destination overcame the discomfort. He wasted no time getting dressed in the frigid mountain air. As he pulled on his shoes, his aching body reminded him of the previous day's exertions.

The next two-plus miles was a constant thirteen-hundred-foot climb. Reaching Kearsarge Pass, he had his first glimpse into the interior. For as far as he could see, there were no roads, nothing but trails hammered out by hiking shoes and horse's hooves. It was where towering mountain peaks gave up their snowpacks to create raging rivers in the deep valleys far below. It was where wildlife had minimal interaction with humans. It was going to be his home.

One last time he looked back into the Owens Valley being faded out by the morning sun. Stepping off the crest he made his way down the handful of switchbacks past Bullfrog Lake following the small runoff stream into the valley. Coming to another trail, he sat down under a stand of trees and took in the peaceful surroundings.

It was only a couple of miles from his destination. How would he be accepted? The information he had received about the community was sketchy at best. Considering the geographical location of the settlement he knew its occupants had to be strong and self-sufficient. Coming into this environment as an outsider would require a lot of trust on their part.

Crossing over a small ridge he descended the trail to Charlotte Lake. The rich aroma of the pine trees added to the crisp fresh air as he approached the lake. He wasn't able to pick out any cabins but could see small wisps of white smoke coming up out of the trees. Making his way around the lake towards the smoke flumes, Ethan walked past a small cabin. He continued, finding more than two dozen cabins scattered throughout the pines.

Coming to a group of log buildings that looked like a common area, he found a bench and sat down. He was at a loss for what to do. If it wasn't for the smoke coming from the chimneys, he would have thought the place was deserted.

Chapter Five

———•●•———

"Good morning, sir."

Ethan turned to find a middle-aged bearded man, standing there with a Bible in his hand.

"You come for the meeting?" the man asked.

"What meeting?"

"It's a church meeting," the man looked puzzled and slightly annoyed at the question, as if Ethan should know.

Others drifted in before Ethan could answer. The men were all dressed in their plain garb and the ladies wore simple dresses and bonnets. Ethan felt he had just walked into the eighteen hundreds. Within fifteen minutes, over a hundred settlers were scattered throughout the clearing. The adults milled around greeting each other while the children respectfully played with their friends. An elderly man with a cane came slowly walking down the path and made his way to the gathering. He made his way to Ethan and introduced himself as Abram. It became obvious that he was their spiritual leader.

Everyone followed Abram into the large log building. If Ethan was going to get to know these people, it would be best to go in as well. The inside of the building, lit with oil lamps, had rugged whitewashed walls. Two rows of rough wooden benches filled the room. A rugged wood table stretched across the front of the room where Abram and two other men were taking their seats.

Ethan settled on the back bench. The men sat on one side and the ladies on the other. Ethan had never been in church outside of funerals and weddings, but somehow he imagined this is not how they did it in New York.

After singing a couple of songs without musical instruments, one of the men stood up and read from the Bible. Ethan heard the words, but they made little sense to him.

Then Abram stood up and started preaching. At first, he spoke softly, and Ethan had trouble hearing him in the back. Before long, the preacher found his wind and rattled the windows as he shared with the congregation words of wisdom from the Bible. All Ethan got from it was that they mostly kept themselves from the evils of this world.

They probably considered him as part of those evils, and maybe he was.

After the service was over, Ethan made his way back outside where he sat back down on the bench. As he had expected, these people skirted where he sat, though several shot curious glances his way. He didn't blame their caution. A stranger in a remote community could be dangerous. Abram, being the last one out, hobbled over and sat down next to Ethan.

"What are you doing here?"

"I was searching for a remote place to live when I came across some vague information about your settlement. Now I'm here, not sure what's next."

Abram stood up and motioned for Ethan to follow. "Well, you need to eat and it's lunchtime. Come on over to my place, and we can talk it over."

They walked along the lake for only a hundred yards before Abram led him up a pathway to a small cabin. The front porch stretched the length of the cabin and held two rocking chairs and a small table. Stepping inside the one-room cabin, Ethan found a clean, well-kept home. The two simple upholstered chairs sitting in front of the stone fireplace were the focal point. A small cabinet and sink, next to a wood cook stove made up the kitchen. On the far wall away from the fireplace was a single bed covered with a well-worn quilt. In the corner, a ladder made its way to a loft.

After stoking the fire, Abram filled the tea kettle and set it on the hot stove. "Tell me about yourself. Where did you come from? What about your family? If we're going to trust you, we need to know who you really are."

Ethan picked his words carefully, "I was born and raised just east of New York City. I served in the army for a number of years before becoming an author and an investigative journalist. While working on a story I discovered a strong link between a local politician and a well-known criminal syndicate. Upon researching this connection, I found a large network of politicians who were taking bribes from these organized criminals. I made the mistake of thinking that if I would just bring these corruptions to light, the justice department would deal with the issue. In hindsight, I should never have written the story. Two years ago, my wife and two girls were brutally murdered because of my revealing publications.

"I have had trouble dealing with this loss and have decided no longer to trust society. I suppose that is why I'm here." Ethan left out the vindictive judgment he placed on the assailants.

Abram motioned for him to sit down at the well-worn table. "Ethan, we are a quiet and reserved people. We work hard at practicing a simple and non-resistant life. One where we practice faith and forgiveness. Internally our association has all things in common. Some folks would call what we have here a commune. None of us have more or less than the other and we all work diligently at the gift God has given us. Due to how we live our lives we do not mingle with or associate with outsiders."

Sitting down at the table, Abram bowed his head, "Thank you God for this wonderful day. Thank you for the food that has been prepared. Thank you for bringing Ethan to our mountain. God, we thank you for sending your Son to save us. We love you God, and we praise your holy name. Amen."

Abram pulled the lid off the pot revealing a stew that if tasted as good as it smelled was going to satisfy Ethan's growling stomach. He was not disappointed as it had been a couple of days since he had eaten real food.

"Did you bake the bread?" Ethan asked his host as he took another bite.

Abram chuckled, "No, that is not one of my gifts. A couple of our wonderful ladies are blessed with that ability, and they do an amazing job."

"They bake for the whole settlement?"

"Oh yes! Each one here is assigned a job based on their God-given ability. It makes for a better community. We found out years ago that your livelihood becomes less burdensome when this technique is used."

"What if someone gets tired of their job?"

"We will work together to find them a new job."

"Surely there are unrewarding jobs that no one wants to do. What about them?"

"We all work together to take care of the less-than-desirable chores."

"What if I would decide to join your settlement? Would you find me a job?"

"First of all, you would need to show your willingness to become one of us. That is not as easy as one might think. You will be treated as an outsider for a long time. Only when you have proven yourself, will the community be willing to accept you as one of the fold."

At his host's urging, Ethan dipped out another ladle of stew and buttered up another slice of bread. "I'm not sure what I'm going to do. I would like to spend a couple of days here just getting a chance to meet the people and explore the area."

"We gather on Sunday evenings to sing and enjoy a time of fellowship. Come along and meet the folks. I would love to show you the area, but as you can see, I have trouble getting around. I will have one of the older boys show you around the mountainside tomorrow after school."

"You have a school here?" Ethan was surprised.

"Oh yes. We raise our children to be simplistic, not unintelligent."

Ethan blushed, "Sorry, I by no means meant to insinuate that. Just being so remote, I didn't think about a school. It does make sense."

After cleaning up the table, Abram said he was tired and needed to take a nap. "You are welcome to spend the night here in the loft. If all works out tomorrow, we will get you into your own place."

Ethan tossed his bags into the loft and went for a walk along the well-worn path beside the lake. Periodically, a side trail would lead up to a cabin largely concealed within the pines. He could hear children playing and now and then caught a glimpse of one running through the trees. It was so different from the constant roar of traffic and the frequent sirens in the city. Past the group of cabins, the path led up to a timber-framed barn, ruggedly built, yet well maintained. Ethan couldn't imagine the work it took to build the infrastructure in this remote location. Beyond the barn, a fenced-in pasture was spotted with cattle and sheep. The braying of mules and neighing of horses came from somewhere inside.

At the west end of the lake, Ethan sat down on a large boulder overlooking the runoff from the lake. He lay back on the boulder and soaked up its warmth from the afternoon sun. To the west, the stream meandered for about a thousand yards before dropping out of sight into the valley. Shutting his eyes for just a moment, the babbling of the water running over the rocks took Ethan into a restful, relaxing utopia.

He had no idea how long he had been asleep when he was suddenly awakened by voices nearby. He watched a handful of teenagers easily traverse the stones placed in the stream for that obvious purpose. Stretching, he followed them just to see where the trail led.

On around the south side of the lake, he saw several other well-hidden cabins and a couple of smaller barns. When he reached the southeast corner of the lake, he came across a path leading up the mountain. He decided to follow this path just high enough to get a good view of the settlement. The climb was effortless without the weight of his packs. Soon he was at the edge of the tree line and sat down on a rock to rest. From this vantage point, he could pick out the cabins far below. *What an interesting place; I think I can live here.*

Looking around he was drawn into the horseshoe crater to the southwest. Checking his watch, he decided to explore this ancient blown-out crater. The surrounding mountains created a sense of security for Ethan. He passed a couple of small grassy meadows and a small pond that was being used for irrigation. Past the pond, he came to a small stone structure on the far side of the six-foot-wide shallow stream. No one was about, and Ethan was not about to interrupt anyone's nap, so he quietly passed the house and climbed a small knoll. Snow still spotted the landscape, but Ethan could see green grass covering the three-acre crater floor.

Ethan felt a chill as the sun dropped below the peak causing him to turn around and head back down the mountain. He'd have to come back here tomorrow.

"Did you enjoy your walk?" Abram asked from his chair by the fire.

"All the way around the lake and up into the crater," Ethan poured a cup of water and sat down facing Abram.

"Didn't meet anyone but did enjoy the walk."

"Did you notice the stone house in the crater?"

"I did. It didn't look as if there was anyone home. The shutters were closed."

"No one lives there at this time. The weather gets a little adverse up there in the winter. The man that lived up there last summer moved down here for the winter and got married. His wife is opposed to living in such a remote area."

Just the thought of calling the stone house a remote area made Ethan chuckle. "I think it is a wonderful location. Yes, it is somewhat removed, but the location and the view are ideal."

Abram stroked his beard before continuing, "Do you think you might like living up there?

"I know I would, can't think of a better place. What is the catch?"

Abram didn't say anything for a couple of minutes. Sitting there with his eyes shut Ethan wondered if he was even awake. Finally, he opened his eyes. "Well, Ethan don't get your hopes up. I still need to get approval from the community. If perchance it is approved, you would be required to take care of shepherding the livestock up there in the summertime."

Ethan had found his dream job. "Is that all? There has to be more."

"Well, at times, if you're not busy, you may be needed to help bale hay."

Ethan tried not to let his excitement show. "What do we do next?"

"You need to meet the folks. Speaking of that, let's

go to the singing."

The clearing was filled with chatter and laughter. Ethan was not that excited about spending the evening singing songs he did not know. He was sure they didn't have a guitar, and his style of music was rock and roll. It just wasn't one of the things he thought about when he made these plans. Abram led him around introducing him to everyone. He tried to make a note of their names but gave up after a handful. It would take time.

The evening air was getting chilly as they made their way into the building. For about an hour or so, Ethan sat there listening to the group sing. He didn't recognize any of the songs, but it didn't take long before the melody and softness of the singing relaxed his spirit and he started to hum along. Just as it was getting dark outside, they stopped singing and spent the next half hour eating their way through a table full of desserts.

The night sky glistened with stars as Ethan and Abram walked back up the path to the cabin. After lighting the lantern, Abram threw a log on the embers and sat down in his chair exhausted.

Within a few minutes, Ethan lay on the thin mattress in the loft with his eyes wide open. Like the flicker of the flames dancing across the rafters were decisions dancing through his mind. Exhaustion tried to drive out the need to make those decisions but could not succeed. Finally, in the wee hours of the morning, he cried out to God to help him understand, and soon he fell into a fitful sleep.

Chapter Six

"I will be meeting with the elders this afternoon," Abram told Ethan over breakfast. "It will be up to them on how we proceed. It's not every day that a stranger wants to move into the settlement."

"What am I to do?" Ethan asked scraping the last of the gravy from his plate.

"Spend the morning getting to know the area and be back here for lunch. This afternoon, I would like for you to stick close by in case they have questions."

Ethan retraced his steps around the lake, but this time he stopped and chatted with everyone he met. As he passed one side trail, the aroma of fresh-baked bread caught his attention. He backed up two steps and, mouth-watering, made his way towards the bakery. Sticking his head inside the door, he found two ladies busy kneading dough. At the end of the small room was a big stone wood-fired oven. One of the ladies looked up and smiled. "Good morning, Ethan, are you enjoying the day?"

Ethan was not surprised they knew him. After all, in a tight-knit community, information on a stranger traveled fast. "Why, yes, I am, thank you. You two look hard at work."

"We have the first batch fresh out of the oven. Care for a sample?"

Eating away at a chunk of fresh bread, Ethan made his way down the trail. His next stop was the woodworking shop. Two gentlemen were busy working on a couple of chairs. With only hand tools to work with, it was obvious that what they were doing was a labor of love. They were happy to see Ethan and took the time to visit, asking a lot of questions, some of which were hard for Ethan to answer. Adjoining the woodworking shop, manned by the two craftsmen, was a hardware store. The stock was different than you would find in civilization. Instead of an electrical section, there were lamps, wicks, and cast-iron skillets.

Shortly after leaving the woodworking shop, Ethan came across an elderly couple sitting on their porch. The lady had a cat purring on her lap as her husband was reading aloud. Ethan stopped to listen but could not make sense of what he was hearing and was just about to move on when the lady motioned for him. "Greetings Ethan, how is your morning."

"How can a person complain when breathing this fresh mountain air," he answered. "I'm sure we met last evening, but I can't remember your names."

"I'm William, and this beautiful lady is Claire," the man stood up and shook Ethan's hand. "We are the Lindberghs."

"I'm Ethan Dawson, the stranger from New York.

What are you reading?"

"It's from the Gospel of John."

The puzzled look on Ethan's face brought an explanation. "It's from the Bible. Am I wrong to assume you haven't read it?"

"You assume correctly. I have very little experience with the spiritual part of my life." It did dawn on him that was what Krystal had asked him to read.

Ethan sat down on a small backless bench as a cool breeze blew up the valley. "What was the 'Go to prepare a place for you'?" he asked.

"The Bible tells us that Jesus has gone to Heaven to prepare a place for His people. That would be those that have put all their faith in Him. At some point in the future, and it could be any day now, He is going to come back and take us there."

"But, didn't He say that like two thousand years ago? Haven't most people given up on that ever happening?"

"It did. And in answering your second question, sadly too many people have given up. Are you one of those people?"

"Well, I can't say I've given up. I just haven't put much confidence in a god that doesn't show himself."

Sadness appeared in William's eyes as he looked up at the mountains that surrounded them. "How can you say that, Ethan? Open your eyes, all around you the mountains and the sky cry out that He is. That is what I will pray for my friend, that God will open your eyes."

Not having a good response to William's declaration of intercession, Ethan just hung his head and looked at the rough sawn floor. His thoughts were on the past couple of days. The life these people are living is intriguing. What would it be like to have the faith that William was talking about? How can someone like William, who has experienced so much, still believe in God? It would definitely give a person a peaceful disposition to believe that heaven awaits them after death. Realization set in as his thoughts moved to his past.

"If God is real," he told William, "there is no way He would accept me. I have done some horrible things. I must accept the fact that I'm doomed to live a turbulent life. I do appreciate you praying for me. Who knows, someday I may be able to believe."

William shook his head, "Think seriously about making that decision, Ethan. Your eternity depends on it."

Ethan thanked his new friends and continued around the lake. At the barn, he met a handful of younger men working with the animals. The large barn was built partially into the side of the mountain. Its timbers were massive, and Ethan wondered how they ever got them into place. A big burly fellow, who appeared to be in charge, crawled over the fence, pulled off his glove and introduced himself to Ethan.

"Didn't get a chance to speak with you last night. I'm Robert and have the privilege of managing the farm. The rumor is that you're planning on sticking around."

"I would sure like to, but I believe it's out of my hands."

"Well, if you do, we could use a young strapping worker like yourself here on the farm."

"Time will tell. Abram is working with the leaders today to get approval for me to stay up in the crater this summer."

"That's a good idea. You okay with being up there?"

"I'm thinking I'll love it. It's got a great view." Ethan withheld his yearning to be secluded from humanity as much as possible.

"Well, if you get the stone house, your job will be to attend to the animals up there during the summer months. What experience do you have in taking care of animals?"

"I had a dog when I was a kid. Does that count?'

That brought on a good hardy laugh, "Not quite. We can train you to take care of the stock, that is if you know how to use a gun. There are times we have to fire warning shots to deter wolves and mountain lions. You a good shot?"

Ethan thought about telling him about his success as a sniper, but decided it probably wouldn't be appropriate, "I'm sure I can get close enough to scare them."

Crossing over the lake outlet, he met a few more folks working up the soil in a garden. He returned their greeting and moved on. A short distance later, he found a large greenhouse full of steaming half-grown plants waiting to be put in the ground.

Halfway up the south side of the lake, he met Doctor Winston carrying his medical bag. Ethan was amazed at finding a doctor in the settlement but not surprised. They stopped and chatted before the doctor hurried on to his house call.

Reaching the trail leading up to the crater, Ethan quickened his pace as he started the climb. He was excited about the possibility of this being his home. On the climb, he noticed other settlers working in another garden on the east side of the lake. *Like a hive of bees going about their job. What a peaceful life.*

Chapter Seven

The half-mile climb was exhilarating. As he walked along the meadow, he paid more attention than he had yesterday. He noticed fences enclosing the meadow. There was a tank by the pond for watering livestock. His focus was on the stone house. He crossed over the creek and walked around the house. A couple of buildings were tucked up against the vertical mountain wall. He recognized the smallest building as the outhouse. Opening the door of the larger one he found it full of firewood and necessary tools. Moving on around the house he stepped up on the porch and out of habit knocked on the door.

He jumped when the door creaked as a young lady wearing an apron opened the door. "Good morning, Ethan, did you come up to see your house?"

That comment caught Ethan by surprise. They may not have modern technology but sure knew how to communicate. The plan had not even been approved yet everyone knew his business.

"Not quite my house, but there is a possibility of staying here this summer. Sorry to bother you. I was told the place was vacant."

"Oh, it is. I'm just up here cleaning the place up a bit. We wouldn't want you moving into a dusty home."

"I don't remember your name but thank you. This is much appreciated."

Holding out her hand, she smiled, "I'm Anna. I saw you yesterday, but we weren't able to meet. Welcome to our settlement. I for one am happy to see new faces. While I like it here, at times the isolation is depressing."

Ethan could not imagine someone with her cheerful disposition could have depressive feelings. "Sorry for interrupting your job. I'm not doing anything, can I help?"

"I would love to have your help. It won't take long with the two of us."

Ethan found the inside of the house simple yet very livable. The living area was the standard combination of living room and kitchen. A stone fireplace was the primary heat source. On the opposite wall next to the separated bedroom was a kitchen cabinet. Next to the cabinet, an old white cast iron sink was adorned with a red hand pump. A wood-fired cook stove was backed up to the opposite wall. He found the only furniture in the adjoining room, was a full-size bed, a straight back chair, and a simple chest of drawers. For the next hour, the two of them scrubbed and mopped and swept and laughed. Ethan found himself enjoying her company way too much. Once they were finished, they sat down on the front porch to rest.

Ethan was going to enjoy sitting on this porch. From here he could keep an eye on both meadows. The sound of the water making its way from the upper meadow down to the pond would assist in many afternoon naps. As Anna was sharing with Ethan trivial information about the settlement, he was appraising her. She was probably ten years his junior and, even with the smudges of hard work on her face, was a beautiful young lady. He thought of Kendra and wondered what she would think of this remote location. She was a city girl and thought Central Park was the wilderness.

After Anna had temporarily run out of knowledge to impart, Ethan took control of the conversation. "So, do you like living here in the mountains?"

Anna looked perplexed for a moment before answering, "Yes, I do. There are times when I miss the convenience of civilization, but overall, the benefits outweigh the negatives."

"What about your family? Is your family here or on the outside?"

"I don't have a family other than my church. I was raised in foster care with no knowledge of my birth parents. I was ten when I was brought up here and have never returned to civilization."

She paused and looking at the ground started shuffling her feet. The pain in her face told Ethan that this was an unhappy subject for Anna. There was obvious pain beneath the happy disposition he had seen earlier.

"You didn't mention a husband. Am I to assume you're not married?"

"I am not married. That's another sad story. Maybe someday I can share it with you, just not today. It's time for me to go." She picked up her backpack and headed down the trail.

Ethan looked at his watch. It was almost noon. *Oh man, I'm going to be late.* He closed up the house and headed down the trail after Anna. He could see her up ahead descending on the switchbacks. His heart went out to her as he thought about all the things she had gone through.

Chapter Eight

"So, why are you here?"

The question by Eli, the youngest of the elders, caught Ethan off guard. He pondered the question as the five men sat staring at him. It had been a long afternoon as he patiently waited outside the meeting house. He had spent the time thinking about his life experiences and reduced it all into a simple composition. He was, as William said, a sad hopeless soul, living a godless life.

"I'm not sure I can answer that question. I have only been here for a little over twenty-four hours, and my reasons for being here have changed. Now I am confused as to why I am here. What I do know is that the more I get to know the citizens of this settlement, the more I feel at home."

"Are you aware of the rules we live by here in the settlement?"

Ethan wasn't sure he had seen a rule book, but it didn't matter, Eli never gave him a chance to answer.

"We do not tolerate any form of electronics in the

community. As you have witnessed, we only use primitive forms of lighting and heating within our homes and buildings. If you have anything that uses electrical power, you will need to dispose of it."

Ethan's mind whirled through his possessions. Here on the mountain the only thing he had that used power was his night vision equipment. He would just leave them in his backpack.

"It is highly recommended that you attend church on Sunday mornings," Eli continued. "If you decide you want to join our fellowship, you will need to be a believer and get baptized. We highly recommend you seriously consider this, as your life in the hereafter depends on it."

Ethan said nothing as he noticed Abram with a half-smile winked at him. "Now Brother Eli, don't go scaring him off so quickly. We don't know much about Ethan yet, but if you run him off, we will never get to know him. Ethan, we do encourage our settlers to join our fellowship, but it has to be your choice. The important question is the one I previously asked and would like you to tell the elders. What is your relationship with Jesus? Have you made the decision to accept His offered terms of mercy? Do you believe?"

He looked around the room and decided to tell them the truth. "No, I have not yet made that decision. Over the last twenty-four hours, I have been evangelized three times here on the mountain. I am not averse to the concept. I just haven't made a decision. Just two days ago I was given a Bible and would like time to read it before making a decision. Please give me time."

The room sat in silence as the depth of the

conversation took its time to find its equilibrium.

Even Eli appeared to understand the spiritual battle going on for Ethan's soul. Yet, he still had concerns. "History has told us that it is wise to be wary when taking strangers into our community. Surely you understand our need to be careful?"

"Yes, I understand. It has been suggested that I might work well up in the crater taking care of the livestock this summer. Would it be agreeable if we did this on a trial basis?"

"That will be all," Abram told Ethan. "You may go now. We will have an answer in a few minutes."

Walking down a worn path to the lake he contemplated his predicament. He was certain he would have problems abiding by their strange rules. What would he do if they sent him on his way? Picking up a flat stone he skipped it across the turquoise water of Charlotte Lake. Maybe the real reason he was here was part of God's plan. He sat down on a log and listened to the children playing across the lake. He heard the sound of an ax somewhere chopping away at a tree. The smell of the pine trees filled his senses. He felt a sense of peace as the water lapped the shoreline.

"There you are." Ethan turned around to see Eli coming down the path. "Brother Abram sent me to tell you we have made our decision. Do you mind coming back to the meeting house?"

Abram motioned for Ethan to sit down, "While it is true that we do not know you, we do know God and he knows you. In the Bible, there is a verse that tells us to be not forgetful to entertain strangers, for thereby some have entertained angels unaware.

"Ethan, we have decided to give you as much time as you need to seek God's will for your life. We are here to help you on your journey. We will be praying that God will open your heart to the truth. You are free to move into the crater house. Eli has agreed to go over with you some of the general housekeeping and supply procedures around the settlement."

Eli led Ethan a couple hundred yards up a well-worn side trail to a stone structure set into the mountainside. The floorboards rattled as they walked across the length of the porch to the heavy oak door. Stepping inside the cool building they were greeted by a woman behind a counter.

"Good afternoon, Eli, I see you brought our new friend. I'm Sarah," she said as she stuck out her hand to Ethan. "Welcome to the storehouse. Are you planning on staying for a while?"

"Thank you, and yes, that is the plan," Ethan answered as he looked around the large room filled with shelves of supplies. In the far corner, two toddlers were playing with toys next to a couple of easy chairs. "This looks like a general store. How do you get all this stuff up here?"

"Have you heard the mules braying at night? They are our supply trucks. Weather permitting, they make two trips off the mountain each week."

"Is Noah around?" Eli asked.

"He's busy in the cooler. Go on back."

They passed through a heavy door and instantly Ethan felt the chill coming from the other side. Closing the door behind them it was suddenly dark. The only light flickered dimly at the other end of the aisle. Walking down an aisle of what looked like bins of fruits and vegetables they found the source of the light.

A man was working over a large slab of meat on a stainless table as a lantern hung overhead. "Good afternoon, Noah. I brought you a new customer."

Turning around Noah smiled at Ethan, "So you have decided to stay? Welcome to Charlotte Lake."

"Yes, for the time being anyhow. Thank you." Ethan eyed the chunk of meat lying on the table. His experience with meat never went deeper than the grocery store.

Seeing the questioning look on Ethan's face Noah smiled, "This is venison. Deer are readily available up here. Have you ever tried it?"

"Don't think so, but I'm sure that's about to change." Ethan looking around noticed several different kinds of meat hanging from hooks on the ceiling of the cold cave. "How many kinds of meat do you have in here?"

"You name it we probably have it. All your wild game, Black bear, elk, rabbit, and of course, venison, are available most of the time. Domesticated animals like beef, pork, lamb, and chicken are available just about year around. Winter weather at times causes a shortage."

Ethan thanked Noah and they made their way back into the storehouse. Ethan took a couple of minutes looking over the fully stocked shelves. "This is better stocked than most small-town grocery stores. How is it priced?"

"Here in our community the price has been paid. A lot of the food items have been grown, raised, or hunted here on the mountain. The merchandise coming from off the mountain is paid for by the settlement. As part of the settlement, you will be contributing to the storehouse through the work that you do and are free to come in here and pick up your supplies. We ask that you only get what you need. You can give a list to Sarah and one of the older children will deliver it after school."

"Even up in the crater?"

"Sure. Go ahead and give it a try."

Looking over a preprinted pad, Ethan checked off a few simple items and handed them to Sarah. It just did not seem right that no money was being exchanged.

"We'll have it up there before supper time," she said looking over the list.

Leaving the storehouse, they stopped by the woodworking shop. "If you need furniture or hardware this is the place you go. They stock many items but can build to order just about anything. It usually takes a couple of weeks on these special orders. Naturally, that is weather permitting."

"I hear weather permitting a lot up here."

"Wait until winter comes, and then you'll understand why we say that."

The humor in Eli's comment did not go unnoticed.

"You said if you need furniture, you can get it here?"

"Yes, they do get caught up at times and build some basic chairs and tables but most of the time they are working on a list. It can take up to a few weeks to get to your request."

"I think I know the answer but have to ask. How do they get paid?"

Eli shook his head, "You're not yet getting it. There is never any money exchanging hands here in the community. Even with the hardware. It is all paid for by the community."

"Where does the community get its money?" Ethan knew enough about economics to know that without a source of income a community could not be sustainable.

Eli shook his head, "That will be for another day."

Leaving the woodworking shop they headed on down to the barn where Eli reintroduced Ethan to his new boss.

"I'll be up in the morning at the crack of dawn," Robert told Ethan. "Have the coffee ready and we'll go over what is expected of you. If the coffee's not ready, you can expect to dig post holes all day."

Ethan didn't know if he was serious or joking. He was sure he saw a grin beneath that big bushy mustache. Regardless the coffee would be ready.

"Well, that about does it." Eli said. "Brother Abram will have a binder with all the rules. It would be best to abide by what it says."

Ethan felt a tinge of irritation at the thought of being submissive to a commune. They may be nice people, but the idea of losing his freedom was going cross-grain against his life.

As Eli headed on down the trail, Ethan still could not understand how such a community survived. He could not comprehend how they managed it, but he was sure it wasn't through exports.

Tapping on the door, he entered to find Abram sitting in his chair reading his Bible. "Well, did you find everything satisfactory?"

"It is amazing what you all have accomplished here on the mountain," Ethan sat down and stretched out his legs.

"How you do it is a mystery."

"The mystery is in the God we serve. He has provided. Are you going up to the crater this evening?"

"Yes, I ordered some groceries and a few other items. I should get up there before they are delivered." Ethan stood and grabbed Abram's hand. "Thanks for giving me a chance. I will stop by in a couple of days."

"I would like that, Ethan. Ever since my wife passed, I have been lonely. Everyone is busy doing their job, not giving too much thought to the elderly. Maybe that's something I should preach on some time."

The thought that Abram could do a little whining, did not slip past Ethan. He patted Abram on the shoulder and picked up his bags.

Chapter Nine

———•●•———

Halfway up the trail, he met a young man coming down. "Good evening, Ethan. I put your groceries on the table. It should all be there."

Ethan recognized the boy from the church but had not met him, "Thank you, uh, what is your name?"

"I'm Jonathan. Abram is my grandfather."

"Your grandfather is a great man, Jonathan. Have a good night."

Ethan made it to the top of the climb and started through the lower meadow. The sun had set behind Mount Bago, and the night chill was setting in. What was it like here on this piece of land when it was a volcano? Was it an enormous eruption or a big earthquake that took out the east edge of the volcano? Whatever it was, it caused a massive landslide to push down into the ravine leaving a flat place large enough for a future settlement. Here in the crater, it left a little piece of heaven for Ethan to call home. He was almost through the meadow when he spooked a deer. He stopped and watched as it bounced across the darkening pasture.

The first order of business was to get a fire burning in the cook stove. Just the sound of a crackling fire brought warmth to the chilly cabin as Ethan unpacked his backpack. Unpacking his personnel items, he realized how few items he now owned.

Opening up his duffel bag, he pulled out his arsenal of weapons and laid them on the table. He reassembled his sniper rifle. A weapon meant to neutralize the enemy may just be a little overkill for a hunting rifle. He wrapped a blanket around the Remington sniper rifle and put it in the loft with two of his handguns. His third handgun, a 9mm Beretta with two extra fifteen round clips, was tucked away under his mattress.

With everything put away, he put a kettle of water on the hot stove and stepped out onto the porch as the twilight was fading. He was deep in thought as the creak of the rocking chair kept time with the frogs croaking by the pond. The moon rising over Kearsarge Pinnacles blocked out stars and flushed the crater floor with a soft glowing light. Even though he was thousands of miles away from New York City, he was struggling with the past.

The time he had spent researching told him that the people behind the crimes he had uncovered, would not let him go. Not only were they evil, but they were also persistent and would do everything they could to hunt him down. He had to remain vigilant and not give away his position. Still, he knew they had inside contacts and if the FBI found him, so would his enemies. He was sure the FBI was looking for him as well, so it probably didn't matter.

Nevertheless, he would stay alert.

The sound of the kettle tooting its whistle broke the night. Ethan fixed a cup of coffee and returned to the porch. Chewing on a piece of bread he thought about Krystal. He sure enjoyed the time he had with her and her children. Was it from the loss of his family or was he genuinely fond of her? He was certain that she would never forgive him for withholding the truth. It didn't matter, she wouldn't have wanted to have any sort of relationship with someone who was labeled a murderer. Even if it was justified, in his opinion. The howl of a wolf somewhere over the ridge brought him back to Charlotte Lake and the stone cabin in the crater.

The sun had not yet come up when Ethan awoke from a night of conflicting dreams. He did not understand his dreams and hardly remembered any details. He knew from the feelings in his gut that they were adverse in nature. As he made his way down the path to the outhouse the glow over the mountains to the east told him daylight would soon follow. Back in the cabin, he stoked the stove. Under the light of the lantern, he sat at the table and opened up the Bible Krystal had given him.

Finding the Gospel of John he started reading. For over an hour he read. So much he didn't understand. As the sun rose above the mountains it shined through the window brightly, lighting up the room. Ethan made a cup of coffee and went out to the front porch. The morning chill was still there, but the rising sun promised to drive it away.

Chapter Ten

The morning mist was still hanging over the pond as Ethan watched the single rider coming through the meadow. By the time Robert had dismounted and tied up his horse, Ethan had a cup of hot coffee on the table next to the rocking chair.

"Welcome to the mountain, boss."

"Thank you. Don't know if it's harder on me or the horse coming up here. But I sure like being here. Would move up here myself if it wasn't for my little lady. She won't hear of it. Say's it's too far away from her friends. Asked me why I wanted to move up here anyhow. I told her I wanted to move up here because it's a long way from her friends. Have to tell you, it got quiet around our place for a while. As you see, we don't live up here, cause she won."

That got Ethan laughing. "Probably for the best, boss. Somehow, I believe she knows how to handle you."

As they walked around the meadows, Robert went over the scope of Ethan's responsibilities. Besides keeping up the fences, he would need to monitor the water and protect the livestock from predators.

"Considering your lack of experience with livestock, it would be best for you to come down to the farm for a few days," Robert explained. "Getting acquainted with the animals will make your job easier once they move up here."

After being assured Ethan would be at the farm the next afternoon, Robert said goodbye and headed down the mountain. Ethan decided his first chore was to take stock of the contents of the tool shed. Opening up the creaking doors, he found it needed to be organized. He pulled everything out and took inventory. There were picks, shovels, posthole diggers, hammers, hand saws, hand drills, bits, and a toolbox with miscellaneous small tools. Besides the tools, there were nails and screws of all sizes. Next, he looked over the watering trough. The winter had been hard and the pipe filling the tank was leaking. By the time he finished repairing the leak and cleaning up around the trough, he was exhausted and ready for lunch.

Sitting on the front porch eating some bread and salt pork he watched the stream making its way down past the cabin. Studying the flow of the stream he came up with some landscaping ideas. He didn't know what Robert would think of him playing in the water, but just a couple of hours of moving some rocks would enhance his view.

Two, maybe three, hours later he sat back down on the rocking chair and admired the cascading waterfall from the rerouted water. Some of the rocks were a little heavier than he cared to move but playing in the icy water was worth it. Soon after sitting down, the sun dropped below Mount Bago, and the temperature dropped with it.

Ethan stoked up the fire in the stove and started heating water for a bath. He had not been out of civilization long and was already missing a good hot shower. After a so-called bath, he fixed a cup of coffee and returned to the porch to watch the evening sky.

Chapter Eleven

Ethan waited patiently from his secured position above the tool shed. Across his lap was his sniper rifle and on his waist his Beretta was ready. He continually searched the meadow and along the ridge to the north and east. It had been the flash of the evening sun reflecting off the binoculars that had given them away. He was certain that they were waiting for darkness to make their move. Once he could no longer see their outline, he lit the lanterns in the cabin and under the cloak of darkness made his way to a defensive position.

The flash of light in his night vision goggles was the first indication they were approaching the cabin. He could hardly believe it when they came into view. It was obviously not well-trained operatives as they had rifles slung over their backs and were using flashlights to illuminate the trail. The closer they got, the more certain he was that they were nothing more than low level gangsters thinking they were good enough to collect a reward. It was a given they were experts at locating him, but that's where their expertise ended.

Ethan found himself feeling sorry for these unsuspecting fools as they made their way across the stream. They had no idea what was about to transpire. He struggled with what he had to do. Too many verses in the Bible he had been reading had softened his heart. He was pretty sure this is not how Jesus handled these situations. Maybe he should just let these guys ransack his home and then leave when they didn't find him. He could live with that if he knew they wouldn't return. He knew that was not an option. They were here only for the money and prestige of being the ones who took him out. They had to be neutralized or his location would be compromised.

Ethan did a final check on the sniper rifle and got into position. He watched as one of the intruders came around to the back of the cabin. When he reached the back door, the hefty intruder used the stock of his rifle to bust the window. The sound of shattering glass broke the silence and verification that these were not good guys. Looking through the night vision scope, he placed the crosshairs on his target and slowly pulled the trigger. The muffled recoil sent minor shockwaves across the crater as fifty percent of the intruders lay crumpled by his back door.

Again, the night was silent as he maintained his position. The other intruder had to know that something had gone awry. He pulled up his night vision goggles and surveyed the area. Ten minutes later he still hadn't seen any sign of the other intruder. Something strange was going on. It had obviously become a game of cat and mouse. *That's fine,* Ethan told himself as he waited. It wasn't his first time he had to outwait the enemy.

Two hours had to have passed before he made his move. Keeping his night vision goggles down, he hung his rifle on his back, pulled out the Beretta and checked the silencer. Slowly he made his way around the west end of the cabin. As he approached a position where he could get a view of the front porch, he heard the rhythmic sound of an occupied rocking chair. Sure enough, there on the front porch sat the other intruder rocking away as if he didn't have a care in the world. *What arrogance!* Ethan thought as he flipped on the laser sight and dropped a red dot on the intruder's chest.

"Greetings Ethan, I wondered how long it would take. Was just about to take a nap, but didn't want to miss this moment."

Ethan froze. *How did this guy know he was there?* Keeping his goggles down and slowly approaching the intruder, he didn't respond. The intruder was up to something, and it would be best to let him reveal it. He stopped when the intruder raised his hands palms out showing that he was not armed. Ethan could now see a rifle and a handgun laying on the edge of the porch ten feet away.

"Do you mind lowering your Beretta? It's kind of making me nervous."

Ethan followed the intruder's request but kept his eyes focused on the rocking chair. *How does he know it's a Beretta? He's not an ordinary thug. Who is he?*

Slowly the intruder took off his hat and smiled at Ethan.

"Steven! What the......." Ethan was at loss for words.

"I was scared you were going to send me to the other

shore with that pea shooter. You haven't changed at all, old friend."

A thousand questions were rushing through Ethan's head as his old sniper buddy was speaking. Nothing was adding up. Apparently, Steven was not here to terminate an enemy, he could have done that all evening from their position on the side of the mountain. What about the guy that was growing cold on his back step?

"What are you doing here?"

"Looking for you."

"Why?"

"I don't know if you're aware of it, but you are a wanted man. On more than one front."

"I figured as much, but didn't expect company so soon. How did you find me?"

"Doesn't matter. What does is that Carlo's found you and recruited me to tag along. He's giving me forty percent to provide cover for his operation. Paid half in advance."

"So, who is he? Or should I say, who was he?"

"He comes from the syndicate in D.C. Has the nose of a bloodhound but that's where his intellect stops. They're not going to be happy when they hear about his tragic death."

"I don't get it?"

"Oh, I am an undercover agent for the FBI. We have been tracking you since you contacted me. That switch up you pulled was a good one. It took us some time to get back on your trail. When Carlos hacked into our system and got your information, we tracked him as well. When we caught him planning a trip out here, I just happened to meet him at a bar. After a couple of drinks and well-placed complaints about settling up scores, he hired me to come along. Needless to say, the word will get back to his people about his untimely demise falling off the trail.”

“So, do you have hopes of taking me in?”

“Why would I do that?”

“You work for the FBI. Isn’t that what they do?”

“Dude! The scum you terminated made this world a better place. You opened a Pandora box with your book, and after you pulled your medieval stunt, a lot of rats came running out of the sewers. We have now indicted over fifty politicians for fraud. That doesn’t mean you’re everyone’s friend. Your official case shows that you are still a wanted man.”

“What next?”

“We need to take care of some housecleaning, if you know what I mean, and then we’ll go over a few things before I get out of here.”

Two hours later they had disposed of the body and had cleaned up the evidence. Sitting at the kitchen table, Steven went over a list of things for Ethan to do and not do when in hiding. “So far I have been able to intercept all your intelligence and keep it in a protected file. I’m just afraid the day may come when it slips through. Just be careful.”

“What about Krystal and her children? Are they in danger?

“Ethan, stay focused. Now is not the time to be falling in love.”

“Are they?”

Steven stood up without answering and pulled on his backpack. Picking up his rifle he nodded to his friend, “I would like to sit and chat, but I need to get out of the area before daylight."

Ethan watched as the light from Steven's headlamp disappeared over the ridge.

Sudden exhaustion overtook his body, and he broke down. *What have I done?*

Chapter Twelve

A heavy frost lay across the meadow just waiting for the sun to rise above the mountain peaks. Ethan was on his way down the mountain to Abram's. Stopping at the top of the switchbacks, he watched as the sun cast its brilliance across the towering Mount Rixford. He deeply inhaled the cool morning air. Having spent too many hectic years in the belly of towering skyscrapers, it was going to take time for this to be normal.

Last night's events still weighed heavy on his heart. He was confident that he had taken out a criminal that was, for all indications, planning to kill him. Still, it was another life lost at his hands. Was he destined to always be a warrior? Could he change? Did he want to change? *I really need to find out who I am. If there is a God, I really need to hear from him.*

Ground squirrels scampered about as he passed the meeting house and somewhere close by a Mountain Chickadee welcomed the morning. *Sure beats the honking of horns on busy streets.*

"I thought you might show up early this morning. I just took the biscuits out of the oven." The aroma drifting out of the door confirmed Abram's statement and the crackle of the fire added to the already welcoming home.

"How well are you adjusting to the mountain?" Abram asked just as Ethan dove into his plate full of biscuits and gravy. "Any regrets?"

"Regret is what transpired in the first thirty-seven years of my life. The mountain is a welcomed distraction."

"I'm glad you feel like that. I will continue to pray for you in hopes that God will soften your heart,"

What's that supposed to mean? Am I hard hearted? If only he knew. Ethan just smiled at Abram and went about consuming his breakfast.

Chapter Thirteen

It was ten o'clock before Ethan arrived at the barn. Robert took one look at his new employee and sent him to the dry goods store. Walking up to the front door of the log structure he wondered how he had missed it on the tour. It was more than fifty yards from the greenhouse but was tucked back in the trees. Inside he found a fairly limited selection of hand-sewn clothes along with just about anything else a person needed to wear. Shelves of boots and shoes of different sizes lined one of the walls, while simple broad brimmed hats and bonnets were neatly displayed on tables and hung on hand crafted hall trees. Ethan was looking at a table piled high with plain colored fabric when a little girl crawled out from under it and ran into the back room hollering for her mother.

A short time later, the mother made her way out of the office and helped Ethan find what he was looking for. Coming out of the dressing room Ethan felt like a changed man. He didn't mind wearing simple home-sewn clothes.

Getting used to suspenders might take some time. He was surprised when they had muck boots his size. Walking away with a bag full of clothes, he still couldn't believe they were included in his residency. He was pretty sure his financial advisor would tell him something just didn't smell right.

"Now you look like a farmer," Robert said giving Ethan a big grin. "Next time you're there get a hat. The sun gets a little rough at this altitude. Let me introduce you to some animals."

First, it was the milk cows. "These are probably the most important of all the livestock. Naturally, they do not migrate up to the crater with the other animals."

"Do we do the milking?" Ethan asked with a concerned look.

"You don't sound too excited. You don't need to worry. There is a team that milks these girls twice a day and delivers the milk to the ice cave." The rest of the barn was filled with newborn calves and sheep.

On the north side of the barn was a large yard enclosed with chicken wire. Hundreds of chickens were busily pecking away at the ground. The netting stretched overhead told Ethan there must have been a challenge with large birds of prey helping themselves to the chickens. Beyond the chicken house was a fenced-in field where the cattle grazed with the mules and horses. A couple of braying donkeys took offense to a stranger in the field and started moving in their direction.

"That's Ricky and Lucy, they think you're a threat," Robert explained.

"Will they defend the livestock?"

"They will take on a coyote or a wild dog, but don't

care much for larger predators. Mainly they just make a racket when danger is lurking about."

Heading downstream along Charlotte Creek, it was obvious to Ethan that the trail was well used. Three more small fenced-in meadows were terraced along the creek before the mountains closed in on the valley. Each of the meadows was occupied by sheep and cattle.

The two men sat down on a boulder overlooking a waterfall where Charlotte Creek dropped rapidly into the gorge.

"Where does that go?" Ethan asked, looking down the narrow valley.

"It eventually runs into Bubb Creek."

"Not the creek, the trail?" Ethan clarified.

"Oh," Robert hesitated before responding, "Some things are better off being left unknown. Because of your position, you will witness men going down the trail in the morning and returning in the evening. Their job is essential to our existence and should not be questioned. In due time, and at the approval of our governing body, you will be told."

Curiosity peaked, Ethan knew he could not let it go, but for now, he wouldn't pressure his boss. It was time to head back to the barn. Some chores needed tending to.

All afternoon Ethan worked at mucking out horse stables. While he was happy to be productive, his thoughts were on the irony. *How did I go from being the author of a bestselling book to shoveling manure? Could it be, because I have alienated myself from society and now, I am paying the price? I can't change anything by lamenting about the past.*

The sun was cradling in the valley over Charlotte Creek when Ethan headed for home. Walking up the north side of the lake on the way to the hardware store he ran into Anna. She looked him up and down before stepping back and holding her nose. "Good afternoon. You must have just come from the farm?"

"Are you saying I may just be in need of a good bath?" Ethan asked feeling a little self-conscious. "I'm headed to the hardware store now in hopes of finding something to build a shower."

"I'll walk with you if you don't mind. I need to mail some letters," Anna held up a couple of envelopes while ignoring his shower question.

"There's a post office up here?"

"We call it a post office. The mule train takes it to Independence."

They walked along together making small talk as Ethan learned more about the community, and Anna got to know Ethan better. They said goodbye where the trail led up to the hardware store.

There wasn't an abundance of parts in the plumbing section. Thankfully, the mountain folks felt personal hygiene was a good thing. Ethan found the necessary parts to make his shower. Putting everything in a plastic five-gallon bucket, he made the twenty-minute hike up the mountain.

Getting a fire started in the stove, he put on a kettle of water to boil. While it was heating up, Ethan cut a hole in the bottom of the bucket and screwed in the adapter, next was the valve, and finally a showerhead. A hook screwed into a rafter on the back porch was perfect for his now completed contraption. For now, he would have to use the cook stove to heat the water. Once it got warmer, he would build a solar heater. A half-hour later the water was boiling on the stove. "At least the water's warm," he noted as the cool evening breeze brought a chill to his shower.

Chapter Fourteen

Ethan awoke to the sound of coyotes howling somewhere in the valley. It was still dark as he made his way out to the privy. The air felt different, and his instinct told him that weather was on its way. By the time he made it back into the house, the kettle was whistling that it was time for coffee. He read his Bible until he noticed the light coming in the window. With a second cup of coffee, he sat down on the front porch to watch the morning. As the sun continued its preparation for a grand appearance, the sky turned all kinds of red. *This is amazing,* Ethan thought. *I just read about discerning the signs of the sky. Red sky in the morning means it's going to be a rainy day.* The cold air blowing down off of Mount Bago made him think that it could be snow.

Before heading for the farm, Ethan brought firewood into the house and stacked more on the back porch. Just perchance, he packed his winter gear in his backpack along with a thermos of hot coffee. Leaving the cabin, he heard the short raspy song of a Western Tanager. "I'm sure you are aware of the incoming weather," he told a covey of quail as they ran down the trail in front of him. On the way down the switchbacks his eyes were drawn to the clouds towering over the mountains to the northwest.

As the day progressed everyone kept their eyes on the sky as the temperatures dropped. It was not uncommon at this altitude for storms to drop measurable snow long after the flowers had bloomed. The feeling in the air and watching the sky was the only source of weather forecasting in the settlement.

On the farm, they had planned on shearing the sheep, but with the oncoming storm decided that would just be mean. "Let the sheep keep their coats on for a couple more days," Robert told the farmhands. "Just clean up the barn and take the rest of the day to button up your homes."

As expected by those who had spent many years in the mountains, snowflakes started drifting to the ground by mid-morning. The men worked with urgency and within twenty minutes were ready to go. A freezing chill hit Ethan when he stepped out of the barn into blizzard conditions. He was not able to see more than twenty feet in the blowing snow.

"You sure you want to go up to the crater?" Robert asked.

"I don't see why not. It's just a snowstorm," Ethan answered as he tightened down the drawstring on his parka. "I'll be up there before it gets too deep. Do you know how long it's going to last?"

"You never can tell with these storms. It may be a day or two. Come on back down when you see the sunshine."

Once Ethan got into the trees the visibility improved. His surroundings were surreal as he walked along the pathway on the north side of the lake. Stopping briefly at the storehouse to pick up a package of meat and a quart of milk, he ran into Abram.

"Surely you're not heading up the mountain in this storm?" Abram asked.

"I'm on my way up there now."

Ethan grabbed Abram's bag and walked along beside him to his cabin. Sitting the groceries on the table, he noticed the concerned look on his mentor's face.

Abram shook his head, "Be careful. We've already lost two of our brothers this winter in a snowstorm. Hurry on now and may God go with you."

The wind was howling through the treetops as Ethan stepped out of the cabin. Shivering, he started questioning his sanity. As he exited the trees, the full force of the icy wind attempted to knock him off his feet. The visibility only worsened with the wind. He was only ten feet from the water before it came into view. The waves from the lake washed up over its shores. "Not a good day for going sailing," he said as his words disappeared into the storm.

Crossing over the footbridge he watched for Bago Crater Trail off to his left. The ground was completely covered with a couple of inches of snow already fallen. Ten paces past the bridge he was able to find the trail between the small flowering floras that were protesting the storm. Starting up the trail he had not gone far before the trail turned to the left and descended. He knew he was already going the wrong way. Just a few more yards brought him to a water tank. "If I miss my trail at this altitude, what's going to happen up ahead?"

Retracing his steps he finally found the trail leading uphill. By now he could only see a couple of steps in front of him, and everything was white. The going was a lot slower than normal as he had to search out every step staying between the bushes. After what he figured was about forty-five minutes, the trail leveled out and he knew he was close to the meadow.

When Ethan left the brush, the trail disappeared completely. He felt his way along as the blinding snow drove into his eyes. It was now about a foot deep covering all of the smaller rocks along the edge of the trail. He pushed on thinking he had to be following the trail. It wasn't until he stumbled over a rock that doubt struck him. His equilibrium told him he had turned south, so turning about fifteen degrees right he pushed his way through the snow for about ten minutes and started an abrupt climb.

"This hill is not on the trail," fear gripped Ethan as he found a rock and sat down. He didn't know if it was the near panic or the exerting energy, but even in this freezing cold, he was sweating profusely. *I should have listened to Robert. What made me think I knew what I am doing out here? I grew up in the city.*

The biting wind swirled around him as he slipped off the rock and laid back on his pack. Looking up into the monotone sky he sighed. *Wasn't I trained to survive?* All of a sudden, he felt very tired and warmth came over him. Slowly he felt as if he was going to sleep. *It's a long time before dark. A short nap would not hurt.* As if an alarm went off in his head he jumped to his feet. *My body is shutting down. I have to stay alert. Think, Ethan, think.*

He tried to retrace his steps but found them blown shut. He walked about twenty paces and didn't recognize anything. It was just a blinding nothingness. *I have to be in the crater, and it's not that big. Okay, shut your eyes just long enough to picture the crater.* He paused for a few seconds as he let his memory work in its hypothermic state.

"Follow the stream." He jerked his head around and could see nothing. Then he heard it again, like a voice speaking softly in his conscious, "Follow the stream."

Following the stream made sense but which way to the stream?

The still small voice spoke again, "A river flows through the valley."

In his delirious state, Ethan understood and continued down the slope. Sure enough, it was only about ten yards before the contrasting dark water of the flowing stream came into view. He struggled upstream along its banks for about a half-hour before he came to the stones he had strategically placed for his viewing pleasure. "Thank you, God," he hollered, trying to be heard above the storm. Even here he could not see the cabin, but he knew the direction and fifteen paces later he slammed the door behind him, shutting out the storm. Setting down his pack, he dropped to his knees and thanked God for bringing him home. Starting a fire in the stove, he went and found some warm, dry clothes before kindling a fire in the fireplace. An hour after being lost, he was sitting by the fire with a warm cup of tea.

The windowpanes rattled Ethan awake in the early morning hours. From the warmth of his bed, he listened to the never-ceasing wind whistling around the cabin. He felt safe. Deep down he knew this feeling was temporary as he could not stay wrapped up in this cocoon forever. He thought about what he had read the night before. Even though he had confidence that God would forgive him for assassinating his enemies, he was sure that the state of New York would not. The day would come when he would be required to plead his case to a jury, but for now, all he had to do was get out of bed and fire up the stove.

By the time the smoldering coals turned into a flaming heat source, Ethan had other challenges. Opening the back door, he was hit by a blast of wind, and he quickly stepped outside pulling the door shut behind him. *Oh for indoor plumbing*, he moaned as he pushed through two feet of snow to the outhouse. Necessity changed to pain when he got the snow cleared away from the door and found the outhouse did not have a heated seat.

Chapter Fifteen

On the third morning, Ethan crawled out of bed to an eerie silence. Opening the door, he found the temperature had risen significantly. Stars sparkled overhead and once again, he could see the glow of the predawn sky. Ethan was anxious to get out of the cabin and as the water heated on the stove he shoveled the melting snow off the front porch. By the time the sun rose above the mountains and reflected its blinding brilliance across the snow-covered landscape, Ethan was sitting on a rocking chair with a cup of coffee.

As the day warmed the melting snow from around the crater walls funneled into the upper meadow overflowing the stream. Ethan had planned on sloshing his way to the farm but was discouraged by the raging water between him and the trail. Giving up on going off the hill for the day, he started looking for projects to do around the cabin. He was intent on getting a safe place for his guns that were easily accessible in a time of emergency. He brought an old wooden crate in from the shed. Cleaning it up and building saddles to hold his weapons took the rest of the morning. *This looks like it was made for an arsenal,* Ethan told himself as he slid the cover over the crate. *But it looks out of place. I need to repurpose it to look like it belongs.*

Sitting back on his chair and propping his feet up on the box, it hit him. He looked through the cupboards until he found a tablecloth and spread it over the box. Strategically laying a few books on the tablecloth he stepped back and admired his new coffee table. *That should pretty much fool anyone.*

Ethan was just about to sit back down when he heard the sound of a lady screaming. His first thought was that it was a bobcat. But when he heard it again, he rushed to the front door knowing this was a woman for real. From the porch, he could see her lying face down in the turbulent stream. She was struggling to get up as she hung on to a rock, but the backpack she was wearing was just too much. Ethan didn't even stop to consider the temperature of the water or the danger of the current as he rushed into the water.

By the time he reached her, he was up to his waist in the freezing water, and it was all he could do to keep from being washed away himself. He had not experienced this much adrenaline since he had been in a firefight in Afghanistan. Getting his footing he grabbed the backpack and pulled the woman's face up out of the water.

Even soaking wet and spitting ice-cold water, he knew instantly that it was Anna. "What are you doing here," he asked dragging her to shore. He could not make out her answer as she seemed very disoriented and confused.

"You're freezing. We need to get you inside and warmed up before hypothermia sets in," thinking it may already be too late. He unhooked her backpack, dropping it on the ground. Anna let out a scream of pain as she tried to take a step. Picking her up, Ethan carried her into the house and set her down on a chair in his room. "You need to get out of those wet clothes," he told her as he handed her a blanket. "I'll make you some tea."

Shutting the door to the bedroom, Ethan put a couple of logs on the fire and then noticed that he was shivering from the cold pants and wet boots he was wearing. By the time he had his boots and wet wool socks drying by the cook stove, Anna hobbled out of the bedroom wrapped in a blanket. Shivering uncontrollably, she came to Ethan and threw her arms around him. "I thought I was going to die," she cried. Ethan held her tight until the shivering subsided and then helped her sit down by the fire. He pulled the coffee table over to her chair for a footstool. With her foot propped up on a pillow, Ethan could see it was already quite swollen.

"I'll be right back," he told her as he disappeared into the bedroom. By the time he had changed into dry clothes, the kettle was whistling. With hot tea in her hand, Ethan filled a plastic bag with crushed icicles and put it on Anna's ankle.

Finally, he was able to sit down and rest. "So, you still haven't told me what you're doing up here?"

The heat from the fire and the warm tea were enough to bring Anna back to her cheerful self. "At church this morning, I heard that you came back up here the night the storm started and that no one had heard from you since."

"So, you decided to do a dangerous thing and check on me?"

"But you have to understand. We have lived up here for a long time and are familiar with winter storms in the mountains."

"Just not experienced at crossing flooded streams?" Ethan asked with a hint of sarcasm.

"Ouch! You know how to hurt a girl," Anna hung her head.

"Sorry, but I just found you in a very precarious situation. You could have died. What happened?"

"First of all, I have had extensive training in wilderness survival and am very comfortable in all kinds of conditions. Everything went as expected on the climb. The switchbacks were the worst as the snow is still about two feet deep. Reaching the creek, I almost turned back but noticed the rocks were just far enough apart that I could get across. Stepping on the second one it rolled just enough to cause my ankle to twist. The next thing I knew I was face down in the water, holding on for dear life."

"You sure scared me. I haven't moved that fast in a long time."

"I'm sorry for getting you all wet, but thanks again for coming to my rescue,"

Anna's smile was disarming Ethan's resolve to not get emotionally involved with this young lady. She just had an undemanding guiltless personality that was driving him crazy. He had to keep up his guard. He watched her as she sipped her tea all wrapped up in the blanket with her now dry uncombed hair and her half-dry clothes hanging in front of the fireplace. Her feet propped up on his coffee table. She set her cup down on the hearth and laying her head against the bunched-up blanket and fell asleep.

How his heart had ached for companionship as she had shared her love for God. He hardly heard what she had been saying as his desire to have someone to share his life burned within him. He just knew it wasn't meant to be. He could tell by the deepening shadows on the window that the day was long spent. It would be extremely dangerous to adventure out into the night with the stream crossing still roaring and the trail covered with snow. Even if his boots were dry, they would get wet again crossing the stream. He knew the answer but did not want to ask the question. She had ignored it, maybe out of desire, maybe out of fear. He knew what had to be done. He let her sleep and stepped out onto the porch to watch the twilight turn into darkness.

Looking up into the night sky, Ethan stared at the Milky Way's broad slosh across the sky. The new moon allowed the millions of stars to wash out the constellations.

Ethan didn't know how long he had been out there when he heard the door open behind him. Anna hobbled out onto the porch still wrapped in the blanket and sat down on the other rocker. "Sorry I fell asleep in there. I must have been tired."

"Yes, you were. You have been through a lot today, but now we're in a pickle. Do you realize you're going to have to spend the night here?"

"I can't go anywhere like this. What are we to do? What will the folks in the village say when they find out I stayed up here with you?"

"They're your people. What will they say?"

Anna did not respond. Ethan could tell she was thinking more about the reaction of the commune than the answer to their dilemma. He offered a solution, "While both of us must stay here tonight, we do not have to act inappropriately. Even in the short time, we have known each other, I have become quite fond of you. Because of that, I need to keep our relationship clear of any regret or even the appearance of wrongdoing. I have been out here thinking it over and have a solution. You will sleep in my bed and I will spend the night out here in my sleeping bag."

"I can't do that to you. What about in front of the fireplace? You can sleep there."

"No, I will be just fine out here, and in the morning, I will go down to the village for help. You had better get to bed before I change my mind."

Anna gave Ethan a sad face as she stood up and started for the door. As she passed him, she grabbed his hand. Leaning down she kissed him quickly on the cheek. "Good night, I'm starting to like you."

When Ethan went in to get his sleeping bag, Anna was fast asleep. After stoking up the fire he extinguished the lamps and stepped back outside. The screech of an owl somewhere in the meadow pierced the night as the rugged wood floor reminded him of how blessed he was to have a bed. He was lulled to sleep only by the water splashing over the rocks.

Ethan awoke to the smell of frying bacon. The sun had not come up, but he could see light from the lanterns flickering through the window. His hunger for the bacon overcame his desire to stay wrapped up in the warmth of the sleeping bag.

"Good morning," Anna greeted Ethan as the rusty hinges announced his entrance. She didn't even turn around from frying pancakes at the cook stove. "Did you sleep well?"

Ethan had no idea whether to laugh or make some smart remark. He decided to be nice and ignore the question. "Good morning, Anna. How does your ankle feel this morning?"

"It feels like a truck ran over it. I did rummage through your cupboards and found some Ibuprofen. At least the swelling is starting to go down. Are you hungry?"

"Now there's a question I can answer," Ethan whispered as he reached his arm around her and grabbed a piece of bacon. She tried to smack his hand with the spatula, but he was just a little too quick. Anna's face was blushing as she spun around and grabbed his arm. "I am so sorry. I shouldn't have done that."

With the biggest grin on his face as he chewed the bacon, Ethan kissed her on the cheek. "Payback," he said turning her back around. "You don't want to burn the pancakes." He sat down at the kitchen table with his cup of coffee and watched her finishing breakfast. *Is this a possibility?* he asked himself. *Would it work?* He could just not do that to her. Not without her knowing his past. She deserved a man without the baggage he carried.

"What are you thinking about?" she asked him as they sat quietly eating breakfast.

"I'm thinking about getting across the stream. It still looks dangerous and with the temperature getting warmer it will not go down anytime soon."

"You mean we're stuck here together forever? That's okay with me," she said with a smile.

"Easy for you to say, you slept in a comfortable bed." Ethan didn't take the bait that Anna was tossing out. He decided instead to ignore it in hopes that it would go away. Anyhow his mind was on finding a solution.

After getting Anna to promise she would get off her feet as soon as the dishes were washed, Ethan headed outside to survey the situation. He walked upstream a couple of hundred yards and found nothing promising. Looking up into the crater he tossed around the idea of walking around the meadow. The deeper snow at the higher altitude discouraged that idea. Sloshing back past the cabin in the rapidly melting snow he started downstream with little hope. Just before the stream dropped off into the lower meadow, it narrowed to only about ten feet across. *If only I had some lumber I could build a bridge,* he thought as he sat down on a boulder watching the stream disappear over the ledge. *Why does something so beautiful have to be so difficult to overcome?* "Are you talking about the raging stream or Anna?" A still small voice answered. Ethan rolled his eyes and walked back to the cabin.

Anna was in her chair with her foot elevated on his favorite pillow. *Oh, she's driving me crazy.* He sat back in his chair with a feeling of helplessness.

"You look defeated," Anna said. "What's the verdict?"

"It just doesn't look good until the water goes down. I did find a place downstream where we could build a bridge if we had the lumber. I looked around, and we have nothing."

"Why not fall a tree across the stream?" Anna asked. "Are there any dead ones near the stream?"

Ethan shut his eyes for a moment before visualizing a two-foot diameter tree that the lightning had struck. It may just work. "That is an awesome idea. I may not have to sleep on the porch tonight after all." He jumped up and headed outside.

Twenty minutes later Ethan was struggling to learn the proper use of an ax as the chopping sound echoed throughout the crater. Stopping to catch his breath he noticed Anna sitting on the porch. Her presence added stress to his lumberjack debut, but finally, he hollered "timber" as the dead pine tree crashed across the stream. Anna's weak attempt to applaud did not escape Ethan's ears.

Anna was still on the porch when Ethan came out of the cabin with his backpack and a couple of trekking poles. "I thought these might help, considering the trail condition. You be careful up here. Go inside and keep that foot up. I'll return as soon as I can." He could see tears swelling up in the corner of her eyes. "What's wrong?"

"I'm just confused, Ethan. I think I'm falling in love with you."

He didn't answer but leaned down and gave her a gentle kiss on the cheek before heading for the settlement. Slowly putting one foot in front of the other he steadied his shaky knees as he inched his way across the log. Looking only at the log, his peripheral vision could see the rushing water underneath. For some reason he silently talked to God as he worked his way to the other side.

Back on the trail, Ethan sloshed his way down the switchbacks. By the time he got to Charlotte Lake, the trail was clear of snow and covered with mud. The crater stream had doubled in size and was splashing over the bridge. He took the trail to the left and headed around the south side of the lake for Doctor Winston's.

Chapter Sixteen

"**I don't think** I'm capable of making it up that trail," Doctor Winston told Ethan. "I do think it would be a good idea if you take one of Anna's friends. It would free you up to get some work accomplished and squelch any rumors that tend to float around."

"That's a good idea. How do I go about finding her friends?"

"My wife will find someone. Do you have any more stops to make before heading home?"

"I need to check in with my boss and would like to speak with Abram."

"We'll have your help meet you at Abram's."

Heading on around the south side of the lake, he came to where the lake discharged into Charlotte Creek. It was over its banks, and definitely not crossable. *I didn't think this one through.* Retracing his steps back around the lake, he stopped at the dry goods store and picked up a bedroll. It wasn't very thick, but he figured something is better than nothing. His next stop was the hardware store where he found a good thick tarp and some rope. It would be perfect for making a shower enclosure on the back porch.

Not much was going on at the farm other than a couple of the men who were cleaning up from the storm. He left word for Robert that he would return in the morning and headed for Abram's.

"Well, thank God," Abram responded to Ethan's news about Anna. "When she didn't return home yesterday, it had us all concerned. She is a very strong woman but doesn't always make the right choices. She must really care for you to do such a dangerous thing." His smile made Ethan's face turn red.

"She may, but one night sleeping on the porch is enough."

"You did the right thing, Ethan. I commend you for making that decision. I'm sorry to say, but as much as we try, our community doesn't do well with rumors. Sleeping on the porch last night is a message to our people that you are indeed a godly man."

Anna's friend, Sandra, arrived loaded down with a heavy backpack. "Sorry, it took so long. I stopped by Anna's for a few of her things."

Once they crossed the bridge and started the climb the trail became a real mess. The wet slushy snow penetrated their boots, and Sandra was floundering. *This could take all day*, Ethan watched her struggle. After about ten painful minutes with minimal progress, Ethan gave Sandra his trekking poles. The poles created stability, but the going was still extremely slow. Halfway there, Ethan began to question whether they would get to the cabin before the sun disappeared behind the mountain. By the time they got to the lower meadow, Sandra was exhausted and on the verge of tears. "I don't know if I can make it," she moaned as she dropped her backpack and sat down on a wet rock.

"We have to keep going," Ethan tried to give her hope. "We only have a quarter of a mile and there's not much more climbing."

Sandra looking down the trail wasn't convinced, "But the snow looks deeper in the meadow."

"Just follow my tracks. Come on, I'll carry your pack. Let's go." Ethan grabbed Sandra's pack and threw it over his shoulder. "Wow! No wonder you're struggling. What do you have in here, rocks?"

"It's just our clothes for a couple of days, and a few other items."

Ethan was pretty sure it was more than just a few items. Heading up the trail not looking back, he had confidence Sandra would follow. As they approached the stream crossing the temperature had dropped significantly and the sun was about to disappear behind Mount Bago.

"I am not going to walk across that," Sandra said with a tone of determination.

"Exactly how do you plan on getting to the other side?"

The silence behind him gave him his answer as he turned his concentration to the balancing act of crossing the log just inches above the rapids. *At least this time it's dry. The added unbalanced weight of this pack doesn't help.*

Reaching the other side, he dropped Sandra's pack and unhooked his. He needed to be ready in case a rescue became necessary. As Sandra started shuffling over the log,

Ethan watched intently. She was shaking way too much. If she went in, he would have to react quickly, or she would go over the falls and that could hurt. He did not need two women laid up in his cabin. She wasn't even a third of the way across when he saw her go.

It was like in slow motion as Sandra's right foot slipped off the upstream side of the log. She overcompensated, her weight shift causing her to fall to the left. Her left foot followed her right, and she fell on her stomach across the log as the trekking poles went flying. With the air being knocked out of her lungs, her scream was without sound.

Ethan was already two feet deep in the water before he realized she was hanging onto the log. He froze as Sandra hung on with all she had while her lungs were struggling to fill with air. Slowly she regained her ability to move and slowly scooted on the log until she reached the far side.

"I am not happy," she whined as she rubbed her sternum. "That hurt."

By this point, Ethan was not sure if Sandra was going to be a help or a hindrance. At least with her there to protect him from Anna, he could sleep inside. "I see Anna has a fire burning. Let's get you inside where you can warm up and rest."

It didn't take Ethan five minutes with the two women before he started thinking of ways to get them home. *And the pendulum swings the other way,* his thoughts went back to the days it was too quiet in the cabin. He let the girls go about fixing dinner and headed out to the back porch. The wind had picked up, causing a challenge with the tarp, but by the time dinner was ready, he had created a fairly airtight room. It would still be cold, but they would get by.

It was Ethan's first experience eating rabbit. But after spending all afternoon climbing the mountain in the snow, any kind of stew would have been good. After dinner, at Anna's request, Ethan filled the shower with warm water and found solace on the front porch while the ladies took their showers. He thought of the evenings he would be sitting in the living room watching television and his wife would be giving their daughters baths. It was supposed to calm them down and get them ready for bed. It instead seemed to make them rowdy. As always, he wished things to go back to the way they were back then.

He heard the door open, and Anna hobbled out wrapped in a warm fleece robe.

"Thank you for building the shower. It sure feels good to get washed up and put on clean clothes."

"How is your ankle doing?

"It's doing better. Sandra brought me some pain medicine from the doctor and this ankle brace." Lifting her foot showed Ethan a wrapped-up ankle.

"We need to get you back to the settlement as soon as we can," Ethan told her in a matter-of-fact tone.

"No hurry on my part. I'm starting to like it up here."

"That's the problem, Anna. I'm starting to like you being up here."

Anna reached over and grabbed his hand, and they rocked in silence.

The squeak of the door caused them to drop each other's hand just in time for Sandra to join them on the porch. It became evident that the girls had a lot in common and soon the conversation quickly left Ethan far behind. It didn't take long before the cold night air moved them back into the cabin.

Long after the girls had gone to bed, Ethan watched the fire burn. He was a little disturbed by Sandra, knowing that taking care of Anna was not her sole purpose for being here. Her primary responsibility was to run interference. That was probably a good thing. He did not come here looking for a companion and it would be best if he didn't find one. As soon as the flames flickered away, Ethan made his bed on the floor and tried to get some sleep. The wind whistling outside reminded Ethan that sleeping on a pad inside the cabin was a whole lot better than on the porch.

For the next two days as the snow continued to melt, Ethan made the trek down to the farm. He didn't know if they needed him on the farm or if it was to get out of the house. The animals on the farm were much easier than the cabin guest.

"We have to do something," he told Robert. "I'm going crazy up there. Do you have any ideas?"

Robert rubbed his shaggy beard for a few seconds, "Has the creek gone down enough for the horses to cross?"

"I'm not an expert at what low enough is, but it has started going down. There's just no way Anna can walk down the mountain."

"Okay, here's the deal. With the colder temperatures at night, the stream will be at its lowest first thing in the morning. I'll be up there at sunrise with the horses, and we can bring them back down. Can you have them ready to go?"

"That early in the morning," Ethan laughed, "One of

them, well, actually they both will complain, but they'll be ready."

Ethan got mixed responses when he told the girls the plan over dinner.

"Can't we wait until it warms up?" Sandra asked.

"Only if you want to cross the log again," he ribbed her knowing she never wanted to set foot on that thing again.

"I have decided I'm staying up here permanently," Anna's underlying tone indicated she wasn't kidding.

This was one of those times Ethan was glad Sandra was there, "We all know that's not happening. I'm tired of sleeping on the floor."

Anna joined Ethan on the porch just as the moon rose from behind Kearsarge Peak. She scooted her rocking chair over next to Ethan and grabbing his arm laid her head on his shoulder. Her forwardness was probably not one that would be appreciated by the elders in the settlement, but obviously her emotions could care less. They sat there in silence watching the moon continue its climb. The few wispy clouds that tried to hide it were soon blown away. The hoot of the owl above was competing with the coyotes down in the valley. In the moon's glow, they could see the stream had gone down significantly and the waterfalls that Ethan had built were again visible.

"Do I really have to go?" Anna asked.

"Don't tease me, Anna. You know the answer."

"I'm sure it's too soon to ask, but is there hope for us?"

Ethan wanted so much to take her in his arms and assure her they could be together forever but knew that wasn't so. "Only God knows that answer. I think we need to give our friendship time to mature."

She squeezed his arm tighter to her, and he could feel her disappointment that he had resisted emotions and embraced reality.

Chapter Seventeen

Ethan was sitting on the porch drinking his coffee when he caught sight of the horses coming through the meadow. Even though the night was cool the snow had pretty much melted off the lower meadow. And once again the birds were chirping about the spring weather in the high mountains. The door squeaked behind him and the girls came out chirping as much as the birds. Sandra sat down in the empty rocker as she complained about having to get up early. Ethan looked up at Anna, who stood there on her bad ankle with a million-dollar smile. *What a difference between these two friends.* He immediately got to his feet and helped Anna to his chair. Her squeeze of his hand was a sure sign of appreciation. He went into the cabin and returned with their packs just as Robert was crossing the creek.

Swinging off his horse, Robert tied both horses to the rail, "Not heading back until somebody gets me a hot cup of coffee."

Ethan looked back at the girls. Sure enough, Anna was trying to get to her feet while Sandra sat tight. "Sit back down, Anna. I'll get it." He returned shortly with a steaming cup, "It was the bottom of the pot, I hope you like grounds."

"A real cowboy eats coffee grounds and spits out the bones," Robert said gruffly as he sat down on the edge of the porch. "Give the horses a rest and we'll be ready."

They visited, or at least the men sat there and listened to the girls talk about everything mountain women talk about. Watching the creek rising, Robert finally broke up their blabbering, "We need to get on the other side of this creek before we get stuck up here." He stood up and started tying the girls' packs to the horses. "Ethan, you take ol' Sawdust here with Anna, and Sandra can ride with me. She'll listen pretty well as long as you let her know whose boss."

"Are you talking about ol' Sawdust or me?" Anna asked as she was up and hobbling towards the steps. Robert was smart enough not to say anything, just nodded his head.

Ethan, seeing Anna trying to make it down the steps, picked her up and swung her up onto their horse. Her response of glee was not missed by her friend, who stopped on the steps waiting to be swept up onto her steed as well. Robert didn't take the bait as he swung up on the horse. Looking down at Sandra standing on the steps looking hopeful, "Your ankle's not hurt. Are you riding or walking?" Sandra mumbled under her breath as she crawled up on the horse behind Robert.

With Anna's arms wrapped around him, it was not easy for Ethan to concentrate on the trail. He needed to get her home and get to work. He had a lot of things he needed to think about, and it did not involve a relationship with her. He really wanted to learn more about this thing called faith. He needed to read more about forgiveness. He had already read about love but was pretty sure it was not this kind of love. At the bridge, Ethan and Anna left the other two and headed for Doctor Winston's.

"Head up this trail," Anna pointed at a trail leading to a small cabin. "This is my place."

Reacting instead of thinking, Ethan followed her command and so did the horse.

"Don't you think you should see the doctor?"

"Yes, I should, but I wanted to show you where I live so you can stop by and see me. Not only that but we can drop off my stuff."

Ethan helped Anna down from the horse but did not carry her to her house. He did let her hold his arm as she led him up to the door. Stopping at the door he turned her to face him. "Anna, I cannot go in there with you. It would just be too dangerous."

Anna grabbed his neck and kissed him before he could react. Pulling back, she smiled, "You're right, we should go."

Ethan swung Anna back on the horse and grabbed the reins. "I'll walk her from here on," he said as he led the horseback down the trail.

Doctor Winston came out of the door as Ethan was helping Anna down off the horse. "I wondered when you would arrive. Thanks for taking care of her, Ethan. We'll get her home once we make sure nothing is broken."

With a cordial goodbye, Ethan swung up on Sawdust for the ride around the lake. Mixed feelings bugged him as he rode. Even though he would miss her company, the last thing he needed was the added responsibility it entailed. Meeting a few folks along the trail he tipped his hat, and they called him by name. He hoped that someday he would get to know them all as well as they thought they knew him. With that, a new fear started to build within him.

Chapter Eighteen

Was it possible that others would find him? He pondered the thought. His knowledge of just how deep the tentacles of the underworld had penetrated the deep state was a real concern. The fact that he had dealt judgment on three of their operatives, and a fourth one disappeared while looking for him, would create a scare within their ranks. They would do everything they could to hunt him down.

His thoughts turned to the safety of the settlement. Unbeknown to this generous God-fearing people, they had welcomed danger into their camp. Based upon Steven's information, he would devise a contingency plan just in case his whereabouts became known. To do that he knew he needed up-to-date information from the outside.

By the time he rode into the barnyard, he had conceived of a plan. He was aware that his plan was in deviation from the ordinances of the commune, but considering that he lived outside the settlement, he justified his plan for the sake of their safety. He still had a few more days helping on the farm before he could proceed. *I'll just have to have faith that their God will protect them. What is the balance between trusting God and devising a plan for the settlement's protection?* He would have to ask Abram that 'hypothetical' question.

The warm sunny day brought life to the valley as the snow continued to melt at a record pace. The lake was full and overflowing as it rushed down Charlotte Creek causing a continuous roar as it dropped into the ravine below the pasture. Working alone on the fences alongside the creek gave Ethan time to reflect on his past and plan for the future. While he enjoyed his time working on the farm, being in the community was not ideal. He looked forward to spending more time in the crater.

The cabin was quiet when he returned home. Sandra was not there to aggravate him and Anna was not there to play with his emotions. Crawling into his bed he let out a sigh, Oh, *it feels good to sleep in a bed.* A scent that had become too familiar hit him. He let out another sigh as he realized it was from Anna's shampoo, *I just can't win.* As his hand slid under the pillow he felt a piece of paper. Pulling it out, he questioned if it was worth lighting the lantern to read. He laid it on the nightstand and tried to go to sleep. Wonder soon drifted into curiosity, which turned to concern and then boiled into anxiety. Finally, he got up and lit the lantern.

He read it twice. Each time shaking his head and asking himself how he could get so involved with a woman in so short of time. He had to put a stop to this before it got out of hand. At least now he knew she was madly in love with him.

For the next few days, Ethan pretty much kept to himself, deliberately staying away from Anna in hopes that she would find greener pastures.

Chapter Nineteen

As he descended the trail to church on Sunday morning, he questioned how he would be accepted. How many rumors had flown around this week about him and Anna? Walking into the clearing in front of the meeting house, he still felt like an outsider, and justifiably so. It was only his third time at the church meetings, and he still only could name a dozen of the church members. He tried to avoid Anna, but she would not have it. All through the meeting, he could see her glancing at him with her seductive smile. He had to stop looking at her and concentrate on the sermon.

As soon as the service was over, Ethan headed for the door, only to be stopped by a couple of ladies who wanted to get to know him better. "We want to let you know how much we appreciate how well you took care of our Anna," one of the ladies told him. "We were so concerned when we heard she was up there with you, being a stranger and all."

Ethan had no idea how to respond to the statement, so

he kept quiet and let them ramble on for a couple of minutes, but unfortunately, that was too long. As he turned to head on out the door, Anna and her crutches were in his path. She grabbed his hand and held on, "Don't think you're getting away without talking to me."

Ethan lowered his eyes and softly responded to her demand, "I really am afraid of our relationship Anna. I thought it best if we didn't see each other for a few days. How is your ankle doing?"

"It would be doing better if I had someone to walk me home," she answered with raised eyebrows.

Ethan shook his head, "You're relentless."

"Please!"

"People will talk."

"I don't care," Anna said as she started for the door.

"Alright, I'll walk with you only to your door. Not a step more."

Anna smiled as she glowed in her victory. "You sure you don't want to have a bite of lunch before you head home? You know I'm a good cook."

"Yes, I do want to eat lunch with you. I want to spend all day with you. I want to spend the rest of my life with you, but we talked this over. It's not going to happen." He gave her the meanest look he possibly could without making her cry. "Anyhow, I told you not a step more."

No more was said about Ethan sticking around. And as soon as they got to her door, he told her goodbye and headed for home. He hadn't gotten far when he met Eli coming at him. The first thing that crossed his mind was that Eli had followed them to see if he could catch them doing something wrong. Just the thought of that caused his blood to boil. Assuming the worst, he took the offensive.

"Good afternoon, Eli. Where are you headed this Sunday afternoon? Shouldn't you be at home with your family?"

Eli stammered a bit as his face flushed. "I'm just out taking care of some church business before going home." Then trying to turn the tables asked, "Where are you headed? Your path home doesn't go this way?"

If he wasn't so angry, Ethan would have laughed. "Has your church business have anything to do with a young, crippled lady that needed assistance getting home, and no one from your church was willing to help?"

Red-faced Eli shot back, "I'm assuming you're talking about Anna. I have you know, she has been one of ours for a long time. Don't you think you can come in here and take advantage of her."

In less than a second Ethan grabbed Eli by his Sunday go to meeting shirt and had him up against a tree. "One more baseless accusation from you, and I'll give you something to talk about. That is, once you're able to talk." Dropping Eli to the ground he continued. "The hypocrisy you portray is not a real drawing card. You know as well as I do that I have never, nor will I, take advantage of Anna. It might do you some good to show a little humility. If you know what that word means."

Eli realized he had been caught and quickly knew he needed to defuse the situation. Hanging his head he confessed. "Yes, I was following you. Please understand, with many rumors flying around the community since the storm, we have to be cautious. The Christian thing to do would have been for me to talk to you and Anna and gain a better understanding of what's going on. Instead, I followed you thinking the worst. Ethan, I understand why you are angry. Please forgive me for doubting your integrity."

Ethan looked down at Eli who had totally surrendered. At that moment, Ethan understood what it was to be a true Christian. Following Jesus did not mean that you would never make mistakes. You are still human and are susceptible to error.

"I do forgive you Eli. I'm sorry for messing up your shirt. I should not have lost my temper." Reaching down he offered Eli a hand to pull him up. "You do have a right to protect your people. I will do my best to avoid, what Abram says 'Is even the appearance of evil'"

Eli stretched out his hand and gladly accepted Ethan's gesture of peace.

Chapter Twenty

By the end of the second week, Robert told Ethan he no longer was required to come to the farm every day. "Spend your time over these next two weeks getting things ready for the summer. We will transfer the livestock as soon as the grass has grown enough to sustain them."

On the way home, he stopped by the storehouse and ordered enough food to last for a couple of weeks. He wanted to stay away from the settlement as much as possible. He stopped by the post office and sent a note to Anna before heading up the trail. Arriving in the meadows, he was happy to see the snow was gone and the grass was starting to grow. It wouldn't be long before the fields would be full of grazing animals. He had to get busy.

It took Ethan two days to walk the fences and make the necessary repairs. On the third day, he fixed leaks in the irrigation system caused by the winter freeze. Each afternoon when the sun would disappear behind the mountain he would sit on the porch and watch the wildlife become active around the crater. These quiet evenings brought peace and contentment. He just wished the underlying ball that kept knotting up in his stomach would go away. He knew where it came from, and inaction would not fix it. Just maybe God is real and would help him. He knew his time here in the settlement, whether it was for the summer or ten years, was only temporary. As Orion became visible above University Peak, he said goodnight to the stars and went inside. Before going to sleep he prepared his backpack for the next morning. He wanted to get an early start.

Chapter Twenty-One

The wind-up alarm on his nightstand banged out an awful sound, and Ethan quickly silenced the annoying rattle. Slipping out of bed in the dark he struck a match and soon the lantern illuminated the room. Not wanting to wait on the wood stove, he used his backpacking stove to boil some water. A cup of instant coffee later, he was crossing the log and heading down the trail. He limited the use of his headlamp in fear of someone in the settlement getting curious about his activities that early in the morning. Fortunately, by the time he came around the corner in view of the settlement, he no longer needed assistance in following the trail.

At the top of the switchbacks instead of heading down to the settlement, he left the trail and made his way along the contour line towards an intercept with Kearsarge Trail. Three hundred yards into the cross-country trek he questioned this decision. It was rugged and boulder hopping in the predawn light was a little unnerving. A mile later he was on the trail and was able to pick up speed. With a light pack, he made good time and met the sun at Kearsarge Pass. Looking at his watch he figured he would be at the trailhead by ten.

Ethan stopped for a brief rest and water at Gilbert Lake. Just as he hoisted his pack, a young couple with an overactive dog came down the trail. They were the friendly type, willing to share more about themselves than ask questions. That was okay with Ethan. He didn't care to devolve any more information about himself than necessary. By the time they made it to the trailhead, Ethan had his ride to Lone Pine.

It was only eleven a.m. when they dropped him off at the Lone Pine Mobil station. He watched them drive away before going inside for an ice-cold soda. That was definitely, something missing up on the mountain. Even though he had scored big time coming down the mountain, he still needed to get home before dark. He wasted no time in getting to the self-storage.

Opening the box, he pulled a few bills out of an envelope. He may not need it in the mountains, but nothing was free down here. He briefly turned on his tablet to verify the battery power before shutting it down. Besides his tablet, he added his hand-held two-way radio and scanner to his backpack. It would come in handy in the mountains if they were being attacked.

Leaving the storage unit, he made his way to the Alabama Hills Cafe. Finding a table by the window with a power outlet nearby, he wasted no time in getting logged into the internet. He had been spending too much time thinking about Krystal and her children. It had only been a few weeks. It was surprising how much things could change in that amount of time. He wanted to get a message to her. He was surprised at how much junk was in his email. He sorted through the junk and found two messages from Krystal. The first one was an acknowledgment of receiving his email and how thankful she was that he was taking the Bible. The second was only a few days old.

Dear Ethan, I pray that you will get this before it's too late. This morning we had visitors from the FBI. They want to know where you are. They have pictures of us together at the train station. I was so afraid they were going to arrest me. I told them everything I knew. Fortunately, I have no idea where you might be. The children and I spend a lot of time praying for you. You were such a blessing to us, and we will never forget you.

Ethan's emotions overwhelmed him to think of the ready-made family he could have had. She had such a strong yet gentle spirit and would have made an incredible companion. He chuckled about the FBI. Sometimes the right hand doesn't know what the left hand is doing.

He typed out a reply.*Dear Krystal, I am sorry for involving you in my run from the law. I pray, and yes, I said pray, for you and the children's safety. I am not as concerned about the FBI, as I am of the associates of those that murdered my family. They have their tentacles deep within the agencies. If they find out about you, they could try to hunt you down as well. Please stay safe and keep your eyes open. I will not give you my address for your safety. I miss the short time we had together and hope that someday we can meet again. Please give my love to the children.*

After pushing send, Ethan verified it had been sent

and shut down his email. Next, he searched to see what was out there referencing his crime. There was an overwhelming amount of information on the search engines and for the next hour, he read as he ate his lunch.

Heading down to the post office he was relieved to find a couple of boxes waiting for him. Next stop was the sporting goods store where he picked up a couple of new trekking poles. Walking across the street to the park he found a table close to a small stream. A birthday party was going on in a picnic shelter and a handful of kids were on the playground equipment. It looked like a good place to empty the boxes into his backpack.

Opening the boxes it looked like it had been sent directly from the FBI's espionage laboratory. Most of the items were things that he and Steven had discussed, but a few were flat out strange. A note from Steven was taped to a user manual. He pocketed the note and went about packing all the items into his backpack.

He was about done when three rough cut young men crawled out of a beat-up low rider and walked into the park. Ethan did not miss that they were talking trash. Instinctively he reached around his shirt and felt the cold steal of the Beretta. *Never can be too safe.* He shoved the remainder of the items in his pack. Hoisting the pack on his back, he headed for the exit. The three who had been just meandering around the park took up a heading to intercept him. Ethan's gut feelings told him they were up to no good, and he reached behind his waist and gripped his weapon and flipped off the safety.

Stopping fifteen feet short, he addressed the trio, "Good afternoon gentlemen, enjoying your day?"

The shortest one and the obvious leader of the gang showed a few missing teeth when he smiled at Ethan. "It's going to be enjoyable when we relieve you of that weight on your back." Pulling his shirt tail to the side revealed a little pistol sticking out of his baggy pants.

"That's alright guys, I appreciate your concern, but I'm okay carrying it. Say, you wouldn't mind giving me a ride up to Bishop?"

"You don't get it. You can either hand over the backpack, or I'll have to make a lot of racket and scare the kids." The would-be thief put his hand on the top of his gun and turned to his buddies laughing. As soon as shorty started to pull the gun from his waist, Ethan had the Beretta at full extension and the tone of his voice meant business in a language the trio could understand. "Drop it now!"

The pea shooter fell to the ground as all three stepped back and raised their hands. This had not been preplanned, and Ethan had no idea what his next move would be. *I need to get out of town fast.* He looked around the park, and people were staring and backing off. "Throw me your keys."

With keys in hand and the trio face down on the grass, he backed his way toward their car. He had just opened the door when the sound of a gunshot coincided with the ping of a bullet shattering the window next to Ethan's elbow. In less than a second, he spun around and located his target and pulled the trigger. Not waiting for verification of results, he jumped in the car and slammed the door. The engine roared to life, and he departed the crime scene.

Fifteen minutes later he parked the car in the handicap spot at the Inyo County Sheriff's Department and walked away. He had to get to the mountain quickly. Dropping his backpack on the sidewalk at the Mobil station, he worked the patrons in hopes of getting a ride to the trailhead. In this part of the country, a backpack and trekking poles would get you a ride, especially if you looked like a seasoned hiker.

It was much later than he had hoped for when he thanked the family for giving him a ride. They were nice enough and wanted to hear stories of his backpacking adventure. He thought about telling them some grandiose story but didn't fccl right tclling outright lies. So, he just told them he had just taken up backpacking and hadn't experienced too much.

It was early evening when he crossed Kearsarge Pass and the sun was getting close to the mountain peaks on the other side of the valley. Climbing over the hill just past the Pacific Crest Trail, he looked down on Charlotte Lake. What a well-organized peaceful place. He did not want to go back the way he came and at the same time wanted to stay away from the settlement. He was not interested in explaining where he had been. "Maybe there is such a thing as guilt," he told the marmot that watched him with curious eyes.

Halfway to the lake, the rocky boulders cleared out, and the terrain became much easier to navigate. Crossing the log with shaky legs, he was again reminded of the need to flatten the top of the foot bridge. Dropping his backpack, he flopped down in his chair exhausted. It had been a long day.

Chapter Twenty-Two

Ethan slept well that night and woke to the sound of the birds acknowledging the predawn morning. It was getting warmer, and he only needed to fire the stove for cooking. After all the years he spent cooking with an electric oven and a microwave, it was still a challenge to get used to this primitive way of living. He tested his satellite radio and was pleased to hear the news channels coming in loud and clear. He indulged himself with a few minutes of listening to an oldies channel before shutting it down and stowing it and the rest of the electronic equipment in the crate.

Today, he planned to climb to the top of Mount Bago just to get an overview of the surrounding area. When his world started caving in, he wanted to be prepared. If the FBI got to him first, he would surrender. If those from organized crime came after him, it would be an all-out war. It took him two hours to climb the south wall of the crater over loose gravel, rocks, and snowpacks. Exhilarated and exhausted, he sat down on the summit and took in the vast awesomeness.

He didn't want to think of the looming danger or his atrocious past. All he wanted to do was take in the scene around him. Before long Ethan caught himself singing songs of praise to a Creator he wasn't totally convinced existed. *Why am I having a struggle accepting this belief?* His thoughts took him back to his turbulent childhood. Could it be that the tragic death of his parents was instrumental in his denial? Yet Christiana lost her father, and she portrayed the perfect faith.

Continuing around the crater rim to the north, he sat on a rock with a bird's eye view of the settlement. A peaceful place that wants to live apart from the world. *If only it was that easy.* He wanted that life, but wasn't it too late? That life has to be for people whose past is not tainted with such violence. He thought of some of the things he had read in the Bible that tried to convince him differently. Yet common sense told him that he must suffer the consequences of his actions. *I may just need to spend some time with Abram.*

Descending the east ridge of the crater Ethan intercepted the trail back through the meadow. With the warmer weather, the grass was growing rapidly and would soon be ready for grazing. He only had a few more days to explore before he would be tied down for the summer.

Curiosity was getting the best of Ethan as he sat on the porch watching the evening develop. He had been thinking of the mysterious workers that passed the farm every morning headed down Charlotte Creek. Where were they going? What are they doing? Robert had told him he would be told in time, but patience is not an attribute of curiosity. It may just be time for a little of his military training to come into play. Tomorrow he would go on a reconnaissance mission.

Chapter Twenty-Three

———— • ● • ————

With his espionage equipment in his backpack along with enough food and water to last all day, Ethan headed down the Pacific Crest Trail to Bubbs Creek. The early morning clouds were low over the mountains and the periodic splatter of rain was not ideal for a day on the trail. Bubbs Creek Trail followed alongside Bubbs Creek which grew louder as the switchbacks descended for about a mile. The southern wall of the valley opened up into another valley. Ethan could only see about a mile up that valley before it was enshrouded by clouds. Curiosity might have drawn him up the trail on a nicer day, but considering the rain dripping from his hat, he must move on.

For the next couple of miles, the trail winding in and out of the contour of the mountain gradually descended with the river. The low visibility prevented Ethan from seeing Charlotte Valley, but he knew that it would be the next large creek coming in from the right. He could hear the roar of a waterfall but wasn't sure if it was a new stream or the echo of Bubbs Creek off the granite walls. The sound intensified as he rounded the ridge and came across a twenty-foot-wide stream tumbling and churning its way into Bubbs Creek.

Climbing a moderate slope upstream for three hundred yards, Ethan came to a shear wall where Charlotte Creek showed her spectacular rage as she dropped almost three hundred feet along the granite face. After searching along the face for a trail without success he concluded it must be on the other side of the stream. The water was deafening as he inched his way across a fallen tree. Back on solid ground, he found the unmaintained trail. Deadfall littered the tread as he switch-backed up the steep slope. As he topped the granite wall, the sun found a hole in the clouds. A little further up the trail, he found a dry spot under an outcropping of rocks. Dropping his pack, he reclined on a nest of pine needles and immediately fell into a REM sleep.

It was nighttime, and he was running down a city street. He continued desperately looking back, just trying to see what was chasing him. Nothing was there, but he felt a ghostly presence. The air was getting thicker, and he heard the scream of despair getting nearer. The sidewalk ahead of him steepened as the buildings around him started to crumble. The concrete sidewalk was now so steep that he was losing his footing. A bright light appeared ahead of him, and as he started to fall, he cried out to God and reached out his hand. The feeling of warm air blew across his hand as the sound of gunfire interrupted his pandemonium.

A grunting sound caused Ethan to open his eyes. The

first thing he saw was the snoot of a black bear two feet from his face. The natural scream that followed caused the bear to turn heals and run. Still shaking, Ethan jumped to his feet and banged his head on the overhanging rocks. Falling back to the pine needles, he rubbed the growing knot on the back of his head. Looking around the area, he realized he was sleeping in the bear's home. That was probably not a good idea.

Laying back down in the pine needles he listened for the bear to return. What he heard was the sound of steel hitting steel. It sounded a lot like someone was hammering something, and it was riveting through the granite behind him. It had to be the men he had seen leaving the settlement. Were they mining for something? Standing up a little more carefully he pulled on his backpack and stepped out into the drizzle.

A quarter mile later he came to a well-worn trail leading up into an unnamed valley. He was no more than a hundred yards up the trail when he heard someone approaching. Quickly he found a place to hide behind a rocky outcrop. From there he watched as a group of men came down the trail with lunch boxes in hand. Was it that late? A look at his watch confirmed his fears. He must have slept longer than he thought. He only had a couple of hours before he needed to head home. Once the workers were well down the trail, Ethan headed up the valley. He was almost to where the trail crested when he again heard the sound of hammering. Leaving the trail, he made his way up around the crest. Whatever was going on in the valley was still hidden from view. He needed to get to a higher altitude.

Crossing the stream, he made his way up the east side

of the valley to achieve a better vantage point and to put some distance between himself and the camp. He was pretty sure they didn't have electronic surveillance, but dogs and donkeys could do the same thing. It took him twenty minutes to get to the top of the granite wall. Lying on his stomach he worked his way to the edge of the ledge overlooking the valley.

Spread out before him a complete mining operation came into view. He spotted the source of the hammering as two men were working on a waterwheel next to the stream. *That must be how they generate power.* He counted five mine shaft entrances entering the northeast face of Charlotte Dome.

Ethan looked at his watch as he considered waiting for the workers to leave before exploring the mines. He really didn't have the time, and for some reason, he was starting to feel guilty for spying on the people that had taken him in and given him a new chance at life. Looking upstream, he planned a route that would take him through a wooded area and down by the mine entrances. *It won't hurt to just take a quick look inside. It's not like I'm going to take anything.* He slowly slid back from the edge and worked his way down to the trees. His adrenaline was pumping as he contemplated actually exploring the mines. *But I said I was only going to look inside. No farther.*

With an eye on the waterwheel, Ethan quietly pushed his way through the brush and crossed the stream. Finding a comfortable place to rest, he waited impatiently for the two men to finish their job. *Is this their source of wealth? Could it be that they have all the riches of the world but chose to live this simple life? Is it possible for a man to remove himself from the greed of great wealth to follow God?* Ethan realized he was witnessing a utopia of sorts where people thought of others before themselves.

Twenty minutes later the workers gathered up their tools and hurriedly took off down the trail. Ethan cautiously moved out of the woods and crossed the clearing. Looking over the waterwheel, he could see it drove a shaft that went inside a shed. It did not take him long to jimmy the lock. To his surprise he found the room well-lit and clean. The shaft coming from the waterwheel was driving a very modern generator. *So much for primitive.* He had to look inside the mines.

The grating of the mine door hinges caused Ethan to pause. The last thing he wanted was for the workers to hear the familiar sound and be alerted that someone was back at the mine. Much slower now he continued to open the heavy wooden door. LED bulbs strung along the ceiling lit the shaft leading straight back into the mountain. *Okay, you have seen inside, now leave.*

A few steps into the mine Ethan started justifying his actions. *What harm is there in just looking around? After all, I am part of the community. Are you really? If they trusted you with these mines, they would have told you. I just won't let them know I have been here.* Ethan turned around and pulled the door shut. He had never explored a mine shaft before, but how hard could it be to walk along a lighted tunnel.

As he moved deeper into the mountain, Ethan was amazed at how a primitive people could excavate a mine shaft with such precision. In regular intervals, unlit side shafts opened up in both directions. *I need to get out of here.*

Pulling out his headlamp, Ethan moved down one of the shafts. *What in the world is that?* Along the walls and across the ceiling, his headlamp reflected veins of highly reflective material. *Could it be?* Wiping off the rock his pulse quickened. *It has to be.* Using his knife, he pried out a couple pieces of the gold. *I may not be a gold expert but this sure looks real. This has got to be what supports the community.*

Deeper into the mine a yellow rope stretched across the six-foot-wide shaft. Shining his light down the shaft, Ethan could see a pile of rubble. Crawling under the symbolic barricade, he cautiously advanced to the loose debris. The reflective gold amongst the broken-up quartz was pulling him in. *I wonder why they haven't cleaned this out. I should not be here.* The temptation was overwhelming, and he started picking nuggets of gold out of the rubble. *There is so much gold here that they won't miss it. What am I saying? It's not mine. But, it's a natural resource, and you have just as much right to it as they do.*

He could hear the rumble before he felt the shake. Fear gripped him as he jumped up and headed for the exit. Hearing a crash behind him, Ethan could see the roof of the shaft collapsing on the pile where he had found the gold. Within seconds a thick cloud of dust surrounded him. Blinded and uncontrollably coughing, Ethan dropped to his knees and pulled off his backpack. Searching through his bag, he found a shirt and tied it over his mouth and nose. The coughing finally stopped, and he was able to get to his feet.

The visibility was still extremely limited, so he walked along the wall slowly moving in the direction of the exit. Red flashing in the haze out ahead of him caused his pulse to race. An alarm had obviously been triggered, and it would not be long before he had company. Throwing caution aside, he raced towards the flashing light and was soon in the ventilated main corridor. With better visibility, he ran for the exit. The squeak of the rusty hinges was hardly noticeable as he pulled the door shut behind him and headed up the valley away from the trail.

The rain had returned, and darkness was setting in as Ethan moved up the valley. There was no way he could go through the village now. *I have to find a way home without being seen.* Shutting his eyes he pictured the valley and surrounding mountains. A nighttime fording of Charlotte Creek would be dangerous, if not impossible. If he could get across, Mount Bago wasshear granite and would be a difficult climb. To go on up the valley was the wrong direction. The only route he could picture was following the contour lines on the north slope. It would take him well above the village but would take hours to get home.

Soaking wet he made his way across the now strong flowing stream and up onto a contour bench about a thousand feet above the valley. He could hear riders coming down the trail. He had no idea how far away they were, but he needed to get as far away from the mine as possible before they arrived. *At least the rain will wash out my tracks.*

It was closing in on midnight when Ethan crossed over a small ridge and into a ravine where he crossed a creek. *This must be the stream that flows by William and Claire's. I need to go see them.* Climbing up out of the ravine he found a contour bench that made easy walking amongst the scrub oaks. Finding a log on the edge of a clearing he sat down. The clouds had broken up, and the moon was casting its reflecting glow across Charlotte Lake.

The community was such a peaceful place. He thought of the people he had met, and how they had welcomed him in. He thought of Abram and his wisdom. William and Claire with their counsel. And then there is Anna and her desire for a relationship that cannot happen. *Is it even possible for me to assimilate to their lifestyle?*

Ethan felt the gold in his pocket, and his heart stopped. *What have I done? I can't keep this.* He pulled the handful of nuggets from his pocket and stared at them. *They were nothing more than cold rocks. What value are these when I already have all I need?* Whether it was from the dampness or the thought of the damage this gold could do, chills ran through his body. *I know what I must do.* He walked over to the stream and slowly poured the gold into the fast-moving water. *Maybe someday someone who has their life right will find it, but it's not for me.*

Walking through the lower meadow his headlamp reflected the glaring eyes of what appeared to be a mountain lion. It was slowly making its way through the grass paralleling the trail. Ethan's heart rate increased as he constantly looked in the direction of the big cat. Sometimes it was there and sometimes, nothing but darkness. He reached around his back and felt the reassurance of the Beretta in the side pocket of his backpack. His attention kept being pulled to the meadow as he worked his way across the log. With a sigh of relief, Ethan stepped up on the porch and found sanctuary inside the stone cabin he now called home.

Chapter Twenty-Four

The thought of safety was still on Ethan's mind as he spent the sunrise on his front porch. He was torn between keeping the rules of the community and the need to know what was coming their way. His inner self kept telling him to trust God, but years of experience kept getting in the way. Maybe a day in the settlement would help clear his thinking.

Yesterday's storm had blown out and the calm water of Charlotte Lake created a reflection of towering Mount Gardiner against the rich blue sky. Passing the spring, the croak of frogs sounding off in the marsh welcomed Ethan to the settlement. The first stop was at the bakery where he picked up three hot cinnamon rolls. As sure as the sun comes up in the morning, William was sitting in his front porch rocking chair.

"Good morning, Ethan. What brings you off the mountain?"

"I was getting lonely and thought maybe you needed company." Ethan answered as he set the rolls down on the table next to William. "Do you have time to give a lesson on remote settlement living?"

"It's all pretty simple to those of us that have spent the majority of our life here."

"Does that include you? Surely you were not raised here in the wilderness."

William scratched his chin before responding, "Not in this wilderness. I was raised in the woods of Minnesota. Carrie and I were in our twenties when we came here."

"What size was the community when you arrived?"

"Well, once we arrived at the lake there were two settlers here, and that included Carrie and me." William chuckled at his hilarious revelation.

"So, the whole community is your doing?"

"I would like to say it is God's doing. We were only looking for a secluded place to call home. It didn't take long before our old community found out about our experiences and started arriving at the lake. One thing led to another, and before long, we had a reasonable number of settlers. What you see here didn't happen all at once. As you can tell by our age, many years have passed since that spring."

The screen door banged as Carrie brought out coffee to compliment the rolls. "It hasn't always been easy, Ethan. That first year it was just the two of us. We spent the first summer building a cabin and storing up for the winter. We underestimated the severity of the winter season here and almost ran out of food. We were new believers back then, and our faith was fragile."

"Fragile sounds like how I would describe my faith."

"Faith grows as you experience God's grace."

"How did your faith grow, considering you were in

such a remote location?"

"Ethan, as you have already experienced, God does not require civilization to show his glory. We not only witnessed His creation, but we also witnessed how He supplied our every need. That is how our faith grew."

Ethan turned when William waved to someone behind him. Four teenage boys were coming up the path. "Good morning, boys," William greeted them. "You headed up to the runoff?" One of the boys nodded and waved back to his elderly mentor as they turned and headed up along the stream behind William's cabin.

"Was that gold pans they had on their backpack?" Ethan asked once the boys had disappeared into the woods.

Ethan thought William didn't hear him as he just sat there rocking in his chair not saying anything. Once Ethan repeated his question, William spoke. "Ethan, what are worldly possessions?"

Giving it some thought, while still hanging onto the question he had asked William, Ethan answered. "Anything that you can physically touch and belongs personally to you."

"Well answered question, my friend. Now, what are your earthly desires, when it comes to worldly possessions?"

"If you would have asked me that just a few years ago it would have been a big list. Things changed after I lost my family. I have lost my desire to acquire things. I'm just happy to have my needs met. Were those gold pans?"

"Yes, they are. The boys enjoy prospecting up along the stream. They haven't found a lot of gold up there, but it gives them something to do."

"Are you not concerned that their search for gold could lead them away from the commune into a more capitalistic lifestyle?"

"Yes, that is a concern. We have trained our children how to follow God's will for their life, and it is our desire for them to stay within the community, but it is ultimately their decision. As you have seen, our system of commonality amongst our people does not lead to poverty, but one of great wealth. Outsiders, which in all practical application you are one, believe that great wealth consists of money. While money is a form of wealth, it is not the only form. We here in the settlement consider the value of time, quality of life, relationships, and basic needs to sustain life, as wealth. More than all of these, we believe that God has laid up for us treasures in heaven that far exceed what is available here on earth. Our children are not for want. They have all they need. Our biggest concern is influence from the outside world. That is why we are ever so cautious when strangers move into our settlement."

What a contrast from the real world. Ethan pondered what William had shared. *Or is this the real world? Could he have been wrong about capitalism all these years? Was this watered-down form of communism really okay?*

"Do you think this kind of community would work in greater society?" Ethan asked.

"Absolutely not! For this, to work there must be a unified faith in God. Each participant must voluntarily submit to serving others, and there must be a form of revenue capable of sustaining the community. That does not happen in most societies. A communistic government tends to erode over time until its leaders have the wealth and the subjects are destitute."

"Are you telling me that there is a form of revenue capable of sustaining this community?" Ethan asked, even though he now knew the source.

William laughed, "I'm not the one that lets that cat out of the bag. Let's just say, we're doing okay."

"Not that I need any gold, but I think I'll go watch the boys at work. It sounds kind of fun. Will they be bashful about showing me how it's done?"

"They will love teaching you. Just as a reminder. We have no currency here, so any gold that is panned must go into the community's treasury."

Ethan hadn't thought of that, he just figured the boys kept the gold they found. It would make sense as there is nothing to buy here on the mountain. Picking up his backpack, Ethan thanked his host and started up the narrow trail.

In and out of the scrub oaks he climbed until the trail leveled off and the walls of the canyon moved in. The stream was only about three feet wide, and the narrow trail did not look like it had been used all that much. About a half mile later, the valley opened up and again he started to climb. He was now above the tree line, and he could see the snowpacks not more than a quarter mile up ahead. It wasn't long before he heard one of the boys holler his name. Looking up to his left he could see the prospectors in a steep crevasse.

Once the boys found out what Ethan was up to, they were more than happy to show him how they went about searching for gold, and like all good teachers, they put him to work with a pick. Two of the boys were pulling pay dirt out of the chasm moving it down to the stream where the other two were panning out the dirt. After about an hour they took a break and sat down to see what they had found.

Ethan took a step back when they held up a pint jar half full of gold nuggets. He did the math in his head and realized it was worth tens of thousands of dollars. Yet the boys did not seem that excited. He was certain they had no idea the worth of gold. He was starting to figure out what made this place tick.

Thanking the boys for their lesson he picked up his backpack and followed the trail up the mountain where it joined the Pacific Crest Trail.

With plenty of daylight left and a lot to think about, he turned north. Glen Pass was only a little over a mile away and this would be a great opportunity to explore more backcountry. Multiple switchbacks later and with burning calves, Ethan reached the top of the pass. There was still a considerable amount of snow on the pass, but he was able to find a dry boulder and soak in the warmth of the early afternoon sun.

Tired from the exhausting climb and the lack of oxygen at twelve thousand feet, he soon fell into a restful sleep, only to be jolted awake by the sound of trekking poles clicking on the rocks. Looking over his shoulder he could see a forest ranger approaching the pass from the north. The last thing he wanted was to come into contact with a law enforcement officer. He could take off to the south and avoid the ranger, but he was getting close and a quick departure would make him look suspicious. He just hoped the guy wasn't looking for him.

As the ranger topped the pass, with a nod Ethan was

the first to speak, "Good afternoon, sir,"

"Good afternoon it is," responded the ranger. "How far do you plan on making it today?"

The question kind of caught Ethan off guard and it took him a moment to respond. How could he answer the question and not reveal where he lived?

"Only as far as these legs will take me," was his generic, nonrevealing response. "Just out patrolling the back country?" Ethan asked.

For the next fifteen minutes, he explained to Ethan about his job here in the interior, and how he lived down at Rae Lakes in the ranger station. He complained about the mosquitoes and the lack of fresh fruit and vegetables. "Speaking of that," he said. "I'm heading down to Charlotte Lake to pick up some vegetables. Did you stop by the village and meet the folks there?"

Ethan assured him he did with a brief nod and let the ranger continue. "They are the nicest folks, kind of strange way of life, but they always have fresh produce and will never take payment for them. How they do it is a mystery to me."

Ethan stood up as if he was ready to take off, prompting the ranger to do the same.

A perplexed look came over the ranger's face. "You look familiar. Have we met before?"

He must have seen my picture in the news. I've got to cut this short. "I don't believe so. Even though I do get into the backcountry often," Ethan lied.

"Do you mind if I take a look at your hiking permit? Just so I can say I'm doing my job."

Fear gripped Ethan. He never even thought of a hiking

permit. How was he going to get out of this one. "Sure thing. I haven't been asked for it before. It'll take some time to dig it out." He didn't even start taking off his backpack, instead he continued the conversation. "You guys must get lonely here in the backcountry. Do you have a family?"

That was enough for the ranger to spend the next ten minutes talking about his family on the outside and the times they had hiked in to see him. In the meantime, it became apparent that he no longer cared about seeing a hiking permit. Finally, he wrapped up the conversation and bade Ethan goodbye.

"Enjoy your hike to Canada," the ranger hollered as he headed south down the switchbacks.

Perplexed Ethan wondered why he said that. He wasn't heading to Canada, he wasn't even headed north, but it might just work to his favor if the ranger came across his picture on America's most-wanted list. He waited until the ranger rounded the corner and was out of sight. Taking his time, he meandered down the trail keeping a low profile. As he approached the Charlotte Lake trail, he spotted the ranger entering the settlement. Taking the long way around the ridge, Ethan continued his stealthy cross country hike up to the crater. He had never considered the possibility of forest rangers visiting the village, but it did make sense. He would just have to stay alert.

Chapter Twenty-Five

The sun was shining, and it was time for an excursion. Ethan studied the map and really wanted to explore the origins of East Creek. He loaded up his backpack with enough provisions for the two-day trip and headed for the Pacific Crest Trail.

Reaching the trail he descended to Bubbs Creek Trail and followed it along the deafening sound of water crashing down the canyon. Reaching East Creek Lake Trail he turned south and crossed the footbridge over Bubbs Creek. The thundering water descending off the melting snowpacks was relentless. It seemed to be telling Ethan that there is a God who controls even this raging river. Just a few degrees cooler and the level of the river goes down. A few degrees warmer and it overflows its banks.

The strong climb up around a waterfall brought Ethan to a bridge. He sat on the edge of the man-made structure and watched the water tumbling over the rocks. The continuous roar of the water rushing to the valley was violent, yet peaceful. It made Ethan think of his life. Could he really ever achieve peace when his past was filled with violence? Was he really even trying to find peace?

Almost two miles later and a couple hundred more feet of altitude along the crushed granite trail brought Ethan to East Lake. Finding a place in the shade along the crystal blue lake, he watched the reflection of the white fluffy clouds move across the still water. Every now and then a fish would break the surface. *What a difference between the raging rivers and this tranquil lake.*

Another mile up into the valley, Ethan came across a narrow footpath that led up the mountain to the east. Starting up the trail, Deerhorn Mountain towered over him. Feeling dwarfed by its magnitude, he continued up the switchbacks along the stream flowing out of the basin above him. Climbing over a ledge Ethan could see a small lake in the basin surrounded by shrubby looking trees. Beyond the lake the terrain rose to another peak that Ethan guessed was higher than Deerhorn. *It really is hard not to believe in a God when you're so insignificant amongst these giants.* For some reason, he continued on. Was it the curiosity of the footpath or was it the underlying desire to follow God's leading? These were questions that continued to challenge Ethan as he climbed towards the distant snowpacks.

Above the lake, the footpath continued along a much smaller stream. The path looked a little more worn and he could make out bare footprints. *Who would be up here barefooted?* Approaching a small mound he came across a no trespassing sign. *I assume the barefooted mountain man doesn't want company.* Ethan checked his Beretta and replaced it in its holster.

Crossing over the knoll, he came upon a small simple log cabin. Its front porch was filled with miscellaneous mining hardware items leaving only room for a single rocking chair. In the rocking chair sat an old grizzly atypical barefooted man with a rifle lying across his lap. Ethan cautiously continued on with hopes that this guy was just unique in nature and not an all-out lunatic. The old codger stared at Ethan and didn't say a word.

Ethan decided it was time to break the ice. "Good morning, sir. Beautiful weather up here on the mountain."

The miner just sat there and looked him up and down. Turning to the side, he spewed a spit of tobacco, half of it made it off the porch. Ethan wasn't sure of what to do but didn't want to spend too much time on this standoff.

"It's been a pleasure meeting you. I'll just be on my way now."

"Ya ain't gone nowhere."

Wow, he can speak. Not so sure I like his tone. Ethan's right hand was resting on his Beretta. *Guess it's time to deescalate this lengthy conversation.* "Sorry to intrude. I didn't realize this was private property. I'll just turn around and head back down the trail."

"Can't ya read or are you just blind?"

"I was just thinking you would like some company." Ethan started slowly backing up.

"I said ya ain't gone nowhere, so sit your tail down there on that rock. We gonna talk."

At least he wants to have a dialogue. Ethan sat down on the rock. *Maybe I will live.*

Another stream of tobacco juice attempted

unsuccessfully to make it off the porch before the old man spoke up. "What ya doing up here anyway?"

"I was just out exploring the surrounding area and had no idea someone was up here. You have to admit, it is kind of remote."

"Ya ever think I might wanna keep it that way?"

"I'm certain you do, and I'm more than willing to let you get back to your loneliness. Anything I can help you with before I leave?"

"As a matter of fact, there is. Ya said you were exploring the area. You're a not one of those communist over at Charlotte Lake, are ya?"

"I'm certainly not a communist, if that's what you're asking. I do live over that way." Ethan had enough problems without letting this crazy know where he lived.

"Well, ya must live with them. They're nothing but a bunch of senseless primitive Jesus freaks."

"You seem to know a lot about them. Do you get over there frequently for supplies?"

With that the old man let out a string of curse words before answering Ethan's question.

"I used to live over there until those greedy hypocrites kicked me out."

"They seem like nice people. If you don't mind me asking, why did they kick you out?"

"In the early days, when there were only a few of us, one of the guys discovered gold above the settlement to the north. I thought we were going to be rich, but the rest decided it would be best if we just used the gold to buy supplies for everyone. Can you believe that? They were a bunch of commies. I say they still are."

Ethan was starting to understand where this was leading. "I'm guessing you decided to leave the group and come out here on your own?"

"I sure wasn't going to stay there and dig up gold for everybody else. They can do their own diggin. I've been up here for forty years now. You should see the gold I've found in these here hills. Shoot, I could take my gold to town and live like royalty for the rest of my life."

"Why don't you? You know none of us are certain of the number of our days."

"Oh boy, it sounds like you've been listening to those Bible thumpers down there. Surely, they don't have ya believing that stuff?"

I really don't know what I believe, but do I want to deny Christ? Ethan recalled reading how if he denied Jesus, that Jesus would deny him. And even though he wasn't sure yet, he just had an uneasy feeling about doing so. "I never did ask you, but are you Sam?"

"I just may be. Has someone down there been talking about me?" he answered angrily.

"Sorry, that's not how it happened. At the bottom of your sign, it said by order of Miner Sam."

"Oh yeah, forgot I put that on there. So now ya know my handle, what's yours?"

Ethan questioned if it was a good idea to give Miner Sam his real name, but it would not take him long in the community to get the truth. After formally introducing himself, Ethan answered the question.

"I don't know what I believe. It sounds good, but I haven't felt that awe-inspiring moment like Apostle Paul had to totally convince me."

"And you won't, because that never happens. It's just a bunch of made up garbage by old white bearded men a couple thousand years ago. None of the Bible is true. You should be smart enough to know that."

Ethan was taken back by the opposition he was experiencing. *This is the kind of thing I used to hear in New York. How is the best way to respond.* He just sat there and thought about the difference between this man and the people he had gotten to know in the community. *What a contrast.*

"I'm keeping my options open," he answered.

"Good, because I have a proposition for you. You see, I am getting older and need someone to take over this mine up here. If you do the digging, I will give you ten percent of the gold. You will be rich."

Ethan laughed at the old man's generosity. "Ten percent. I thought you were opposed to greed. How about fifty-fifty? That makes more sense considering I'm doing all the work."

A few more nasty words came out of Miner Sam's mouth before he settled down. "I have done all the work, and you want half of what we find."

"If you did all the work, than you don't need me. If the gold mining up here is as good as you say, why haven't you mined enough and moved to the city where you can rest and enjoy that luxury life you talked about?"

"Ya don't believe me. Come inside and I'll show ya the gold. Just don't try any funny stuff with that there pistol."

Ethan stood up and stretched his sore muscles. Following Miner Sam into the dark dingy cabin the first thing that hit him was the stench. *This guy must never take a bath.* Hanging from the smoke-filled ceiling an old lantern gave off a dim light. A rugged table sat in the center of the room, flanked by a cot on one side and a makeshift kitchen on the other. The old woodstove was belching out smoke.

Miner Sam banged on the stove a couple of times which seemed to subdue the belching. Reaching up on a shelf, he pulled down an old coffee can and unscrewed the lid. "Look in here and tell me this isn't a lot of gold."

Ethan had no doubt that the can was filled with gold, but even so he took a peek. What he was not prepared for was the mesmerizing yellow that looked back up at him. The hypnotic effect of a half a million dollars of gold pulled him in. It was the same feeling he had experienced in the mine shaft just before the ceiling caved in. *Why am I doing this? If you take this gold, you can undo all the things you have done wrong. Really? That's not true. But it is. Just think about how you could use gold to buy justice. You could be free to go anywhere and not worry. That's not true, riches here in this world are only temporary. They will fly away. Turn and run away from this place. This guy is evil. But he will make you rich. Turn and run, do it now, or I will never know you.* Ethan looked away from the gold and into the eyes of a demonic individual with a satanic smile spread across his face.

"Now you will join me in our search for more gold. All the pleasures of the world are ours for the taking."

Ethan looked around the room and noticed that Sam's rifle was leaned up in the far corner. He would have plenty of time to get out the door before the old man could reach his weapon. It was time to make his move. "Thanks for the offer, Sam, but I have to pass. You see, when I look at your gold, all I see is a sad, lonely old man, nothing more."

As hateful foul words screamed out of Miner Sam's mouth, Ethan ran out the door. The sky above the mountains had grown dark with thunderous clouds sending streaks of lightning crashing into the granite rocks. *What happened to the nice day?* Ethan knew he only had a few moments before the crack of the rifle would echo the lightning strikes. He had just crested the knoll when the ping of the bullet off the rocks told him Miner Sam had made it to the door. He ducked as he ran praying that Sam's aging eyesight would fail. Another shot rang off the rocks. He was just about below the ridge. Only a few more yards. He felt the thud of something hitting his backpack as he heard the crack from the rifle. He knew what had hit him, but he felt no pain as he descended out of sight of the cabin. Not knowing how fast a madman can run, Ethan kept up the pace.

The sky was continuing to darken. Ethan looked at his watch. It was only two-thirty. *This is a really nasty storm. Is this a sign from God? Was this what the people outside the ark witnessed when the floods came? Is God trying to tell me that I am outside the ark? If I would only believe in Him and accept Jesus that I would be inside the ark?* He had to find shelter, but where? The only shelter for miles was occupied by a demonic mad man.

The torrential rain made it difficult to follow the footpath as Ethan made it down the mountain to East Creek. Reaching the stream he found it already raging. He had to get across and find shelter amongst the overhanging boulders up on the west side. Making his way upstream towards Lake Reflection he came across many downed logs. None of which looked safe. Eventually he came to the lake where a pile of downed trees had choked off the outlet. He found himself crying out to God as he made his way across the slippery logs.

Climbing up the jagged edge of the granite wall Ethan came to the outcrop he had faintly seen from the stream. Remembering his encounter with the bear, he inspected the shelter before taking off his backpack. He was soaking wet and cold. *What a miserable mess I've gotten myself in.* Pulling out the stuff sack that held his clothes he discovered a hole in one side. Digging through his clothes he found what he had felt on that last shot. *Someone must be watching over me.*

He needed to get dried off and warmed up. It would be hard to do without a fire. Yet, if he built a fire, it could reveal his location. Peeling off his wet clothes, he shivered as he used an extra shirt to dry off. His hands were shaking from the cold as he pulled on dry clothes and slid into his sleeping bag. It might not be real comfortable under the overhanging rock, but it was dry, and he was warming up.

The rain continued to pound the mountain as visibility dropped to near zero. All Ethan could do was curl up in his sleeping bag and recount the day's events. He started to feel sorry for Sam. Living all alone up here, it was apparent he was totally consumed by greed. Ethan thought of his close call in the gold mine. The unexplained drawing power of gold had almost taken his life. Now this. He shook with fear of how close he had come to succumbing to enticing power of riches. *How was I able to resist? Was it a spiritual intervention? Is God really watching over me? Has He determined that I will believe in Him? Is He even giving me a choice?* Ethan continued to struggle with a lot of unanswered questions, but one thing he did know, it was no longer just a physical battle.

Sometime in the middle of the night, Ethan woke to the sound of a mountain lion emitting a blood-curdling scream. Just a little unnerving, he felt for his Beretta under his stuff sack. Just the feel of the cold steel in his hand gave him some assurance. The rain had stopped, and he could see the stars shining over the mountains. He was considering packing up and heading for home, then he heard the sound of rushing water. It would be best to wait until morning.

Daylight brought with it the dismal revelation of an uncrossable overflowing stream. The trail was no longer an option. Packing up, Ethan moved down off his slippery perch and started rock hopping along the west side of the fast-moving stream. Without a trail the going was treacherous and slow. Once he made it down past East Lake, he came to a rock face that dropped into the stream. It was just too steep to make his way across.

Climbing straight up the mountain two hundred yards he found a fissure in the rock face. Using his trekking poles as anchors he made his way across the moss-covered granite face. Reaching the other side, he decided to stay as high as possible until he was able to descend to the bridge. About a quarter of a mile of slipping and sliding across the rocks brought him to an area of vegetation and he was able to descend towards the stream. It was almost noon before he arrived at the bridge and sat down for a rest.

Looking up at Mount Bago, his soul longed for the peace and contentment that was living on the other side. Behind him, greed had destroyed a man who had at one time lived a contented life. Ahead of him was a community of peaceful people who loved God and wanted to live at peace with all men. *I want to be like them. I have no need for wealth. All I want to do is have someone to love and a place to call home.*

With five miles to go, Ethan swung his backpack over his shoulders and headed down the trail. Bubbs Creek was louder than ever as he switched back up the trail towards Mount Bago. The sound of a peaceful nature welcomed him into the crater, and by the time darkness closed in around the mountains, a fire was burning in the cookstove, and Ethan was comfortably unwinding in his favorite chair.

Chapter Twenty-Six

It was a couple of hours before daybreak when Ethan stepped out onto the porch. Other than a couple of liters of water his backpack was empty. It felt strange hiking without a full backpack. He had been trained to always be prepared for every contingency. He questioned his decision to leave his Beretta at home, but really wanted to quit depending on his weapons to save him. Like the last trip, he knew he would be returning with a full pack.

Crossing over Kearsarge Pass the eastern horizon slowly turned from a dark slate blue to deep pink. Somehow in his bones, Ethan felt that the clouds now being revealed in the early morning sky would be rain later in the day. He needed to hurry. The last thing he wanted was to climb back up the mountain in a storm.

Arriving at Onion Valley trailhead, Ethan was happy to find the friendly camp host making his rounds. Twenty minutes later he was sitting at the bus stop. The pink sunrise had now turned to a fully overcast dreary-looking sky.

Looking over the bus schedule, he knew his time in Lone Pine would be limited. On the plus side, he could easily be mistaken for a long-distance backpacker.

Boarding the bus, he found that he was the only passenger headed south and took advantage of the situation by starting up a conversation with the driver, who was happy to have someone to talk to. By the time they reached Lone Pine, Ethan had talked the driver into dropping him off on the north end of town. Ethan slipped the driver a twenty-dollar tip and waited for the bus to leave before heading to his storage unit.

He was relieved to find the box untouched. He soon had the contents all tucked away in his backpack. Not that his military uniforms and the cash were necessary on the mountain, but he needed to be ready to pick up and run at a minute's notice.

Walking back south to the bus stop he stopped in at the outfitters and purchased two flexible solar panels which pretty much filled his backpack. He ordered a sandwich to go from McDonald's and made it to the bus stop with five minutes to spare. It was starting to get hot in the valley, and for more than one reason, he was anxious to get to a higher altitude.

It was noon when he stepped off the bus in Independence, and it was starting to rain. He had no luck at all getting a ride up Onion Valley Road, and it was five p.m. before he stumbled into the Onion Valley campground soaking wet. He badly needed a break before heading up the trail. Finding shelter under a pine tree and using his backpack as a pillow he fell into a troubled sleep. He was in a very vulnerable situation. Waking up fifteen minutes later, he assessed his condition. He was cold and tired, and he had a six-hour hike to make it to his home in the crater. "I would be happy to trade the money in my pack for a warm dry tent and a hot meal," he muttered as he clinched his wet backpack on over his tired shoulders.

As he walked through the campground on the way to the trailhead, he noticed two less than desirable guys and an unsightly woman watching him closely as he walked by. *I need to keep an eye on that group.* He kept glancing back as he headed for the trailhead. With dreaded anguish, he started up the trail. It was wet and muddy, and the rain was coming down hard. A mile and a half up the trail, he stopped for a brief break. He had just stood up to pull on his backpack when the two despicable guys from the camp showed up. He knew they had only one reason to be there, considering the knives they were wielding. Reaching behind his back for his Beretta, Ethan remembered he had left it at the cabin.

"We'll take that," the obvious leader of the two stated in a matter-of-fact tone. Whether it was the high he was on from smoking weed or sheer stupidity, he made a fatal mistake. Reaching out his hand for the backpack while lowering his knife was the opening any trained expert needed. Simultaneously he threw the backpack down the hill behind him and grabbed the assailants' outstretched arm and with a quick twist caused excruciating pain. As the assailant's other hand started to raise, Ethan intercepted it as he had done in training many times. The only difference this time is that he turned the knife 180 degrees and drove it home. With his life draining from him, the assailant crumpled to the ground.

Instinct told Ethan to roll to his right as the other attacker was coming in fast. It was too late as he felt the sharp pain slice across his left shoulder. Ignoring the excruciating pain, he spun around and tripped his attacker, who lacked any form of ability to maintain balance on the muddy trail. Crashing down the hill the guy came to rest in the brush along the stream. His knife was nowhere in sight. Within seconds Ethan was on him pummeling him with whatever strength he had left. Something inside him was telling him to stop, but the adrenaline that filled his body was driving him on. Finally, he realized the attacker was no longer a threat and stopped.

Back up on the trail, Ethan found the lifeless body of the first attacker. *What have I done, what have I done?* He sobbed. *This is not at all what I wanted to happen. Why did they have to follow me?* He felt a warm sticky sensation running down his left arm and that's when the adrenaline left his body, and the pain returned. Checking out his arm he could see that he had lost a lot of blood. He needed to stop it quickly. Ripping off a piece of his shirttail he one-handedly wrapped a tight makeshift bandage around the wound.

Knowing he could not leave the dead assailant on the trail, he dragged him to the edge of the ravine and rolled him down the steep hill. The heavy rain would soon wash away the signs of struggle on the trail, but it would always leave its ugly stain on his soul. All he could think about was the Bible verse he read where it talked about the man that lives by the sword, dies by the sword. It was true for these two, and he was sure it was meant for him as well.

Injured and exhausted, Ethan found his backpack and

started up the hill. He had no idea if he could make it, but he had to move on. He knew he needed medical attention, but where was he to go. All he knew was he had to keep going, one step at a time he made the grueling climb as the rain increased and he heard thunder in the distance.

It was dark by the time he crossed over Kearsarge Pass. It was all Ethan could do to keep walking. He was starting to become delirious as every shadow became the enemy waiting to attack. He had lost relevance of time as he stumbled down the trail leading into the village. He should go see the doctor, but some underlying guilt convinced him otherwise. There was only one place he felt safe. He pounded on the door with what strength he had left before collapsing on the porch.

Chapter Twenty-Seven

Anna was just about to call it a night when she heard a thumping followed by a thud. Pulling back the drapes, she could see a bulk lying at her door. *What could that be?* Cautiously she unlocked the door. "Ethan!" She screamed as she recognized the motionless form lying at her feet. Dropping to her knees she was relieved when she felt his pulse. She tried to wake him up, but could not get any response. Taking off his backpack she pulled him inside and shut the door. The first thing she had to do was get him warm. Removing his shirt, she found the makeshift bandage and panicked. Just from the look of it, she knew he had lost a lot of blood. Removing the blood-soaked bandage and seeing the wound confirmed her fears. He needed to be sewed up, but that was not the worst of his problems. She needed to go get the doctor. She wrapped the wound with strips of clean cotton and tied the ends. That would do until the doctor could get there.

Covering Ethan with a blanket, Anna pulled on her coat and made the muddy trip in the pouring rain to Doctor Winston's home. The doctor was full of questions as they hurried down the trail. All Anna could answer was what she had seen. Ethan was unconscious, so they knew nothing of how he had been injured.

Arriving at the house they found Ethan semiconscious and trying to sit up.

"Just stay down Ethan," Doctor Winston said softly as he knelt beside him. "Let's take a look at what you have done. Anna, please get some water boiling. Ethan needs some hot tea, and we need hot water to clean things up."

Looking over the shoulder wound, the doctor determined that even though it bled like a stuck pig, it had done little damage to the arm.

"Ethan, I'm going to sew up the wound, and it's going to be painful. I would like to give you a shot of Morphine but am hesitant to do so until we get you stabilized. Can you handle the pain?"

The soft moan in the affirmative was not convincing. One stitch at a time the doctor closed up the wound. He said nothing, but from years of experience knew that this was no accident. With the wound closed up and bandaged, the next step had to be taken.

"Anna, what blood type are you?"

"O positive. Why?"

"Good, that's compatible with most types. Are you willing to donate a pint?"

Anna thought of her blood flowing through Ethan's veins. "I will do whatever it takes to save him."

"Pull up a chair. We only have a short time." Doctor Winston instructed as he pulled the equipment out of his bag. Within minutes they had a pint of blood and were feeding it into Ethan's deprived veins. Slowly Ethan came around; by midnight he was sitting up drinking herbal tea and eating some leftover stew.

"I suppose you want to know what happened." Ethan finally said.

Without saying a word, both Anna and the doctor nodded their heads.

Ethan had to tell them the truth. Could he trust they would keep it confidential? He was sure Anna would do anything for him, but the doctor was one of the commune leaders. He might feel convicted to bring it to the others if he knew all that Ethan had done and was doing.

"I went to Lone Pine to clean out my storage unit. Two guys tried to rob me on the trail. One stabbed me in the shoulder. I wrapped the wound the best I could with my shirttail. At first, I thought I could doctor it myself, but by the time I got back I knew I needed help."

"Why didn't you come straight to my house?" Doctor Winston asked.

"I guess I wasn't thinking straight. It would have made more sense."

"It's late and I have a busy day tomorrow." Doctor Winston stood up. "You will be hurting for a couple of days but should be just fine. I'll warn our pack mule team to keep a lookout for robbers. We wouldn't want anyone else getting hurt."

Ethan kept it to himself that these would-be robbers would not be hurting anyone else. He felt it would not be beneficial for that information to be devolved.

After Doctor Winston left, Anna came and sat down beside Ethan grasping his hand. Laying her head on his good shoulder, he could feel she was shaking. "I thought we were going to lose you," she whispered. "There's something else you would like to tell me. Isn't there?"

"What do you mean?"

"I don't know. It's just that I felt you were holding back from telling the whole story with Doctor Winston. Can you tell me?"

Ethan remained silent as his thoughts processed the necessity and importance of what information he should share. What knowledge would put her in jeopardy? While he knew at some point it would be necessary to confess, he wasn't sure it should be to Anna.

He decided to start by asking her a question. "What do you know about me that I haven't told you?"

"Well, I know you used to be in the military and have a lot of weapons."

"Who told you that?" Ethan asked as he tried to process her response.

"When I was injured and stayed at your place, I was looking for a blanket and found your weapons inside your coffee table. I was shocked and scared at first, but somehow, I felt you are a good man and wouldn't hurt anyone."

Her brief moment of silence brought Ethan to push her on. "And then?"

"After I had pulled you out of the rain, I brought in your backpack. It was so heavy I thought it might be something important that needed to be dried, so I opened it."

"What did you find inside?"

"I emptied it, Ethan. I am so sorry. Now I wish I had left it in the rain."

"What you have seen cannot be undone. What are you going to do now?"

"Nothing but hope to show you enough love, that you will eventually reveal who you really are. What hurts worse than what you have done is your hesitancy to trust me."

"So, you do not plan on telling the others what you discovered?"

"I really don't know. I'm an emotional wreck right now Ethan. My heart aches for someone that I have grown close to only to find I really don't know him.

Anna's statement slammed Ethan to the core. The pain he was now feeling was far greater than the one in his shoulder.

Taking her hand in his he looked into her teary eyes. "Everything I have told you is the truth. I have not lied to you at any time. Yes, there are times I have not told you everything, as I was afraid it could put your life in danger. I am who I told you I am, and only came here to live a peaceful, non-assuming life. It is my desire to remove any veil of secrecy between us."

"So, are the feelings you have for me genuine, or is there someone out there keeping you from truly loving me?"

"Anna, I have told you from the very beginning that our relationship would not work. I care about you, but I have lived through some disturbing and violent things. My past would not be an acceptable match to your serene life."

"Just tell me one thing." Anna said as she wiped the tears from her eyes. "Did you steal the money in your backpack? Is that why the men tried to kill you?"

"I did not steal the money, and the thugs did not know

it was in my backpack. In the outside world, I was a very prosperous man. What you found in my bag was only a small portion of my wealth. I felt with summer coming on, it was time to empty the storage unit and bring everything up here. Even though up here there is no need for money, someday I may be asked to leave and will need it."

"That explains it enough." Anna said, "What do we do now?"

"For now, I feel strong enough I need to head on up to the house before the sun comes up and folks start asking questions."

"Ethan, you just about died. I can't let you go."

"Yes, you can. Come up in the morning and check on me if you want, but for now, I need to go." He slowly stood up and let his equilibrium catch up. "Where is my pack?"

The rain had stopped but continued to drip from the trees as Ethan walked along through the settlement in the predawn hour. The pressure on his shoulder from the pack caused a lot of discomfort. He knew morning would come soon as the glow from lanterns burning inside cabins showed through the windows.

Up on the side of the mountain, he looked down at the wakening village. A wisp of fog drifted slowly across the calm water of the lake. On the far side of the lake came the crow of a rooster announcing the arrival of a new day.

Chapter Twenty-Eight

"It looks like you've done a great job preparing the pastures," Robert told Ethan as they sat on the front porch overlooking the stream and the meadow. "The fences look as if they will keep the livestock confined to the field. Have you noticed any wild predators lurking about?"

"I spotted a mountain lion stalking me one night coming up the trail. Other than that, I haven't seen anything." Ethan took a sip of coffee and silently moaned as pain shot up from his shoulder."

"You will once the animals get up here. The younger ones are easy prey. You'll have to keep an eye out for the way they act. They will warn you. Just be ready when they do. Think you can shoot straight enough to deter these four-legged poachers?"

Not wanting to be egotistical Ethan just shrugged his shoulders and said, "I've shot a gun a time or two. I do have a scope on my rifle, which should help."

"Well, if you need any lessons, we have a couple of

sharpshooters in the village."

Ethan chuckled softly. He looked forward to practicing his skill on something with more than two legs.

With cups in hand and God's creation stretched across the sky, Ethan asked Robert the question he had asked a lot of the residents of the Charlotte Lake community. "Robert, I have never heard your story. How did you end up here?"

Robert stroked his big bushy beard and looked deep into the recesses of his memories. "Ethan, like most of the folks who have migrated here, my story is unique. I was born and raised on a ranch in northern Arizona. My parents were good godly folks even though we didn't attend church much. I do recall a few times a year we would get up early on Sunday morning and make the fifty-mile drive to town to attend services. My momma tried to raise us right, and the Lord knows, she read the Bible to us every day. Despite her trying, I never accepted the Lord. When I was twenty my dad and I had a falling out, and I packed up my stuff and headed west in my old pickup truck."

Pausing in thought Robert sipped his coffee and soaked in the brisk fresh air blowing in over the crater walls. "For the next four years, I worked at a ranch in Southern California along the Mexican border. Then one day I was out riding the fences when I came across a young couple who were hiking the Pacific Crest Trail and were lost. I had never heard of the trail, which ended up being only a half mile from the ranch. Between the three of us, we figured out where they went wrong, and I watched them walk away. That was a turning point in my life.

"I gave my two-week notice and started preparing for an adventure. Sold my truck and everything I couldn't carry on my horse. So, to shorten this story, I spent that whole summer riding from Mexico up to here on the trail. I arrived here in the village in mid-July looking for some real food, and my horse needed shoes."

"Did you finish the trail?"

"No, I got sucked into this vortex and haven't left. I don't suppose I ever will."

"How did that happen?'

"Well, like happens to a lot of free-spirited men, I met a lady here, and one thing led to another, and now we have six children."

Robert stood up and untied his horse. "This cowboy isn't going anywhere, except back down this mountain."

"You have a good day, boss. I'll be down in the morning to help bring up the livestock."

With Robert gone, Ethan unpacked his backpack and turned on the satellite receiver. Within a few minutes, he was connected to his tablet and was scrolling down through the news. So far, there weren't any articles about the two guys he had taken care of on the trail. It would come up soon enough. Their friend in the camp had surely reported them missing by now. Checking that the battery was fully charged, he shut it down and stored it away in the crate. He would have to limit his sign on time to reduce the chance of being detected by the folks in the settlement and the outside world.

Ethan was walking the fences one last time when he noticed Anna coming up the trail, being followed by a black and white medium-sized dog.

He intercepted her at the stream. "What brings you up here this sunny afternoon?"

"I brought you a present. His name is Growler."

"You brought me a dog?"

"He will keep you safe. You like him?"

"It's a dog. What is there to like?"

Anna frowned and hung her head, "I am just trying to help. I thought you would be happy to have a dog. After all, it has to be lonely up here."

Ethan could see she was about to tear up. Taking care of a dog wasn't high on his list when he was already dealing with livestock.

He forced a smile to his face. "Of course I like him. He will be of great help up here."

A small smile formed on her lips. "I knew you would. You shouldn't mess with me like that. He's a border collie and will help you with the animals. You're going to love him. He will warn you if anyone comes into the crater. I thought maybe, you know, considering your secret stuff, you could use an early warning."

Ethan hadn't thought about a dog to warn him of someone approaching the cabin. It might be an added layer of security he could use. He knelt and petted Growler, who responded with his namesake growl. "Come on, Growler. If we're going to get along, you need to be friendlier than that."

Once inside the cabin, it didn't take Growler long to find a home on the rug in front of the fireplace. And it didn't take Anna long to find her favorite spot in the overstuffed chair. With her feet comfortably resting on the footstool, she didn't even have to ask. Ethan brought her a cup of coffee and sat down on the crate/coffee table.

"What's the motivation for your trip up the mountain

this afternoon?" he asked.

"I just wanted to bring Growler."

"Come on! You know I'm smarter than that."

Anna looked down at her coffee and swirled it in the cup a couple of times. "I want to know about us. We have only known each other for a couple of months and have gone through a lot. I actually think God wants us to be together. What do you think?"

"I think nothing has changed since the last time we had this conversation. Other than that, you snooped through my backpack and found things that would confirm what I have been telling you about the odds of our relationship working. Why would you want someone like me when you have seen the trouble I bring to the community?"

"You're right about the questionable actions you have engaged in. For sure, there are things I would like to see you change. I can't expect you to be just like us when you have only been here for a short time. I guess, to answer your question, I really can't get enough of being with you even with all your faults. Guess that's just how love works. Speaking of how things work. Someday I would like you to show me how all these electronic toys you have work."

"I need to get back to work. The things in my backpack don't concern you. Please forget about them."

Ethan walked out, leaving her sitting in his chair. He worked his way around the upper meadow, checking every inch of the fence and looking for any weakness. A lot easier to fix it before it involved chasing animals around the crater. The sun had hit the top of the crater when he kicked his boots off on the front porch. He had just sat down on his rocking chair when he heard noises coming from inside.

Surely not.

His doubt was confirmed when Anna opened the door and with a sheepish smile sat down in the empty rocker. "Sorry, I fell asleep in your chair. I must have been tired."

Ethan shook his head and rolled his eyes. "I'm beginning to think you would like for us to get married and make this your home as well."

"Thought you would never ask." She grinned.

"You're welcome to come up here, but for now, quit trying to make it something it's not. You'd better get headed home before you get stuck on the trail after dark."

Acting like she was pouting, which she kind of was, Anna grabbed Ethan's hand and squeezed it. "Sadly, you're right. Be careful up here."

Chapter Twenty-Nine

From the switchbacks Ethan could see the activity on the far side of the lake. The livestock had been herded into the upper meadow for the trip up the trail. Fifty-five steers, over a hundred goats, a herd of recently sheared sheep, and a couple of donkeys. A handful of seasoned farmhands on horses and a dozen more men milling about preparing for the drive.

As Ethan approached the crowded barnyard, Robert rode up from the back of the lot and gave the order to move out. Opening the gate, the lead horseback rider started down the trail leading an old steer with a rope. All the others seemed to know what to do and followed the leader single file. Every so often a farmhand would join the procession as they moved along the trail. Once the cattle had all left the lot, the sheep happily followed along. Not so much single file, as they ran all over the place but seemed to make progress. At last, the goats, being naturally rebellious, tried to make a run for it heading in the wrong direction. The experienced and quite capable farm hands quickly got them back on track and walked along with them heading around the lake. All Ethan could think about was the children of Israel as they left Egypt and how that must have looked with all the livestock. He could see that the settlers had this under control and there was nothing for him to do, so he headed cross country up the mountain, staying clear of the overcrowded trail.

Ethan made it to the lower meadow as the first of the steers were reaching the top of the switchbacks. He opened the gate and found a good observation point to watch his charge entering the crater floor. Once through the gate, the cattle seemed at home in the lush green meadow. While some wanted to stop and graze, others wanted to run around the meadow testing its boundaries.

The goats had no interest in going through the gate, but the farmhands had done it before and with a little heavy-handed coaxing they made it into the meadow. Ethan was sitting on his perch being schooled on the techniques of handling livestock. The sheep, not happy with sticking to the trail, had the handlers running all over the mountain. They were being assisted by a couple of sheepdogs, who did an excellent job of turning them back towards the destination. He just hoped someday Growler would be up to the job. He would take the canine out to meet the animals later in the day.

They were just getting the last of the straggling sheep through the gate when Ethan noticed the movement up on the southern slope of the canyon. Pulling his field glasses out of his backpack he focused them on the movement. A mountain lion was intently watching the meadow below its position. It was now in a frozen position with only small systematic movements of its head. As it was weighing out the opportunities it was observing, Ethan was intently studying the predator. *What the...* Another mountain lion entered his vision. *There are two of them. This is getting interesting.* Just as he was about to put the glasses away his attention was drawn to a flash up on the mountain to the southeast.

Turning the glasses that way, he focused in on the spot, only to find someone with binoculars looking back. He watched as the individual appeared to be studying the village below. The man would look through the binoculars and then write on a notepad. Ethan had seen this kind of action many times, and it brought a sense of panic. *Surely, it's not the U.S. military getting ready to invade the settlement.* Ethan searched the sky looking for any sign of drones. If it was the military coming in, they would have eyes overhead watching everything. From where he was, it looked like the sky was clear, at least to the naked eye. He needed to know who was spying on the village.

Chapter Thirty

Ethan was certain the man behind the binoculars would be leaving via Kearsarge pass. He made a note of his features and what he was wearing. Blending in with the farmhands returning to the valley, Ethan cut off across country once they were in the trees. If he hurried, he would make it to the trail and backtrack towards the scout. He had no idea what he would do when he met the scout, but he would figure that out on the way. Checking his backpack for his Beretta, he briefly pulled out the cold steel and inspected the chamber.

Twenty minutes later he had intercepted the trail and was silently making his way up the mountain towards the ridge. Approaching the ridge, he spotted the guy sitting with his back against a tree, eating a sandwich and looking through binoculars. He silently slid the safety off the Beretta and approached the tree from the man's blind spot.

"Don't move a muscle," Ethan whispered as he pressed the barrel of the gun to the guy's head.

The man tensed before dropping his binoculars and a half-eaten sandwich.

"Where's your weapon?" Ethan asked.

"I don't have a weapon."

"Don't lie to me. I watched how you were doing recon on the village. Nobody doing that goes anywhere without a weapon. Where is it?"

The man's shoulders sagged. "It's in my pack. I wasn't expecting company. How did you know I was here?"

Ethan kicked the backpack away from the man and moved in front of him while keeping the Beretta pointed at the man. "Who are you and why are you spying on the village?"

"Cody Turner. I used to live in the community."

"Give me some reason to believe you."

"My grandparents are the ones that started this community, William and Claire Lindbergh. I don't even know if they are still living. They were elderly when I left six years ago."

Ethan lowered his weapon allowing Cody to relax a little.

"So why are you up here?" Ethan asked again, "Why not just return to the community and find out for yourself about your grandparents? In answer to your question, they are alive and well."

"I'm glad to hear that. I look forward to seeing them. I have a lot of reasons for not just marching into the village. I made some enemies when I left. Even my parents may not want to see me."

"What were you writing in your notebook? It sure looked like military recon work."

"That is scary. Where were you watching me from? I was just jotting down the names of people I remembered. You want to see?" He tossed his notebook to Ethan. Ethan picked up the notebook and found a dozen names written down. He tossed the book back to Cody and holstered his Beretta.

"Okay, you can get up and stretch if you want, but you're not done answering questions."

Cody slowly stood not taking his eyes off Ethan. "Did the community hire you for security? Surely, they haven't changed that much."

"No, they didn't. I'm ex-military and am on my own. Where did you serve?"

"I just returned from Afghanistan. I spent a lot of time doing recon for our team. That's what made me comfortable to come up here and scout out my old home before my mission."

"You're starting to make sense. What is your mission? Naturally, I expect nothing but the truth."

"I'm missing my past. As I told you this was my home. My parents brought me here when I was three. It was all I knew until..." Cody's voice drifted off.

Ethan could tell the conversation alone was hurting this fellow veteran.

"Please continue."

"I had it all. It was only two weeks before our wedding. Everyone had come together and built us a cabin. It was going to be the place we would spend our life raising our family. My fiancé and I had grown up together here in the village. We were the best of friends. Then one day I made a really bad mistake that ruined my life. I not only hurt, my soon-to-be wife, but my parents, grandparents, and a lot of other people in the community."

"What did you do that was so heinous that would cause you to leave here and join the military?"

"When I walked out of here six years ago, I didn't have a plan. I knew that I would come back someday, but did not know when. One thing led to another until I found myself in the military killing terrorists. It was quite a change from my non-violent upbringing. After getting out of the service, I decided I was ready to return to my roots. The problem is, it may just be too late. I may no longer be welcome, even if I repent."

"You still haven't told me what you did."

"It's a complicated story.

"Go ahead. I have the time.

"I was a miner down at the Charlotte Mountain mine and was good at my job. We had discovered a large vein of gold and were diligently working to recover it all. Having grown up here I never concerned myself with the value of gold, other than I was taught that it provided all we needed to live comfortably here in the village."

"So, what changed that?"

"I guess you could say that it's the sinful nature of man. I started thinking that if the commune had more than enough gold to last for many generations, why shouldn't I keep some for myself and my future family. I started taking just one little nugget a day home and burying it in a jar under a floorboard in my house. Throughout a couple of years, I had accumulated a few jars of gold. I started feeling guilty, but for some reason couldn't stop. That was when I started getting greedy and instead of one nugget, I would take two or three.

"One day someone must have watched me put the nuggets in my lunch box. As I was leaving that day, the elders were waiting for me in the village and made me open my lunch box. I was caught. They took me to the meeting house and called all the community together. I was scared standing in front of the congregation as they read off the charge against me. Stealing anything in the community is a serious crime. Stealing gold was much worse. It showed that I had lost my way, and that greed would lead to even more serious sins. I could see my fiancé crying in the back of the church. I cried for forgiveness and leniency. While I heard compassion from some, I heard things coming from some of the elders that night that denigrated my soul."

Ethan was starting to see the picture, "So, is that when they decided to make you leave the village?"

"I never gave them a chance. When they made me step outside so they could vote on my demise, I left. I walked through the night until I came to the valley. I had nothing but the clothes on my back. The six years since then have been a living hell for me. I want to go home."

"I can understand," Ethan was starting to feel compassion for the outcast. "Have you dealt with the greed issue?"

"The roots of my upbringing run deep, and the time came when I realized I had all I ever needed here. Sure, money can buy you things, but we had all the things we needed here. What money can't buy are relationships. I miss all the people I ever knew from my childhood, especially Anna. I'm sure she's moved on and has a family by now.

"Are you saying Anna is your fiancée?" Ethan was

not surprised. This must be the sad story she had not been able to share.

"She was! As I said, I'm sure she's married and has a family. Do you know her?"

"I have met her a time or two. She is still unmarried at no fault of her own."

Cody's eyes lit up for a moment before reality set in. "I doubt if she would have anything to do with me after I left her as I did. I never even tried to contact her."

"You just never know," Ethan told him. "The first thing you need to do is make things right with the community, so they will let you stay. Come on down to my place in the crater, and we'll work out a plan."

Chapter Thirty-One

Late into the night, the two men sat on the front porch of Ethan's cabin discussing the situation in the valley and their time in Afghanistan. Ethan with his night vision glasses on his lap had been keeping a watch over the livestock. He had little experience with mountain lions, but was certain they would at least attempt to score an easy meal or two.

By the time they called it a night, Ethan was comfortable with the plan. Cody would keep an eye on the livestock the next morning while Ethan paid Abram a visit. The kind old elder would have the wisdom on how to handle the order of restoration.

Trying to sleep with a stranger in the house was part of Ethan's restlessness. The other issues were the sounds of the animals in the meadow and the emotional ties he had with Anna. He was glad he had pushed back. It was going to be an interesting few days. Not to mention the outside threats that he hadn't forgotten about. He needed to continue working on a contingency plan. He had just drifted off to sleep when the donkeys started baying loudly in the meadow. Grabbing his sniper rifle and his night vision glasses he headed out onto the porch. Cody was already there looking through his.

"It looks like we have two guests on the hill. They are just outside the fence."

It didn't take Ethan long to spot the two predators he had seen earlier in the day.

"What do you think?" Cody asked. "Should we take them out?"

"We could, but I would like to see if the donkeys will deter them. If we kill these, more will take their place. It would be better if they are scared off."

The mountain lions walked along the fence line for a couple of hundred yards. All the time the donkeys made all kinds of racket and stayed with the lions on the opposite side of the fence. The livestock had all moved away from that side of the meadow and was milling around nervously. Finally, the mountain lions turned up the hill and disappeared into a ravine.

"Go get some sleep," Cody told his host. "I'll stand watch the rest of the night."

Exhausted, Ethan was soon fast asleep and was only awakened at the sound of a skillet on the cookstove and the smell of bacon frying. Coming out of the bedroom he found Cody holding a cup of coffee and making flapjacks.

"Any more excitement?" he asked.

"Not until I found the bacon," Cody smiled. "It sure feels like I've come home. As a teenager, I did spend one summer up here with my uncle."

Chapter Thirty-Two

Ethan sat silently watching Abram stare into his coffee cup. He had just broken the news about Cody's return to the mountain. It was a lot for the spiritual leader to work through, and it looked like he had no intentions of hurrying the process.

Finally, he looked up at Ethan, "Lest we become rash in our words and do damage to the road of reconciliation, let's ask God to give us wisdom."

The authenticity of Abram's prayer was filled with straightforwardness and humility. When he had finished praying, he pulled out a piece of paper and started writing. When he had finished, he folded the paper and slipped it into an envelope. "Give this to Cody. If he seriously desires to make things right, he will follow these instructions. Thank you for letting him into your home, but from now on, it is imperative that you remove yourself from the process."

Leaving Abram's, Ethan had one more issue weighing heavy on his mind. Stopping by the bakery and the store he picked up a few things for lunch and made his way around the lake. It took some doing, but he finally found her working in one of the gardens.

"What brings you down here this morning?" Anna asked.

"I needed to see Abram and have lunch with one of my friends. That is if she can stop hoeing weeds. Are you ready for a break?"

Putting down her hoe, Anna followed Ethan to a clean shady spot under a tree.

"So now we're friends?" Anna commented between bites. "What a move forward for our relationship. What's next?"

"What's next is that you're going to tell me about how you almost got married."

"What if I'm not comfortable with doing that?"

"Then I would say you are hiding something."

Anna's half-hearted laugh revealed her discomfort, "Says the man who has a closet full of skeletons."

"And one that is not looking for a lasting relationship," Ethan added to Anna's sarcasm.

Wrenching, Anna's downcast eyes showed her sadness. She fiddled with her food for a couple of minutes and with tears slowly making their way down her beautiful, yet distressed, face she told Ethan about Cody. Wiping away the tears as she finished, she shared how devastated she had been and had not allowed anyone to get emotionally close to her until she had met him.

"So, when this guy Cody rides into town someday in search of his fiancé, what will you do?" Ethan bated Anna just to see what she was thinking.

Anna laughed at the possibility of that actually happening. "I would let him swing me upon his trusty steed and we would race off into the sunset. Seriously, I have never been asked that question. We were best friends before he took off. I don't know what I would do."

Ethan stood up and pulled on his pack. "I need to get back up the mountain before the mountain lions decide it is lunchtime. Thank you for sharing, I know it was hard for you."

Anna jumped up as well, to not let Ethan get away without a big hug. "I'll come up and see you after work tomorrow."

"I'm sure you will. Be prepared to see God at work."

Why did I say that? Ethan asked himself as he headed for the crater. *Now she's going to think I'm going to get serious with her. Oh well! She'll know soon enough.*

Chapter Thirty-Three

As Cody read the letter from Abram, his face was tight, and his hands were trembling. Whatever Abram had written was an emotional tsunami. Pacing around the room mumbling incoherent words, he started banging his head into the door. Ethan recognized this as signs of a battle-hardened veteran who had hit emotional overload and was having difficulty processing. He had to deescalate the situation. Abram had told him not to get involved but had no idea what Cody had experienced.

Grabbing a resistless arm, Ethan dragged Cody out the door and down to the creek. Snatching the instructions from Cody's hand he shoved him face-first into the water. Coming up sputtering and madder than a Banty rooster, Cody came at Ethan with intentions of doing bodily harm. By now, Ethan was laughing so hard that all he could do was take the swings Cody was determined to deliver. After a few wild swings, Cody gave up and sat down on the edge of the porch, soaking wet and exhausted. Ethan sat down next to Cody and opened up Abram's letter.

"We're going to go over this together Cody. It's quite obvious, you started perceiving things that were a lot worse than what you were reading."

"I really don't know what happened. I was just reading the letter, and something snapped. You sure know how to bring someone back. That's some cold water."

"As you know, it's nothing but melting snow."

Ethan silently read the letter. About halfway through, he spotted the trigger.

"So, you were not aware of your parents' deaths?"

Cody's head jerked up with a puzzled expression. "I don't remember reading that. Does it say anything else about my family?"

"Doesn't look like it. He just writes that your parents were instrumental in formulating these instructions before their death."

Cody was shaken but able to comprehend what was going on. "It is sad that I didn't make it back to tell them goodbye. I'm sure my grandfather will be able to fill me in. I should get started on the list. Finding Anna and apologizing to her will be the hardest. Just maybe…."

Ethan knew what Cody was thinking and kept it to himself. It was not his battle to fight. With Growler sitting at his feet Ethan watched Cody head down the trail to the settlement.

Chapter Thirty-Four

Ethan scanned through the news. It was amazing how in such a short time he had become detached from the outside world. He was beginning to understand the mindset of a remote settlement. A good way to destroy peace and contentment was to be bombarded every waking moment with the evil that ravages society. He questioned his decision to bring technology to the mountain. He would have to stay focused on the task at hand and not get caught up on things over which he had no control. Looking up from his laptop he surveyed the surrounding mountains and meadow. God had blessed him richly by bringing him here.

An hour later Ethan had scoured the internet and had found no evidence that anyone had a reliable lead on his whereabouts. Some articles told of witnesses sighting him at different places around the country. The funniest was the news report of a raid on an Amish farmhouse in northern Indiana. He felt a little guilty for that one but got over it quickly.

He was about to give up when in the dark corner of the search engine he found a report of a single mother who had been questioned about her interaction with Ethan. The report did not mention her name, but Ethan could tell by the article that it was Krystal.

Scrolling down through his emails all he had was spam. Not a single message from Krystal. Maybe she'd moved on. Deleting the spam one page at a time, he came across a message that caught his eye. The name of the sender was *Sleeper car guest* and the subject was *Looking for you*. Opening the message he began to read. *Ethan, I need to talk to you. For our safety, we have left my parents and are staying at an undisclosed location. We have reasons to believe that the people you warned about know our connections. Some stranger has been inquiring about us in town. I got scared and ran. I do have the children with me and, for now, at least, we are in a safe place. What should we do?*

Looking at the date Ethan could see that Krystal had sent the message fourteen days ago. No telling what has transpired in two weeks.

He typed out a response. *My dear Krystal, while I will never be sorry for getting to know you, I am sorry for the problems our short relationship has caused. The only advice I have is for you to come here. It's the only place I can protect you and the children.*

After reading the response he questioned his motives but knew it was the only thing he could do. Hitting send, he shut down his laptop and disconnected the satellite receiver.

He had just finished eating his lunch when Growler jumped to his feet and approached the door. The deep-throated growl communicated that it wasn't just time for a necessary trip to the nearest tree.

"What is it Growler? Is there something out there?" Ethan grabbed his Beretta and opened the door to see Anna coming up the trail. "Thanks for the warning, Growler. I guess I won't need this." He put the gun back on the shelf.

By the time Anna was crossing the log, Ethan could see her tear-stained face and the way her chest heaved with sobs. It must have not gone well.

Anna's distress quickly evolved to full throttle crying as she climbed the steps and started pounding Ethan's chest with her harmless fist. "I hate you, I hate you!" she screamed. "I really hate you!" He let her beat off some steam before he wrapped his arms around her where she sobbed on his shoulder.

Finally, Anna got herself under control, and he let her go, even though he could tell that was not at all what she wanted.

Sitting on the porch, Anna kept reaching out to take his hand, one which he was not offering.

"So, why did you come up here?" Ethan asked after an uncomfortable amount of time.

"You know."

"Do I?"

"How long have you known about Cody?"

"I spotted him up on the ridge the day we were moving livestock. Thought he was someone coming looking for me, so I tracked him down. Once I found out who he was and what he had done, I let him come here temporarily. Back to the real question, why are you here?"

Anna squirmed in her chair and again reached out for

a hand to hold only to find rejection. It tore at Ethan to see the sadness in her normally cheerful disposition. She didn't seem to have a clear-cut explanation.

"I really don't know. I was hoping you could tell me what to do. I'm still in shock and am not sure I can forgive Cody. I have always loved him, but…." She stopped in mid-sentence as if she was about to reveal something profound.

"But what!"

"Cody has been gone a long time and I was resigned to the realization that I would live alone for the rest of my life. Then, you showed up and caused a lot of ruckus."

"Ruckus? Not even sure I know what that means."

"Well, you lit a fire in my heart, and once again I had hope. I know, you kept telling me that it would never work out, but I was certain that God had brought us together and eventually you would see that. Then, this happens."

"So, you're saying, your challenge with your ex-fiancé is my fault?"

"Yes and no!"

"You're impossible."

"Are you saying, you want to terminate our relationship?"

"From my standpoint, our relationship was purely platonic. I told you it would never work out. I do hope for the best for you and Cody."

Anna's cheeks flushed, and her eyes darkened, "Who said Cody is going to be part of my life?"

"You told me you always loved him and if that's the case, in time you will forgive him."

"You're impossible!"

"That was my line. Tell me something new, like when

are you going to forgive him and move on with your life?"

"Augggghhh! Can you at least help me make sense of the fiasco my life is in? As much as I shouldn't, I trust you."

"Sure. Start by getting your little fanny back down the mountain. Considering the two of you need professional counseling, I recommend you two don't spend time alone. Get together with his grandparents, their lasting loving relationship is filled with good godly experience."

"Sounds like you're passing the buck. Can't you help us?"

"You know my past; do you really think I'm the one that should walk you through this mess? Not hardly!"

Ethan stood up, indicating this conversation had come to an abrupt conclusion. "I'll see you on Sunday. Be careful."

Ethan watched as Anna shuffled along the meadow. "What am I doing? All I would have to do is say the word. But that is not fair to her or the community. My past has become a liability. Maybe someday God can fix me."

Chapter Thirty-Five

While Ethan was spending two uneventful weeks in the crater keeping watch over the livestock, the settlement was a beehive of complex activity. One of their own who had gone astray had returned. A plan of reconciliation was put into place by the commune leaders and approved by the church. Cody made a public apology to the entire settlement and privately met with individuals he had personally hurt.

Ethan, feeling he would only be the catalyst in creating additional anxiety and commotion in the village, decided to stay away. His only contact was an occasional farmhand who would come up to assist with the animals.

Late each night he would fire up the satellite internet and read any articles about his whereabouts. So far, all leads led to dead ends. He prayed it would stay that way. One night he received a message from Krystal. She did not use her real name, but her alias stood out.

We have made it to Utah to an old friend's home. It is

very temporary accommodation, as the home is small and crowded. I wish we could talk on the phone, but I know that is impossible. If you can help us come to where you are, I would forever be indebted to you. Please hurry as we are running out of resources. I'll love you always.

Utah! An idea came to Ethan. He clicked on a few web pages and found what he was looking for. Sure enough, Junior had a social media page that displayed his flying experiences. Scanning down through it, he was happy the trip to Independence was not mentioned. Finding the link to direct messaging, he shot a message off to Junior. As expected with the younger generation, it didn't take but seconds to get a response. *Just tell me when and where, and I will be your pilot,* the message read. *I am now flying higher-performance aircraft. It'll get you there quicker but cost more dough.*

Next, Ethan typed out a message to Krystal. *I need you to let me know where you are without revealing your location on the internet. Send me the compass direction and distance from the last place we said goodbye, and then start making preparations to leave.*

Ethan felt he had been online long enough and shut down the equipment. It was late at night, and he did not expect Krystal to respond anytime soon. Throwing another chunk of wood in the cookstove, he filled the water kettle. A half-hour later he was taking a lukewarm shower contemplating how he was going to break the news to the settlement that Krystal and her children were coming to the mountain. Even though the chain of events had already been put into play, he still needed their approval. He knew the community would never approve of Krystal and her children living with him. He didn't know if it was the breeze blowing in around the tarp, or the thought of the two of them together that created the chills that he was experiencing.

Chapter Thirty-Six

Early the next morning Ethan made his rounds, checking the fences and the livestock before heading down to the village. Arriving at Abram's in time for breakfast would make the old man happy. Not that he took anything for granted, but it seemed that Abram always had enough for two. As expected, Abram was happy for the company but sensed there was an underlying reason for Ethan's visit.

"So, tell me my brother, what brings you to the valley this morning? They say the eyes are a window to the soul and by the looks of things, yours is shrouded in mystery."

"It's a blessing just to be called your brother," Ethan answered. "You are correct. My life is shrouded in mystery, and God is removing the shroud at a rapid pace. I can hardly keep up. Can I start at the beginning?"

"Please do. I have all day."

"Well, do you remember me telling you about the mother and children I met on the train?'

"Would that be the one whose daughter asked you

about your faith?"

"It is. Anyhow we have been corresponding and to make a long story short, she is on her way here." Ethan watched for an adverse reaction from his elderly mentor and found none. After a moment Abram looked up at Ethan with the 'go on' expression.

"I'm not naive enough to believe that it is okay for them to live in the crater with me"

Stroking his thinning beard like he was used to doing when things needed to be thought out and taken as gospel truth. "Why is she coming here?"

Why does he have to ask the questions I don't want to answer? Ethan looked down at the scars on his now rugged hands. "Our time together on the train was enough to convince her that she would like for us to spend more time together in hopes our relationship can grow. I have to admit I have the same desire. Even though I have doubts, considering my turbulent past."

Abram poked around at the coals in the fire. "Ethan, in the couple of months that you have been here, you have had a lasting effect on the community, not all of it has been bad. Your friendship with Anna has changed her life. I know many expected you two to get married, but as we see, God had other plans. Without your loving care for her, she would not have accepted Cody's return. You may not have heard the two of them are to be married in a few weeks. It's a little fast for me, but I was not asked."

Ethan found himself reacting with mixed emotions to the news but kept his silence.

Abram continued, "Nevertheless, you have even won over Eli who was your biggest skeptic. Robert says you're doing a fine job with the animals.

"All I can promise is that we will welcome this family into our community and give them a place to stay. For how long we don't know, but her and the children's safety is of primary importance. You can tell her that. When is she getting here?"

"I will be going to the valley tomorrow with hopes of bringing her and her children home. I may be gone for a couple of days as we don't know for sure when they will make it to Independence." Ethan was deliberate with his words, so as not to mislead Abram.

"God speed, my brother. Bring them here when you return, and in the meantime, I will prepare the community."

Arriving at the farm Ethan found his boss still feeding the animals in the barn. "What brings you down here so early, problems in the crater?"

"Guess you could say that," Ethan responded. "I'm just checking to see if I could get someone to relieve me for a couple of days. I need to make a trip into town."

"Sure, that's not a problem. Are you expecting a mail-order bride?" Robert joked not knowing how close he came to hitting the mark.

"Ouch, you know how to hurt a guy. Thanks, boss. I should be back in a couple of days."

Ethan continued around the lake. He had thought of finding Anna and congratulating her, but an inner voice kept telling him that was not a good idea. The last thing he wanted was to plant any more doubt in her head. Not only that but he was anxious to get back to the crater and check his email.

"We are ready to go anytime you get here. We are two

hundred and thirty miles west southwest (258 degrees) of the previously mentioned location. I hope you can find it."

Ethan pulled up a map and soon pinpointed her location and relayed the message to Junior. *"Once you pick up the passengers bring them to the location you dropped me off a few months ago. This is classified and will remain a need-to-know operation. Thanks again for your help."*

Within minutes a reply came in with an estimated time of arrival and the identification of the aircraft. He hammered out one last message to Krystal.

"Be at the municipal airport southwest of town at 2:30. Go to the ramp where you will find a gas pump. Your aircraft will be a white and green twin-engine Piper Seneca. It would be best for you to stay in the car until you see the aircraft arrive at the gas pumps. Once the pilot has finished fueling the aircraft, drive out to it. He is expecting you and will help transfer your bags and the children. I'm praying for your safe travels." Ethan hesitated before adding, *"Your sleeper car friend."*

Shutting down the system he grabbed his backpack along with his Beretta and headed out the door. It was already afternoon, and the flight would be arriving in a little over five hours. His only hope was to get a hitch to town from the trailhead. The adrenaline he felt propelled him forward and two hours later he was crossing over Kearsarge Pass. It was three-thirty when he walked into Onion Valley trailhead and not a soul was in sight.

Reading the bulletin board, he noticed a flyer looking for anyone that had information on a double homicide that happened upon the trail a few weeks back. *Who might have that been?* Ethan asked sarcastically. All he could do was head on down the road towards the valley. The temperature was rising rapidly as he descended, and he had just made the turn at the third switchback when a pickup truck came by and hit its brakes. The ride in the back of the truck wasn't ideal but a far cry better than walking. Fifteen minutes later, the generous day hikers dropped him off at the Chevron station an hour before the flight was due to arrive.

Grabbing a cold drink, Ethan made his way over to the Independence Courthouse Motel where he secured two rooms. Turning on his tablet he connected to the wifi and checked his email. No new messages, which was a good thing. Bringing up Flight Tracker he typed in the call sign. Ethan spotted the Seneca a hundred and ten miles northeast of Independence. Ethan's clicked on the call sign and read the data. Altitude 12,500 feet, airspeed 160 knots, course heading 210 degrees, destination Lone Pine.

Lone Pine? Why is he going to Lone Pine? Did he forget where he dropped me off? How am I going to get to Lone Pine? Ethan took a quick shower and returned to the Flight Tracker. He noticed the Seneca was in a descent thirty miles northwest of Independence. It still said Lone Pine but looked like it had turned right and was heading for Independence. Ethan was pulling on his shoes when the data block disappeared. *Now what?* He wasted no time getting out the door into the late afternoon sun. He could only hope that nothing had gone wrong as he practically ran the half mile to the airport. It was still over 85 degrees, but the sun was shortly going to be dropping behind the mountain range.

He didn't see any plumes of smoke to the east but did hear the droning of the twin-engine aircraft. The sun flashed off the wing as it entered downwind revealing its position. Ethan ignored the tightness in his chest as he was relieved to see the aircraft under control. *Looks like he pulled a fast one in making the cyberworld think he was going to Lone Pine.*

As the propellers came to a stop the door opened and the first person out of the plane was Ethan's little friend, Jonah, quickly followed by Cathryn and Christiana. They all had spotted Ethan and were running to meet him. All three jumped into his waiting arms. It was as if he was their long-lost father. How that strong connection happened in only a few days on the train was a miracle. One that Ethan could literally wrap his arms around. His eyes were drawn to the children's beautiful mother as she crawled out of the aircraft. He gave the children one last quick hug and stood to embrace Krystal. The strong lasting hug was only interrupted by the children's impatience.

Ethan let go of Krystal only to help Junior unload the luggage. Looking at the number of suitcases and duffel bags on the ground caused Ethan to moan. How much of this needed to go up the mountain? With an empty airplane and an envelope full of cash, Junior was soon airborne, and Ethan led the family down highway 395 to the motel.

The excitement of the three children in the motel room was a little overwhelming for Ethan, but he knew he could adjust. They had done so well on the train that he just had to give them time to settle down. All he wanted to do was have some alone time with Krystal to discuss their future. Finally, they became exhausted and went to sleep. Alone at last, Ethan and Krystal were sitting at the little table sipping on a cup of motel brewed coffee. "It will get better than this," he told her as he held up his cup.

"Do you mind expounding on that statement?" Krystal asked as she too held up her cup.

"A lot has changed since we said our goodbyes at the Grand Junction train station."

"You're telling me. I had a lonely, yet peaceful life before I met you."

"Sorry, I never meant for you to be dragged into this, but here we are, and all I can say is I am happy you are here."

Reaching across the table Krystal took hold of Ethan's hand and squeezed gently. The soft smile and the little dimple said it all before she even began to respond. "The children were so excited when they found out we were coming to meet you. They asked if you were going to become their daddy. Oh, for the innocence of little ones. As for me, I am very fond of you and with certainty feel you would do everything in your power to protect us. I just don't know how our relationship will develop until you have reconciled your past. What are we going to do?"

"Krystal, where we are going tomorrow is a long and difficult trip. It will be all the children can do to handle it. Once we get to the settlement there will be a place for you and the children to stay and you'll be well taken care of. In answer to your question, I don't know. What I want to do is marry you and adopt the children. I too am concerned about how that can work as I am a wanted man. I'm not so sure it's a good idea for you to be under that bondage."

The tears in Krystal's eyes told Ethan that he was hurting her badly. "I am willing to move forward with our relationship as long as it includes counseling from a godly couple I deeply respect and admire. That counseling would entail my revealing all of my past."

"Is there anything you need to tell me about that would hinder our relationship?"

"Yes, are the children asleep?"

Krystal stood up and checked the little ones. Returning to her seat she nodded. Ethan unbuttoned his shirt and pulled back the collar. "See this scar?"

"Ouch. That looks new. How did you manage to get that?"

Ethan went on to share with Krystal what transpired on his last trip down the mountain. "I know it was self-defense, but I can't even go to the law and tell what happened. That's part of being a wanted man."

Shaking her head Krystal was at loss for words. Finally, she responded to the revelation of Ethan killing his attackers. "Jesus was pretty clear about those that used the sword would die by the same. I don't condone what you did in New York, yet I understand why you did it. What I don't understand is how you were able to do that to your attackers? I guess we are made different. I find you as a loving patient man, who wants to do the right thing. I am not at all concerned about how you will treat me and the children, but I do agree, that we need counseling and a lot of prayers before we move forward. I really do want this to work."

He squeezed her hand and agreed. "Let's get some sleep; we have a big day tomorrow."

Chapter Thirty-Seven

"We can't carry everything you brought on the plane," Ethan explained to Krystal and the children. "Separate the things that are important to you from the replaceable things. We have everything you need up in the settlement."

Jonah was clutching his teddy bear with a big frown. "Can I take Henry?"

Ethan ruffled the youngster's hair, "Of course, you can. Take the things that remind you of home."

With that information, everyone went to work and by mid-morning they had it whittled down to two large and three small packs. A cheerful motel clerk who just loved the children rambled to Ethan about how nice it was that the whole family was going hiking. Ethan didn't care to correct her but used that opportunity to employ her to find someone to take them up to Onion Valley trailhead. It wasn't but a few minutes before a minivan pulled into the parking lot with the clerk's husband at the wheel smoking a cigar. He was gracious enough to snuff it out as he rolled back the door and helped his passengers get it. Ethan could see Krystal wrinkle her nose as she crawled in. *Nasty smell, but we would all smell nasty if we had to hike up this road.*

Thanking their driver with a fist full of money, they were soon on their way. Ethan, who was used to backpacking and always found the trail tough, was certain it was going to be nothing but pain and agony for the other four. It would only be a matter of time before he would be carrying Jonah. He made them stop and rest frequently to keep from getting blisters. They were all excited and the imagination of where they were going was enough to drive them on. Arriving at Gilbert Lake at noon, they stopped for lunch. Where normally the children would be running wild, they took this time to take an unexpected nap.

"Surprising what a lot of exercise and thin air will do," their mother said.

"It's going to get thinner as we continue to climb. We're only about halfway to the pass, so we had better move on." Ethan answered as he got to his feet.

Reaching down he helped Krystal to her feet and wrapped his arms around her. She was quite content with maintaining this position for a few minutes as they watched the children sleep. Finally, the reality of the climb ahead overpowered the here and now. "Come on children, it's time to go."

The complaints increased with altitude to the point it was right down moaning by the time they reached Kearsarge Pass. The kids shouted for joy as they dropped their packs and plopped to the ground. Up ahead they could see Bullfrog Lake and a lot of mountain peaks.

Ethan let them rest for twenty minutes before he rousted them up. "We have three more miles to go, and once that sun drops below the mountains, it gets cold."

The sun was below the mountain, and they were shivering when they walked into the settlement. Knocking on Abram's door he was surprised when it was opened by Eli.

"Good evening, Eli. Surprised to see you here this late in the day."

"We were expecting you, just didn't know when. Come on in out of the chill." Eli led them into the small room, which became smaller with the additional five visitors.

Abram slowly got to his feet to show respect to his guest and to greet the newest visitors to the settlement. Grasping Krystal's hand with both of his he had a twinkle in his eye. "You're even more beautiful than Ethan could describe. Welcome to our community."

Krystal blushed and introduced each of the children to Abram and Eli. "We are honored to visit and possibly live here. Ethan has shared as much as he can about his new home, and we are excited to assimilate here as well. You must thank God each day for the blessing he has on display here."

"We sure do, my darling young lady. He has been so good to us. It looks like he has blessed you with some wonderful children. They look like they have had a long day. Eli will take you to the home of one of our dear sisters who has beds for you and your children. Tomorrow we will work on a long-term plan. Good night children, may the Lord go with you."

Once Ethan was assured Krystal and the children were taken care of, he headed up to the crater. It had been a tough and grueling day, but one of promise. He still had a lot of concern about outside forces invading the settlement. Already his actions had disrupted Krystal and her children's life. Not only had theirs been disrupted, but now it was certain the grandparents were missing their grandchildren. Ethan pondered the thought, *It's amazing how a person can affect the lives of so many others, some of whom they have never met. I really need to be more conscious of these consequences.*

The glow from the cabin window was a beacon pulling him home as he walked along the meadow. The night was still, and the stars showed bright overhead. An occasion audible from one of the livestock and the shuffling of Ethan's hiking boots against the trail was all that could be heard.

Crossing the log, he could see the shadow of someone sitting in his rocking chair on the porch. It didn't take long for him to recognize Hugo. Hugo Tozatulp had migrated to the United States from Eastern Europe as a child and as a young adult stumbled upon the settlement while on a backpacking trip. Now, thirty years later, he was happily married with five children, and his leadership was considered a great asset to the community.

"Good evening, Hugo. Did the livestock miss me?"

"No, but I did. It's awful lonely up here."

"Yes, it is. Isn't it awesome?"

"Speaking of lonely, I heard you were bringing back a bride. Where is she?"

"Awe, come on Hugo," Ethan said with a big grin.

"You know you wouldn't approve of me bringing her up here. All unmarried and such, just wouldn't be right. Now, would it?"

"I reckon you're right, Ethan. You did the right thing. I suppose we'll all get a chance to meet her soon. Well now that you're here and don't need me anymore, I'll head on down the mountain to my little lady."

Once Ethan watched Hugo's light disappearing below the rim, Ethan petted Growler's head. "Come on boy, it's time for some shut-eye."

Chapter Thirty-Eight

Finding a suspect in *triple homicide is within reach,* read the headline. Ethan scanned down through the article to see if there were any clues to their reasoning. Most of what the authorities had revealed was a lot of hogwash, but what bothered him the most was the statement issued by an unnamed source that said their daughter was friends with a lady that was on her way to meet the suspect. What was even worse was the comment that she had turned over her computer to the FBI. *That is trouble. If that is Krystal's friend who took her to the airport, they would have access to her emails. It's a good thing I didn't give her Junior's contact information. Hopefully Steven was still running block.*

He scrolled over to the email address used in communicating with Krystal and deleted it. The footprint would still be there but at least he would not somehow use it and get the FBI any better leads. It would be best if he limited his time on the internet. It was time to play it safe.

It was still early morning when Ethan completed his chores and headed down the hill. It was late summer, but the days were already getting shorter and the leaves at this altitude were already showing signs of the coming fall.

Krystal stepped out on the porch at Ethan's knock. "The children are still sleeping. The good news is that Elena has said she would care for the children, so you could show me around." The glow on her face as she took hold of his hand communicated to Ethan what his plans were for the morning.

"Wait right here, and I'll get my jacket."

Ethan led Krystal west around the lake until the smell of baking bread turned them up the side trail.

"The first thing we have to do is pick up some cinnamon rolls and go see some friends of mine,"

Krystal could have spent all day in the bakery. "Just maybe I could help here," she commented as they walked back down the path with a paper bag full of rolls.

"Up at three every morning? I'm thinking your responsibilities will focus on three little ones for the time being, at least until they are in school. Let's just take one day at a time."

"That's one of the attributes I love about you," Krystal said as she pulled him closer to her as they walked along. "Who are we going to go see now?"

"I want you to meet William and Claire. They were the first settlers to arrive here at the lake and their experiences make them more than qualified to help us through our challenges." Ethan led Krystal up the side trail.

For over an hour William and Claire lovingly grilled Krystal on all things relational. Not just with her first husband, but with her children, her parents, and most importantly with her God. They never even mentioned Ethan. Krystal's meek and loving character shined as she humbly and without prejudice answered their questions. While not devolving more than necessary, she never left them wanting.

They both left the Lindberghs with a feeling of happiness. Somehow, they felt they were doing the right thing. Yet in that feeling of ecstasy, a gut-wrenching realization of New York arose. Pushing it aside, they continued around the lake stopping at the farm where Ethan introduced Krystal to his coworkers. Robert did a little ribbing before privately speaking with Ethan about his responsibilities in the crater. "We'll help you when we can, but it is still your responsibility."

"I appreciate your concern, and now that they are up here, it shouldn't be a problem."

"Have you told her about Anna?"

"Nope, but it is at the top of my to-do list. Fortunately, in that department, I have nothing to be ashamed of."

"That is a blessing, but the conversation must happen before they meet. Does Anna know about this young lady?"

"Yes, she does. I told her all about Krystal and the conversations we had on the train."

"Well, with Cody coming home and her getting married to him, it's a closed issue anyhow. I hope you all can be happy and bring nothing but peace and harmony to the community. Do well, my brother."

Crossing over the outlet they came to the big flat rock, that not so long ago, Ethan had rested on that Sunday afternoon. "Let's sit for a while. I have something I want to share that could take some working through."

"What may that be?" Krystal queried as she leaned back into his arms. Looking down the stream where it disappeared into the valley, she wasn't sure she wanted to hear anything else that might take away the utopia she was feeling. She tried to shut out any preconceived ideas about what else could destroy what she was experiencing. Krystal hadn't felt this since before her husband died not so many years ago.

Ethan chose his words carefully. "Our time together on the train did something to me that will last a lifetime. It lit a fire where there was no desire. It made me think that there was the hope of having a family again. It is a family that I had grown to love in only a couple of days. Rolling out of Grand Junction, I cried with the emptiness that I left back in the station. To simplify what I'm trying to say, emotionally you messed me up big."

Krystal had a big grin on her face as she tilted her head back to look into his eyes. He took that as a sign and kissed her gently.

"That all sounds good, but I have a feeling this conversation is going to change to something less humorous."

"It all depends on how you take it. Some parts are, but we will get to that. The day after I arrived, I hiked up to the crater to see where I was going to be living and met a young lady cleaning the house." Ethan expecting an adverse reaction paused briefly. Not even feeling a twinge from Krystal, he continued. "We became close, and she was all into us spending the rest of our lives together. I will admit I had a lot of feelings for her but told her it would never work out. She grew up here in the community, and I did not. Probably the biggest reason I said it would not work was because of the time you and I spent together. Even though I question my own faith, I still prayed daily that God would bring us back together."

"How far did you two take this relationship? I'm certain you know what I mean."

"Emotionally, we took it too far. There was minimal physical contact. Seriously, we did nothing that I am ashamed of."

"How did it end?"

"I consider it an answer from God, as I had no idea how many times I could resist. One day a man who had been her fiancé six years ago returned to the valley. I gathered there were still some embers burning for that old flame. Just two days after his return was when I received your email wanting advice on what you should do. It was like an answer to my prayers. Please believe me when I say you have never been an afterthought."

"That's an interesting revelation, my man. So why didn't you tell me about the girlfriend in one of the emails or down in Independence?"

"Our emails were not like ongoing love letters. I seriously never expected to see you again."

"What are your feelings for her now?"

"My feelings for her are the same. I could not let go of the dream of spending the rest of my life with you. It kept my relationship with her, as they say, platonic. I'm sure you will have more questions, and I promise without reservations to answer them honestly."

Krystal again tilted her head back for another kiss, as

a way of accepting his terms without saying a word.

As they stood up to continue their walk, Krystal asked if she could meet Anna.

"Sure, I think that would be a great thing to do. She's probably working in the garden now."

Anna had seen them coming before they spotted her. Pulling off her garden gloves and wiping the sweat off her brow, she met them at the edge of the garden. Ethan warily introduced the two women who had tried to steal his heart. He listened as they exchanged niceties. He was relieved at the lack of hostility in either one's tone.

They were a hundred yards down the trail when Krystal spoke, "I can see why you were drawn to her. She's a beautiful woman, inside and out. I now feel blessed that you chose me." She grabbed his arm and rested her head on his shoulder. "Let's go get the children and you can show us where we are going to live as a family."

"Does that mean you want to get married?"

"Only if you ask." She smiled.

He squeezed her hand and reassured her not to give up hope.

Crossing over the bridge at the east end of the lake, the children were again full of excitement. Even though they had not been told what was going on, the joy was somehow transmitted through their mother. Cresting the switchbacks they could see all the animals in the meadow and the stone cabin in the crater.

"Are we going to live here?" Jonah asked.

His mother patted his shoulder and didn't say a word.

Krystal took one look at the log and chose to cross the rocks. "You will need to square that thing off if you want me to cross it,"

The children didn't seem to care and ran across the log and up onto the porch. From the far side of the stream, Ethan looked at Krystal sitting on the porch with the children laughing and playing. A lump filled his throat.

After a tour of the cabin, they returned to the porch where the adults watched the children playing in the stream. Krystal reached out and took Ethan's hand. "I think we should tell the children."

"Krystal, I'm thinking it's a little premature. We still have a lot of issues to work out before making that lifetime commitment. I don't want to hurt you again."

Chapter Thirty-Nine

"**We need to** talk." Ethan's face showed signs of anxiety.

Krystal grabbed his arm, and they walked a short distance away from Elena's cabin. "What's the problem?'

"I just heard from the mule train driver that someone in Lone Pine was asking about me. It was through a third party, and he had no details. That in itself is not a big issue if it wasn't for the other thing he told me."

"Which was?"

"I don't want to scare you, but I want you to keep your eyes open. It has been reported that a large number of gang members have been spotted in Lone Pine and Independence. They have been causing a lot of problems. I'm concerned that somehow, they got wind that I'm here, and they're just trying to figure out where here is."

"Did you tell Abram and the other leaders?"

"I just found out myself. I'm on my way to tell them now. I may need to leave for a while."

"Not without us."

"It could get dangerous. I need to go talk to Abram."

Ethan could see by the intensity on Abram's face that he was trying to process the information. All the time Ethan had been revealing the details of his criminal life of vengeance, Abram hadn't said a word. It was when Ethan had told Abram of his plan to leave the community that Abram broke his silence.

"Not so fast Ethan." Abram stroked his beard.

"Don't you think that if I left it would deter the criminals from coming up here?"

"Not necessarily. Only God knows the hearts of men. Running is not the answer. Something you're not aware of is the security team we have that handles these types of situations."

Security team. Ethan could imagine a half dozen primitive people with pitchforks. *Do they really know the brutality of these gangs?* "You actually have a security team up here? What do they do?"

"You will find out. I will call an emergency meeting with the leaders for tonight. In the meantime, we will bring our security team up to speed on the potential threat. Don't be alarmed and please don't go to the valley. We will send a messenger for you once a plan is in place. It may be a couple of days."

"What am I to do in the meantime?"

"Go about your business and be aware of your surroundings. Oh! Keep this under wraps. We will put out a bulletin to the community when we have the plan in place." With that, Abram put on his jacket and hat while ushering Ethan out of the cabin.

Not wanting to leave Krystal in suspense, he made the trip back around the lake to Elena's. She was relieved to hear what Abram had to say and squeezed Ethan's hand to let him know she was there with him. "Come see me tonight if you can. We can talk after the children go to bed."

"I would love that." Ethan leaned down and kissed her briefly before heading down the trail. He needed to get busy and stop thinking about the looming danger.

Chapter Forty

Back in the crater, Ethan busied himself with maintenance chores around the cabin. It was getting into fall, and winter came quickly at this altitude. He wanted to build a real bridge across the stream. With chores complete, he decided it was time to cut down the old tree by the pasture and get it moved up next to the one he had never squared off. His ax swinging skills had improved and twenty minutes later the fifty-foot pine tree crashed to the ground.

Now what? he asked himself before starting to clear away the branches. He spent the rest of the day working on cleaning up the log and cutting it to length. The activity helped keep his mind off of the potentially upcoming encounters. He had formulated a plan which would take the fight away from the commune. What he had not planned on was a docile community to have a security apparatus in place to protect against hostile outsiders. He was learning something new about this place every day.

The log was too big for him to handle. What he needed were a couple of horses and a long rope. "The boss will surely understand the necessity of a bridge," he told Growler who was watching him intently.

He had just sat down at the table to eat his supper when Growler warned of an incoming human. Grabbing his Beretta, he opened the door in time to watch Jonathan dance across the log.

"I have a message for you, Ethan. Grandpa said to make it quick. I practically ran up the mountain."

"Thanks, Jonathan, you want something to eat or drink?"

"Thank you, but I got all I need here." He tapped his water bottle on the side of his backpack. Jonathan played with Growler while Ethan read the message.

"Tell your grandpa, I'll be there shortly. I have a couple of things to wrap up here before heading down."

"Sure will!" With that, Jonathan was across the log and running back down the trail.

Ethan grabbed his backpack and loaded it with essentials, consisting of his tablet, weapons, ammunition, and cash. Not that he would need any of these, but he had to be ready for what may come. Walking down the trail, he found strength in his resolution. Accepting the possibility that he may not make it out of this predicament. He prayed that all would go well, and he would not hurt Krystal.

The clearing was bursting with hushed voices as the settlers made their way into the meeting house. Ethan could feel misguided judgment being transmitted in their behavior. He was okay with that, as he was doing what the elders had advised. If it was up to him, he would run, but where would he go? Who would he hurt? He thought of Jonah and how happy he was when they were together. Did he have a choice? Standing there at the edge of the clearing as the eyes of the community were upon him, Ethan shut his eyes and begged God to give him wisdom and strength to do the right thing.

At the front of the room, the elders sat around the table. The benches were filled with uncertain folks that had made their way in from the clearing. He felt a hand on his arm and turned around to find Krystal with a scared smile on her face. "Are you going to be alright?" she asked.

"Oh, course. Remember, they are on our side."

"I just don't know. It seems so strange. It's like a tribal council."

"That's exactly what it is. They are the only law up here. You don't think the forest ranger would consider taking them on. There are too many of them, and they are well established. It'll be okay darling. Are you sitting with Elena?"

"No, she stayed home with the children. Anna is saving me a spot."

Ethan felt comfort in knowing those two were becoming friends. It was all the better for long-lasting peace in his future. *If there is a future.*

Abram motioned for Ethan to join them in the front of the room where he took a seat in the empty front row.

Abram called the meeting to order with prayer. After he had prayed for wisdom, they sang a song and Eli stood up and read the first chapter of James. Once he had completed the chapter, he looked around the room at the faces of a mystified congregation.

"My brothers and sisters, we greet you in the name of our Lord and Savior Jesus Christ. We have come together this evening with heavy hearts. At no time do we search out conflict, for the twelfth chapter of Romans verse eighteen tells us to live at peace with all men as much as it depends on us. There is much more in this chapter instructing us on kindness and compassion. We are not to repay evil with evil. That can only lead to destruction.

"James the brother of Jesus starts out telling us to count it all joy when we fall into various trials. That is what has brought us together this evening. This isn't the first time we have had trials. Satan is alive in this world we call our temporary home. Peter tells us to be sober, be vigilant, because your adversary the devil walks about like a roaring lion, seeking whom he may devour. Resist him, my brothers and sisters. Remain steadfast in your faith. James told us in the chapter we read that when we lack wisdom, we are to ask of God who gives to all liberally and without reproach, and it will be given to us. But we must ask in faith, without doubting. Tonight, we need wisdom that can only come from our Creator as we undertake the situation at hand. I pray we all approach the issue with humility and grace. I pray that our only aspiration is to find peace and reconciliation within our brotherhood."

Once Eli had taken his seat, Abram stood and, putting his shaky hands on the table to support himself, addressed the people. "Tonight our community has come under attack. We have experienced many adversaries over the years and have found refuge in our God. He has delivered us from the mouth of the lion. He has delivered us from the fiery furnace. He has delivered us from Pharaoh's army. He has delivered us from many storms in this life. Our God is real, and He is with us tonight.

"The attack we are under is one that I alone take responsibility. We have been deceived in a way that was not malicious. It happened not because this individual wanted to do us harm. It was done out of fear. It was not fear that our brother Ethan had of self-harm but fear of the danger that could come upon us. We have gathered all the facts and have reached the conclusion that Ethan's only crime is one of omission.

When he arrived, he was only looking for what all of us were looking for when we moved here to the settlement. He wanted to get away from the world and live a peaceful quiet life. What he failed to reveal was that before he left civilization, he enacted justice on three criminals that had taken his family's lives and had to defend his own life on more than one occasion. Our brother served as a Special Forces operative in Afghanistan. He is trained to, what they call, 'neutralize the enemy'. While that is not the way God has instructed us to live our lives, we can empathize with our brother. We have asked our brother to share his thoughts with you."

Ethan stood and turned around. His first impulse was to run. He now understood why Cody had fled the village six years ago. Many times, Ethan had faced the enemy in times of war. It was not near as frightful as facing the hundred plus stone-faced settlers in this small commune.

"In the spring when I arrived here, I came without any form of prejudice or malice. As Abram stated, I did come with some heavy baggage. When I arrived here, I was a lost human being living with the guilt of sin. I know the end of

Romans chapter six tells us that the wages of sin is death. It doesn't stop there; it goes on to say the gift of God is eternal life in Christ Jesus our Lord. This is all knowledge that I have gained from being here in your presence. I was able to tell myself that I was only dishing out justice when I repaid the men who had ravenously killed my family.

"When I came into your community I was lost, wandering aimlessly about. What I found is a community of believers who live the life they proclaim. You took me in when I was lost, and you gave me hope. God is using you to bring me to Him. I am eternally grateful for your hospitality. In first John, it tells us that if we confess our sins, He is faithful and just to forgive us of our sins and cleanse us from all unrighteousness. Do I believe this? Most certainly! I also believe that even though God will forgive me of these crimes, the State of New York will not.

"My fear is not with the authorities. If they find me here, they will do you no harm. It is the associates of my family's murderers that cause sleepless nights. They are ruthless and will not stop with just killing me. They will ravish this community. They, as we heard earlier about the devil, are like a roaring lion, seeking whom they may devour. Abram started by telling you about the attack on the community. I am the one that has brought this evil upon your doorstep. I am at your mercy and will be willing to leave upon your request. Whatever your decision is, I will understand and am forever grateful for my time here."

Abram again stood to his feet as Ethan finished. "Ethan has spoken from his heart. As this is not an accusation, but a confession, the elder board has agreed that now is not the time to open the floor for questions. Once he has left the room, we will allow you to have your questions answered by one of the elders or the security team. We now ask that Ethan and Krystal to leave the meeting, so we can converse freely. You will be called in as soon as we are through. Thank you."

Ethan and Krystal were happy they wore their jackets as they huddled together on the bench in the clearing. He wrapped his arms around her as the waning daylight gave way for the darkness to envelope them. Ethan could feel Krystal shaking as he pulled her tightly against him. "Are you okay, my dear?"

"I'm scared."

"I'm scared too, but I do know that God is in control and what is going on inside that building is by design. One thing they cannot take away is my love for you. Right now, that is all that matters to me."

"I don't know. It seems as if Satan is attacking us right now, and the darkness only makes it worse. Where are we going to go if they make you leave?"

"They won't make you leave. You and your children are safe here."

"I let you go once. It will not happen again."

Krystal's determined statement brought a lump to Ethan's throat. He turned his face down to the best friend he had in this life and kissed her passionately. Their embrace was interrupted by the sound of the door opening just thirty feet away. They stood as Jonathon motioned for them to come in.

"Well, here goes," Ethan whispered as he squeezed Krystal's hand.

Chapter Forty-One

Ethan did not let go of Krystal's hand as they walked back to the front of the meeting house. *If she will not leave me, we are in this together.* Reaching the front, they were asked to keep standing. Abram leaned over to Eli and asked him to read the verdict. Eli stood to his feet with a piece of paper handed to him by one of the church deacons.

"We, the congregation and citizens of Charlotte Lake community in response to the revelation of crimes committed by Ethan Dawson as confessed by his own free will, through unanimous consent agree to the following. While only God can forgive sins, we as a community will hold no ill will of his past transgressions. He has without doubt shown remorse. We ask that he strives to live a life of humility and gratitude. This body recommends that Ethan makes restitution to the authorities of the locality of his crimes. No time attached to this recommendation, it is to be when God moves him to do so. We pray that his conscience will be his guide." Eli sat down and Abram motioned for Ethan and Krystal to take a seat.

"At this time brother Arnold will explain the security procedures."

At that, a younger chiseled-faced gentleman at the other end of the table stood up and faced Ethan. "Ethan, I've hardly met you but know a lot about you. Upon your confession, to our leaders, my team and I have done our research. It is a strange and evil world outside the protection of these mountains. That is why we live here. As head of security, we make it our job to acquire every piece of knowledge we can about each person who enters our community.

"Most people come in here and are here a couple of days and move on down the trail. No pun intended, but that is the case. We don't even bother with them. Others that seem to meander about the community cause us concern, and we activate our resources. You were different. You came in here wanting nothing but a place to stay. You weren't looking for handouts, you were willing to assimilate into our culture and do your share of work. You still triggered our security apparatus, and we initiated our background check. Even with our widespread security network, you were almost impossible to find. It wasn't until you brought Krystal and the children up here that we were able to connect the dots and locate your real identity. We briefed the elders on the situation and at their request we were restrained from further action while they spent time in prayer. While they were praying for a solution, you came to Abram and confessed. The timing of this confession is important because we had just received a message from our contacts that gangs were starting to arrive in Lone Pine and surrounding communities asking where they could find you. Fortunately for you, you did not use your real name anywhere in the valley and all the perpetrators have are rumors of your existence."

Ethan humbly held up a hand. At the nod of the security chief, he asked, "Would it not be better if I left the community? It could draw them elsewhere."

"That idea has surfaced, but we don't throw our brothers into the lion's den. If the government comes looking for you, we are impelled to have you turn yourself in. When it comes to heinous criminals attacking our village, we will protect our own. We do have a plan and would like you to temporarily join our security team. You have information we need."

Ethan was perplexed and even though he didn't speak up, Abram could see it in his face.

"Ethan, I understand your confusion. If you stick around after the meeting, we can discuss covering them in a more intimate setting. But before we go, I would like to address the rest of our congregation."

Looking over the congregation at a now overwhelming compassionate body, he admonished them on gossip and backstabbing. "There is no place here in our community for discord and division. Please continue as you always have, showing love and compassion to all. God has seen us safe this far, and He will continue that protection as long as we trust Him."

After prayer, they sang a song and were dismissed.

Chapter Forty-Two

"An intrusion is imminent. There are about a hundred and fifty known gang members in the lower valley." Arnold told Ethan once the room was cleared. Krystal's gasp was audible, as the security chief continued. "Law enforcement knows they are there, but they are only meeting in small groups and are not doing anything illegal at this time. Don't worry, ma'am, we have all our team on full alert and will know as soon as they start up the trail. While your safety is our responsibility, we asked that everyone stay aware of their surroundings and report suspicious activity."

"Would it be safer if we moved Krystal and the children to the crater?" Ethan asked with hopes of an unexpected approval.

"That is not a good idea. The security we have down here can not cover the crater. You would be on your own. We know you have weapons, but please remember, this is a team. You are not the Lone Ranger or a superhero. Any form of individuality is contrary to our nonresistant principle."

"That's another thing I don't understand. How can we defend the community if we are nonresistant? It sounds counterintuitive."

Abram held up his hand for the others to let him explain. "As an individual, it is imperative that we follow the biblical principle of turning the other cheek. As a follower of Christ, we do not repay evil for evil. When it comes to the community, we are a self-governing people. Something that you may not know is that we have our own governing body. Our community elects officials that handle the legal proceedings. They are the ones that have established our security team along with all monetary transactions. While they consult with the spiritual leaders, they are not controlled by the church."

Ethan was starting to understand, "So you are saying that as a member of the security team, I have the authority to secure the area?"

"Yes, but if you go outside the scope of your authorized instructions, you will be in the wrong. Such as, getting revenge for something that has transpired in the past. Do you understand what I'm saying?"

Ethan winced slightly, knowing that he was telling Ethan he could not go Rambo on the adversary. "I do understand and will abide by the guidelines given to me by my superior." He was certain they took a page out of his military handbook. He was really surprised at how well they were organized.

They stood up to go home and Abram told them to gather around. He put his hands on Ethan and Krystal's shoulders and offered up a prayer of protection for them and the community at large. "Go in peace, my brother and sister. May God be with us." With that, they walked out into the night.

Chapter Forty-Three

***

The next morning Ethan was on the front porch sipping a cup of hot coffee. The hazy fog reminded him of the oncoming winter. At his feet, Growler was lazily looking at nothing in particular when he all of a sudden jerked his head up and looked down the trail.

"What is it Growler? Is someone coming?" He reached under the blanket on his lap where he felt the cold steel of his Beretta. *Now remember, no individual retaliation.* To his relief, Hugo appeared out of the haze.

Crossing the log, he spotted Ethan on the porch. "Good morning, Ethan, anything left in the coffee pot?"

"Oh, there may be a cup or two. Have a seat, and I'll get you a cup."

"So, what brings you up here so early this morning?" Ethan asked as he sat back down.

"Robert sent me. It seems that Arnold has requested your presence at his office. And we all know here in the community that when the S.C. asks for something, it's not optional."

"He seemed like a pretty nice guy last night. Where's his office?"

"Oh, you don't know? Go to the storehouse and tell Sarah that S.C. wants to see you. She will help you."

"I will do that, thanks. Sure a lot of mysteries around here."

"I'm sure after last night you can understand why. Considering our remoteness and lack of outside law enforcement, we have to use caution and be prepared."

"It may be a shot in the dark, but I assume you are on the security team?"

"What makes you think that?"

"If I was in charge of security and we had a suspicious individual, I would use every opportunity I could find to get an agent close to that person. Having you come up here to help while I was gone was that opportunity security needed to search the cabin. What did you find?"

Hugo's reaction told Ethan that he had hit the target. "I did not search your cabin."

"Who did?"

"Arnold will have to answer that question. I cannot devolve that information."

"What did they find? Nothing was missing."

"Can't tell you that either. All I will say is they are not concerned about your ability to protect yourself up here. You had probably better get going. Arnold doesn't like to wait. Oh yes, he did want me to have you bring your tablet."

Pulling on his backpack Ethan gave Hugo a couple of instructions concerning unfinished chores and headed for the log.

"Oh, and they also like repurposed furniture." Hugo hollered as Ethan almost lost his footing on the log. Tomorrow, he needed to finish the bridge.

Arriving at the storehouse, he waited patiently for Sarah to finish with another customer.

"That was an interesting meeting last night Ethan. I just want you to know Noah and I have been praying for you and Krystal. She seems like a nice lady. What can I do for you today?"

"Thank you for your prayers. They are much needed and appreciated. I was told to let you know that Arnold sent for me. Do you know how I can find his office?"

The sheepish grin on Sarah's face told that she knew. "Hold on, let me check." She headed through the big oak doors into the ice cave and was gone for what seemed a long time. Finally, she returned with Arnold in tow.

"We wondered how long it would take for you to get here this morning. Must of been a lot of traffic." He grinned and stuck out his hand. "Welcome to the team. Let me show you around."

Walking through the oak doors the temperature dropped significantly as they walked deeper into the cavern. Walking in behind the hanging meat Ethan could hardly see where they were going. "Hold up!" Arnold stopped at something hanging on the wall. Lifting a flap revealed a dim emerald light. He stuck his thumb on the light, and Ethan heard the sound of deadbolts being pulled back. The stone wall started moving as Arnold pushed open a hidden door flooding the meat locker with light. "Wow!" was all he could say as the room beyond was a clean brightly lit modern facility. Walking into the room he could see this looked more like a command center than a primitive settlement. A sign hung from the ceiling that said, 'Welcome to City Hall'.

"You seem to be a little taken back by what you're seeing. You didn't expect us to use sticks and brooms for security, did you?"

"I seriously had no idea how you managed to keep the settlement safe. This is unexpected. I know you didn't bring me here to destroy my perception of this backwoods community, so why am I here?"

They walked by a row of computers where workers were busy monitoring several different things.

"How many hidden security cameras do you have here in the village?"

"That's classified information, but I can tell you that we know about you going into the mines, and we know that you poured the gold in the stream. That move probably saved your bacon."

"What don't you know about me?"

"There is not much that we don't know about you. That's why you're here. You did bring your tablet, right?"

Ethan pulled his backpack around and slid out his tablet. "That's another thing. How did you guys know I had a tablet? It was not in the cabin when you searched it."

"We have our ways. Once you learn more about this side of the community, you will see it is more technically advanced than most American cities. Here we are, give these ladies your tablet. You'll get it back when you leave."

"Why do they need it?"

"How do you think the mob has honed into your location. The security on your tablet has been breached, and they are constantly monitoring each time you connect to the satellite. The ladies here will scrub your hard drive and set you up on our network. From what we have seen remotely, you don't have any personal data other than a few love letters to Krystal. By the way, that was a nice job on not revealing your location. It saved us a lot of heartaches."

Ethan followed Arnold into a conference room where a long hand-crafted table was surrounded by men and women who were intently looking at their tablets. They all put them down and stood as Arnold took his seat at the head of the table and motioned Ethan to sit to his left. Ethan looked around at the intent faces and recognized a few from last night's meeting.

"Okay everyone; let's finish the issue we were working on before we get into Ethan's case. Where were we?"

A lady in her mid-thirties spoke up. "We were dealing with the threat from the California BOE."

"That's right. Did you get it solved?"

"Providing they rely on automation as we think they do. We will no longer be on their radar. They were easy to hack, and the file has been removed and in its place is a memo that shows we passed inspection and have met all requirements."

"Sometimes you guys amaze me. Nice work team. Now, let's go back over Ethan's case and bring him up to speed. Who's got the file?"

A younger man with a full beard slightly raised his hand. "I do, sir."

"Thanks, Oliver, go ahead with the latest report."

"Sure! As of nine this morning, the number of

confirmed gangsters was just over a hundred and sixty. By the undercover photos we have of eighty percent of these adversaries, we don't expect they will be able to make the pass. They are overweight and under-motivated. Nevertheless, we will continue to monitor them for signs of movement."

Arnold held up his hand, "That is still thirty plus that could inflict harm. As far as the rest, keep an eye on them. Sometimes drug-induced stamina will surprise you. Has the militia been ordered up?"

"Yes, we have twenty activated and another twenty on standby. We have asked all other ready-bodied men to be ready for an AW1 code if necessary. Considering the amount of time it'll take for them to get here, we have plenty of time to get armed."

Arnold showed his approval for the call-up plan but had one concern. "What defense plan are you using?"

"Depending on how many are climbing the pass. If the numbers are low enough, we'll send out six agents to apprehend them as they pass through the wooded area just below Bull Frog Lake. If the numbers required a more lethal approach, we will set up a line along the PCT and use the RPG's"

"Sound like a little overkill but do whatever is necessary to keep them out of the community. As you have been trained, apprehend all of the perpetrators. The first priority is to capture. Those that are not inclined to be captured, terminate. It will be their choice."

Ethan was listening to every word and found it intriguing yet alarming what they were planning. They were setting up war plans where they would be largely outnumbered and yet have the advantage. He wondered where he fit into the plan but figured when they wanted him to know they would tell him.

Arnold picked up his tablet and studied it intently for a few minutes. "Ethan, it looks like we have you on the south ridge. With your sniper abilities, we have decided you will be our cover when the incursion transpires. I assume you want to use your weapon?"

"That would be preferable sir, considering I'm used to it."

"That's what we have heard. Stop by the armory on your way out and pick up some ammunition. Oliver will show you where it's located. Are there any questions on this subject before we move on?" A glance around the table showed no response. "Great! Be vigilant, folks. As you know, this is a real-life situation. Let's move on to the gold transfer. Damien, looks like you are in charge of that?"

A red-haired man with a full beard looking like he was in his early thirties responded, "I am. We are scheduled to make a run on the first of next week. Considering the circumstances, I would like to postpone the transfer until the threat level subsides."

Arnold turned to one of the two ladies in the room. "Loraine, where are we standing on the supply account?"

Loraine scrolled through her tablet for a moment before responding. "It looks like we still have just over a million in that account. We should be fine for a couple of months."

"That brings up the question of the supply chain. What are we doing about protecting the mule train? It could come under attack if these hoodlums are on the trail."

Arnold looked around the table for an answer.

Probably the oldest of the group spoke up. "Well, the driver always carries his gun for protection against wildlife. I recommend we have at least one of our guys ride with him."

Arnold nodded, "Make it happen. As for the gold, I agree with postponing this month's transfer. The biggest challenge we have with that is the oncoming winter. We only have another month before switching to winter procedures. The good news is winter will keep the bad guys away."

The meeting ended, and Ethan followed Oliver to the armory. Sliding back a heavy steel door, Ethan was surprised to see a climate-controlled cavern. Walking past racks of assault rifles, they came to shelves of ammunition.

"Your rifle uses the three thirty-eight, doesn't it?" Oliver asked as he looked over the ammunition."

"You know your weapons. That is the ones I use."

"It was easy. That was what we found in your cabin. Sorry, we had to do that. Hopefully, you understand."

Ethan didn't respond as he still wasn't thrilled at the idea that someone had searched the cabin. He made a note to inspect the cabin for bugs and cameras. It just might save some embarrassment. Heading for the exit with a backpack full of bullets he passed another pallet of cases marked RPG. "What kind of adversary are you preparing for to need these?" He asked his escort.

Oliver brushed off the question, and they continued to the exit. Stopping by the technology office, a young lady with a cheerful disposition handed him his tablet. "It's all cleaned up and connected to our network. It should be safe now." Ethan thanked the girl and headed for the exit.

Ethan had planned on stopping by and updating Krystal but felt it best if he processed it first. Some of the information he was now privy to was classified. He headed west around the lake and made his way up the trail. It didn't take long before he noticed fresh horse tracks. Who would be riding a horse up here and what are they after. Reaching the meadow, he was surprised to see a couple of horses and a few of the men doing something up by the cabin. Over the last knoll, it became obvious. They were pulling the log for the bridge over the stream. He made it to the stream crossing just as they were finishing putting it into place.

"Boy, you sure know when to show up." Robert ribbed.

"These days, I'm just doing what I'm told." Ethan tossed back.

"You told me you wanted to use some horses to pull this log. We figured the best way to keep you out of trouble is to help you. Just forgot you had a meeting with the big guy this morning. Speaking of the big guy, how did it go?"

Ethan pulled off his hat and scratched his head. "The more I learn about this place, the more confused I get. I would tell you how it went, but I was told not to talk about City Hall out here."

Robert motioned for the other men to head on down the hill with the horses. He wanted to stick around and talk to Ethan. Once they had their cup of coffee and were kicked back in the rocking chairs on the porch, Robert answered the unasked question.

"How right you are about City Hall. Hopefully, you understand the reasoning."

"Well, I can see how bringing City Hall into the village would destroy the community. I haven't grasped the complexity of the overall operations. When I got here, it didn't take long to realize there was an underlying operation. I just never expected anything as elaborate as what I have seen. What level of security clearance do you have?"

"Let's just say, I've got a lot higher clearance than you do, my friend."

"I imagined that. Then I have a few questions, and if I get out of line, please stop me. I mean no harm, just curious. Why the facade?"

"What do you mean by facade?"

"When I came into the community, I saw a very special place where people live without electricity and running water. They dress plainly and cook their food on wood stoves. There is a bakery fired by a wood-powered bread oven. A carpenter shop where everything is crafted by hand tools. Your food is grown in short-season gardens, and your meat hangs in an ice cave. You have a doctor who runs around with a medical bag doing house calls. And, I might add, does an incredible job. You have cowboys that wrangle mules up and down the mountain a couple of times a week to resupply the storehouse. I could go on forever, but you know all this.

"Yet, under the surface, you have a high-tech, practically sterile environment where computer fans whine and bright lights drive away any form of darkness. There at City Hall, you have everything the modern world has and more. Back to my question, what keeps the people working in City Hall from rebelling? They leave the high-tech workplace and go to their homes where snow is blowing in under the door, and they have to pee outside? Just seems strange."

Robert stroked his beard in thought before addressing the questions. "A few months ago if you would have walked into a modern community where the church had a steeple and all the homes had running water, electricity, and a large screen television, would you have stayed?

"I doubt it."

"Not only that. We have a tight-knit community because we all live a common simple lifestyle. No one is greater or of lesser value than someone else. We work together for a common cause. If we let City Hall creep into the community, it would only be a matter of time before the world and all its sinful pleasures would take over our lives. That is why we keep City Hall underground. It is only there to provide infrastructure to the community. Without it, it would be difficult to sell our gold."

"Trust me when I say I don't want anything to change." Ethan replied. "One day I witnessed some of the boys pull a half a pint of gold out of a crevice, and they were disappointed they didn't find more. They have no idea how much it is worth. They only do it for the enjoyment of being productive."

"Again, you are on the right track," Robert said. "The community is wealthy enough to provide for many generations, but to sustain our remote lifestyle we need much more than monetary wealth. We need a functioning community that works together. Otherwise, we would have to depend on those from the outside."

"But don't you depend on the outside for a lot of

things? Mule trains are coming up the trail a couple of times a week."

"Yes, to some extent. The essentials we need to exist are here in the mountains. There are things like shoes, cookware, medication, and scores of other items that we do not manufacture up here. It just doesn't make sense to do so."

Ethan was starting to better understand the philosophy of running the mountain complex. While he still wasn't sure whether the tail was wagging the dog or the other way around, he could see the value on both sides of the coin. The simplistic lifestyle hid the gold operation, and the gold operation provided for the simplistic lifestyle. They needed each other. Obviously, God provided all the needs they had in His way. It still amazed him how they downplayed wealth to keep greed in check. "Where does the electricity come from for City Hall?"

"That's a simple one. You ever notice the steam vents coming out of the south wall of the canyon?"

"Yeah, that's from the volcanic activity underneath us, right?"

"Yes, it is. Should make you feel comfortable. There is a pipeline that runs from one of the steam vents to an underground steam-powered generator. The electrical grid underneath the city hall is an engineering marvel. You should take a tour someday."

Robert stood up, "Guess I had better get back to work. Thanks for the coffee."

Ethan had a lot on his mind as he watched his boss walk away.

Chapter Forty-Four

With an undercover agent camping out at Onion Valley Campground and another at the top of Kearsarge Pass, the security team was active flying infrared drones up and down the trail monitoring the foot traffic. The remainder of the forward defense team was stationed at intervals along the Pacific Crest Trail. All of them dressed like hikers and were heavily armed. They were confident that the community was secure and that everyone should go about their daily activity.

Sunday afternoon a chill was rising in the air. It was as if something was about to happen. In the village, people seemed to be on edge. If you asked, they couldn't really tell you why. By late evening, it was as if panic was setting in. It was like watching the birds when a thunderstorm was imminent.

The first sign of trouble was the western parameter where infrared cameras caught a group of armed men coming up the trail along Charlotte Creek. They were only a hundred yards outside the village and security had only two agents on patrol in that area. The monitors automatically sent a message to the agents.

Receiving an alert message on their watches, the two agents moved towards the trail. As they crossed over the rocks, they never heard the muffled recoil of the assault rifles. Their lifeless bodies hit the water, and the current carried them downstream. The community was at war.

The Sunday evening singing was over and only a few had left the building when the door opened, and four men dressed in black burst in. Each of the intruders carried a semi-automatic assault rifle. One of the men raised his gun in the air and yelled for everyone to get on the ground. At once, the churchgoers obeyed the commands. On the ground, they started praying.

One of the intruders walked among the people looking for someone. After he had checked the whole room, he returned to the others by the door. "Where is he?" he yelled. No one answered. He angrily repeated his demand and again with no response. Finally, he yanked a woman to her feet and yelled into her face. "Where is he?"

"Who are you looking for?" The woman nervously asked.

"You know who I'm looking for. He came here from New York."

Trembling, the lady answered, "I don't know, but I pray that God will forgive you for the evil you are doing."

With that, the man backhanded the woman, and crumbling, she fell to the floor. "Does anyone else want to get mouthy," he yelled. "Everyone get up and move against the wall." With the help of his friends, he started shoving the worshipers to the far wall.

Among the hostages, Anna kept low-keyed and moved to the rear next to the wood box. She was certain the attackers knew nothing of the trap door used to resupply the wood. Hopefully, it hadn't yet been filled for winter. As people packed in front of her, she slowly slid the door open, stopping each time a scraping noise emitted from the ungreased wooden door. A cold breeze drifted in across her legs. She needed to make her move before the rustling stopped.

Dropping to the floor Anna squeezed herself through the door and opened the outer door slowly looking for danger. Seeing none she slowly crawled out and made her way around the meeting house. Looking around the corner, she could see two armed men guarding the door. Turning around she retraced her steps to the other side and made her way down to the lake. By instinct, she knew she needed to tell Ethan. She was certain she had not seen him at the singing, so he must be at home. As quick as she could, without making any noise, she made her way around the shore of the lake to the trail. She had just started up the trail when a voice interrupted the night.

"Stop or I will shoot!"

For a moment Anna hesitated and then saw the dark figure appear in front of her. The man set down his gun and grabbed her around the waist and pulled her to him. Feeling a sharp object against her side triggered reflexes that were far faster than her out-of-shape assailant. In a heartbeat, she inflicted soul-wrenching pain in parts of his body that wouldn't soon recover. He crashed to the ground, and she took off running up the trail. She could feel a burning pain on her side. Her hand went to where she felt the pain as she ran up the hill knowing that her assailant would soon be coming after her. Her dress was torn and she could feel something warm and sticky. She could only pray that her injuries were minor and that she wasn't losing much blood.

Topping the hill, she heard gunshots behind her. The sound of bullets ricocheting off the rocks only made her run faster. It was hard to see in the dark. Her many recent trips up the trail had prepared her for this moment. Then the thought came to her. *Was she leading the gunman to Ethan?* Ethan was always on alert. Surely, he would be hearing the gunshots. Topping the crest, she could see the small light shining from the window. *I must hurry on.* And then she cried out to God.

On the porch with his field glasses in hand, Ethan had heard shots coming from the village and knew something was going down. Lying next to him, his sniper rifle was cleaned and loaded in preparation for the upcoming mission. It had been a while since he had lain in the rugged terrain of Afghanistan waiting for the target. Did he still have it in him? Now that he had plenty of ammo, he should shoot a few practice rounds. He would do that tomorrow. A gunshot echoed around the crater, and Growler stood to attention. *That sounded close!* Ethan stood up with his glasses and looked towards the trail. Nothing was there. He scanned the meadow and around the crater walls. Not seeing anything moving but a few marmots he returned to the meadow. Movement at the corner of his scope redirected his attention to the trail.

Someone was running fast. He could only make out that it was a woman wearing a dress. Soon the night vision scope auto-focusing feature kicked in and the clarity of Anna came into view. She was definitely in trouble and holding her side as she ran. He was processing her actions when another figure crested the hill. Ethan refocused on the chaser and could tell he was carrying a gun and running a slow trot. A few seconds later, the gunman lifted his gun and started firing. That's when Ethan could see the guy had night vision goggles.

Ethan had to act fast. He dropped to a knee and rested the Remington on the edge of the chair. It only took two seconds for the night vision scope to focus on Anna's assailant. He was closing in on her fast. If she stopped for only a second, she would be dead. *God has put me here for such a time as this,* Ethan whispered as he put the crosshairs on the chest of the gunman, who at that moment made a fateful decision. He stopped to get a better shot. Pulling up his rifle was the last thing he did before the sting of the high-speed projectile cut through his chest.

Ethan watched the man drop and moved his sight back up the trail to see if there were any more. He held the crosshairs on the center of the trail until Anna reached the logs crossing the stream. Setting down his rifle he felt the reassuring cold steel of his Beretta in his waistband. Running down to the logs, he grabbed Anna as she stumbled off the logs into his arms.

"They have hostages in the meeting house," she sobbed as he helped her onto the porch.

"Are there any others coming up the trail?"

"I don't think so. I ran into this guy after I escaped the meeting house. He was right at the crater trailhead."

"You did well coming up here. Where's Cody?"

"He's helping guard the east ridge."

"What about Krystal and the children? Were they at the singing?"

"They were at the singing but left before the attack."

A gnawing sensation started to grow inside Ethan.

He had pulled on his combat vest and was loading up additional ammunition in the pockets. He handed Anna his secondary 9mm handgun. "Do you know how to use this?"

"I have only shot a rifle, but I can figure it out."

"Good. You stay here with Growler and don't let anyone in unless you recognize their voice. I will be back." With that Ethan was out the door and heading for the village. Coming to the now-deceased gunman, he pulled the night vision goggles off his head and adjusted the strap to fit him.

Stopping at the ridge he scanned the valley below. If he could spot any of the intruders from here he could reduce their numbers. He saw a lot of movement coming in from the east side which told him that was most likely the men on patrol heading into the village to help. Scanning back through the village he picked up two individuals with weapons coming eastbound on the south side of the lake. Pulling up his sniper rifle, he focused the scope on the two gunmen to verify they were not part of the security team. Ten seconds later, they moved into a clearing just as the moon gave additional light. They were dressed in all black with a black stocking cap and night vision goggles. *They are, without a doubt, the enemy and this is not for revenge,* he told himself as he slid a bullet into the chamber. *If I do it right, I can get two for one.*

Ethan waited until the one gunman was standing in

front of the other and pulled the trigger. The two men dropped out of view as the small missile went through the one's torso and lodged in the heart of the other. *Two down.* He didn't stop to admire his kill. He scanned over the village with no more results. It was time to engage. He had to find Krystal.

He had thought about descending cross country into the settlement, but speed was more important at this time. Using his night vision goggles he scanned the trail from the switchbacks down to the village. Not seeing any movement, he made his way to the trail and practically ran down the mountain. Stopping a hundred yards above the spring, he again carefully scanned the area ahead. It was time to move cautiously. He had to assume that all the perpetrators were equipped as he was and could see him in the dark. He shouldered his sniper rifle and pulled out the Beretta. He wished he had taken the assault rifle from the gunman up in the crater. It would have been handy in this close-in situation.

He started hearing shots being fired in the direction of the eastern flank and figured the security forces had encountered the assailants. He had to make his move quickly to free the hostages. Reaching the meeting house without incident, Ethan could see the two armed guards at the door. They did not have night vision equipment and were nervously walking around. He needed to neutralize them without warning the ones inside.

Ethan moved a little further into the trees and whistled softly. The heads of the gunmen jerked his way. He whistled a little louder this time, and one of them started his way peering around the corner of the building to see what was making the noise. Ethan picked up a small stone and tossed it to the back of the meeting house. The gunman slowly inched his way towards the noise with the gun up and ready to fire. Another stone landed just a few more feet back keeping the now scared gunman inching along his way.

The gunman's internal senses felt the presence of another human being, but it did not register from where it was coming until it was too late. The strong hands that grabbed his head and the snap that followed left him paralyzed. He gasped for his last breath, and his neutralizer lowered him quietly to the ground.

Moving around the other side of the meeting house, Ethan could see the second guard was staring intently in the direction his buddy had gone. That was enough for Ethan to quietly approach from behind. Just five feet from the other guard, Ethan stepped on a stick causing it to snap. The guard spun around just in time to see Ethan before he too was neutralized.

Looking through the window, Ethan could see the hostages were still against the far wall where Anna had escaped. It looked like about forty or fifty settlers. Two of the gunmen were sitting on chairs on the far side along the other wall with their weapons on their laps. The other two were pacing in front of the door. There was no way he could break down the door and get all four before they shot him. *How could he get in there without alerting gunmen? How did Anna say she got out?*

He circled back around the building passing the now expired guard. That's when he saw the door next to a stack of firewood. It would be difficult, but he had to try. Slowly opening the door, he started meticulously removing the few pieces of wood one at a time. With the wood box completely empty he could see through the crack in the inner door. Several legs and the benches were partially blocking his view, but he had a clear shot at two of the gunmen. The noise suppressor on the sniper rifle would give him a couple of much-needed seconds to get off a second shot. Pulling back, he dropped down the night vision goggle to clear the area before proceeding. Through the trees, he saw four figures methodically moving in the direction of the meeting house. Their movement was not that of erratic invaders but of confidant soldiers that knew the terrain. It had to be security agents. He moved in their direction and positioned himself to intercept their approach.

As they passed, he could see it was as he expected.

In a hushed tone, he alerted the agents. "Friend here, don't shoot."

All four spun around, and Ethan found himself staring down four assault rifles. Raising his hands in the air, he showed himself to the agents. "We have a hostage situation in the meeting house. I have neutralized the parameter and was getting ready to move in when I saw you coming."

"We got word that was the case," the team leader responded. "Most of the team is scouring the community. Have you devised a plan? Do we need a negotiator?"

"No need for that. These people are trained combatants and do not negotiate. They must be taken out."

"Are you sure? That's pretty violent."

"I can assure you, they will have no problem killing you if they have the chance. I am really surprised they haven't murdered everyone in the meeting house. It's only a matter of time. Here's the plan."

With the plan explained, Ethan returned to the wood box, and with the sniper rifle in place, he was happy to see the legs had shifted slightly to give him a better view. The problem with that is it had one of the gunmen looking right at the door. Ethan needed just a couple more inches to get a good shot at the second target. He waited for the gunmen to get distracted by something in the room and took that opportunity to carefully slide the door. He could now hear who appeared to be the leader telling the hostages about their plans.

"Once we get everyone here, we're going to lock you in and burn this place to the ground. You'll get to meet your Jesus sooner than you thought you would," he sneered.

"Shut up!" one of the others yelled. "Don't give away the plan."

"Doesn't matter, they're going to be dead anyhow."

"Still, just be quiet. We don't need to hear it."

That was enough. It was time to turn the tables and let these hoodlums explain their actions to an Almighty God. He tapped the ground two times with his left foot, signaling the team ten second warning. With the gunmen leaning back in his chair looking right at him, Ethan had his crosshairs looking right back at him. At three seconds to go, the gunmen started registering what he was seeing between the pairs of legs along the far west wall. At two seconds, he started to lift his hand and point while simultaneously starting to jump up from his chair. Ethan, seeing the expanded eyes of the alerted gunman, gently pulled the trigger. Not waiting for a response, he moved to the second gunmen and with a clear shot removed him as a threat. He could hear the crashing of glass as he shoved his rifle aside and with Beretta in hand shoved open the door and slid through the opening, knocking hostages out of the way as he went.

The security agent at the window with one of the gunmen in his sights, watched the first gunmen jump to his feet only to fall hard to the ground. *One second early. He* smashed the glass and took the shot. Not having a silencer on his handgun, the sound echoed around the valley. As the other three were crashing through the door Ethan was unloading his Beretta in the fourth and final gunmcn.

Chapter Forty-Five

While to some it seemed like time stood still as they witnessed the carnage exploding around them, it all happened in five seconds. There was no time to waste. They had to get the people out of there and to safety. Once Ethan was assured the agent in charge had it under control, he headed out the door. The enemy was still out there. He continued around the north side of the lake where he met a dozen agents who were going from cabin to cabin looking for assailants. They told him they had neutralized eight, and Ethan shared about the six at the meeting house and the three he had dealt with earlier.

"Word from the command center is that the western parameter cameras picked up twenty coming up Charlotte trail," the security team leader told him. "That would mean we are still looking for at least three." He had just crossed rocks at the outlet when he thought he heard something coming from the barn beside the garden. Not picking anything up in his scan he raised the goggles and worked his way up the path. He was just about to enter the garden shed when a voice behind him stopped him in his tracks. "Don't move a muscle or you're dead."

Ethan froze. "Who are you?" He asked.

"That is none of your business, Ethan Dawson. What matters is that I have finally found you."

"Why were you looking for me?" Ethan asked and knowing the answer threw in a distraction. "What agency do you work for?'

"I'm not telling you anything, but one thing for sure, I don't work for any government."

Ethan thought he recognized the voice from a news clip he had watched during the trial. "Okay, I understand. Sorry about your brother, but he deserved it."

"Shut up! My brother was a good man. He didn't deserve to die like that."

Again Ethan had guessed rightly. The man with the gun behind him was the brother of one of the men who killed his family.

Ethan sensed the gun not too far from his head.

"Drop your guns on the ground and step forward." The voice was starting to sound hurried and nervous. Ethan slowly took his sniper rifle off his shoulder and lowered it to the ground.

"Now your handguns. All of them!"

Ethan, again not wanting to cause the assailant to shoot out of fear, slowly removed his Beretta and set it on the ground. His head was spinning looking for an opportunity and a plan to get out of this situation. Now without a firearm, he only had the knife strapped to the inside of his boot.

"Walk, you maggot." The over-demanding criminal shoved Ethan towards the garden shed. "Open the door."

Sliding back the door, the aroma of fertilizer and garden tools drifted out to meet them. "Get in there." Again, he was shoved from behind as he entered the dimly lit building.

"This will be a good place for you to rot. Right there with the fertilizer. Now turn around, I want to see the torment on your face as you die."

As Ethan turned around, he could dimly see the figure of the man who was about to take his life. His only regret was that he would be leaving Krystal without a husband and her children again without a father. And then it hit him. "Do you know Jesus?"

The gunman shuffled for a few seconds. "I went to church. It's a bunch of bull."

"I just want you to know that when you kill me, I get to go to Heaven. It's going to be awesome. You could go there too if you want."

"Shut up! It's not me that's biting the big one, it's you."

"Yes, I understand, but someday you too will die, and then what? Don't you want to go to Heaven? I don't think you would like the misery of hell at all."

"There's no such thing. It's all a lie, and you know it. You think God exists and you're going to Heaven, fine. Say your last prayer, and at amen, you are history." He lifted his handgun to Ethan's head.

Ethan obliged by closing his eyes as he lifted his hands towards heaven. He slowly started talking to God as he had read Stephen did as he was stoned. "Lord Jesus, please receive my spirit. Do not charge this man with my death; he doesn't know what he is doing."

"Shut up! I know what I'm doing." As he stretched out his arm to shoot, Ethan saw a small flash from the woods, and his assailant dropped to the ground. Ethan grabbed the gun and dove for cover. He pulled down his goggles and could see a figure slowly coming towards the shed. "Oh, my goodness! He saw the outline of her skirt."

"Ethan, are you okay?"

"Yes, I'm okay. What are you doing down here? I told you to stay in the crater."

"You're welcome. We'll discuss that later. Right now, Krystal needs your help."

"Where is she?"

"Her and the children are being held hostage in the clothing store."

"Let's go." Ethan grabbed his weapons and ran down the trail towards the store. Was it anger or fear that drove him as he ran? He could not bear the thought of losing another family. If what the security team had discovered was true, only two more invaders were still a threat, and both were assaulting Krystal.

He soon overtook two agents who were cautiously approaching the store. "Does anyone have any information from inside the store?" He asked.

"Not much. They did toss out a message on a stick a few minutes ago with demands."

"What kind of deal are they looking for?"

"As expected, they want to trade Krystal and the children for you. But, as you know, we don't negotiate with terrorists."

"Yes, and expect nothing less. In this case, we may want to consider the trade. We could get four innocent individuals clear and insert a special force operative. I'm all in."

"Nice gesture, Ethan, but it is not your call."

"May not be my call, but let me tell you this. My future wife and children are being mercilessly held in there, and I'm only going to give you about three minutes to come up with a plan, or I am the plan. Time starts now, gentlemen."

The two agents were still chattering with someone on their radios when Ethan said, "Time's up. Cover me, I'm going in." He moved around the building under cover of darkness looking for all the egress and ingress opportunities. There were three, the first option was the front door, heavily barricaded, and the back door was too obvious. The third and last was the single window which would create a lot of noise. There had to be something else. He moved in closer and once again circled the store. At only four feet from the structure, he was not worried about the enemy as they were keeping themselves pretty much hidden.

On the far side of the building, Ethan tripped over a wall and landed flat on a wooden platform. It was still extremely dark behind the store, and he had no idea what he was on. Finding a flashlight in his combat vest he turned it on to see a wooden door covering something. *Could it be?* He answered his question by finding a handle and lifting the panel to reveal steps leading under the building. *Thank you, God.* He whispered as he slowly made his way into a dusty spider web filled basement. "Now, all I need is a way to get upstairs quietly." Shining the light around he did find an old rickety set of stairs that led to the first floor. Looking them over, Ethan was certain they led directly into the main storeroom. He could hear the creaking of the floor directly overhead.

He shut his eyes and pictured the inside of the store. Besides the main room, he remembered there were two rooms at the back. An office and a fitting room were positioned in the back left corner. Ethan moved that way looking for loose floorboards or some kind of door. Under the fitting room, he found nothing, but he did hear voices above him. Listening intently, he tried to make out what he was hearing. He couldn't make out any words, but he could hear a lady crying. That had to be Krystal. The fire inside Ethan burned hotter as he pictured Krystal in all her beauty being abducted by some godless immoral thug. If there wasn't anything in the office, he was going in the door guns a-blazing.

Under the office, he found a shelf on which sat several boxes. Checking the floor above the boxes affirmed his suspicions. A trap door in the floor allowed the clerk to store the records under the floor. After clearing the shelf, Ethan took off his combat vest. Easing himself up onto the shelf, he lay flat on his back with the floor only a couple of inches above his face. Pushing up slightly the floor creaked before giving way to his force. A beam of light from a lantern in the other room flooded into the hole.

Up just enough to peek out, he could see one of the gunmen in the main room pacing back and forth. He could hear the girls crying but heard nothing of Jonah. Ethan was certain from being under the fitting room that Krystal was in there with the other gunmen. Just the thought of it brought tears of anger to his eyes. He had to move quickly. He lifted the trap door and rolled out onto the floor holding the door, so it didn't slam shut. Easing the door shut, he pulled the knife from his boot and quietly approached the doorway into the store.

It was time to set a trap. He found a jar of buttons and tossed one of the buttons into the room. It clattered as it rolled across the floor. He could hear the gunman move his way and then stop. He rolled another button through the doorway. It smacked into a display and spun to a stop.

"Who's in there?" The gunman asked.

Ethan stood quietly in the shadows and waited. Finally, the gunman felt the need to do his job and with his gun drawn stepped into the dark office. His biggest mistake was he took one step too far. The knife found its mark and silenced another killer. Ethan eased the gunman to the floor so as not to alert his comrade.

How do I keep the children quiet while I save their mother? God, if you can shut the mouths of lions, surely you can do the same with children. He slowly peeked around the corner and found the girls on the far side of the store asleep on a pile of linens. To the left of them, Jonah looked as if he had been sleeping for a long time. Ethan raised his hands to God and softly asked, *Why did I doubt?*

The last of the assailants were behind the fitting room door with the woman he loved. He silently prayed that he wasn't too late and crashed through the door. The first thing he saw was the look of anguish on Krystal's face and her torn dress. The marks on her face told the story of brutality. Standing over her was a monster of a man with a long ponytail all dressed in black. He held a leather belt in his hand and was about to minister another blow. In a split second, Ethan processed all his eyes could see, and his brain could comprehend. He plowed into the man with all the strength his adrenaline-filled body could generate.

They flew across the room and crashed into a mirror on the back wall causing it to shatter. The man screamed as Ethan grabbed his ponytail and yanked, the assailant's head jerked around, and he went to the ground. A swift kick to the stomach caused vomit to spew from his cursing mouth. Ethan pulled the Beretta from his waistband and was about to finish off this blight on humanity when he heard the voice of Abram. "Don't do it, Ethan. His life is not yours to take."

Ethan turned around to see his old friend standing in the doorway with a couple of security agents behind him.

"You said it was City Hall's job to protect. Right now, I'm working for them."

"Are you? This man is lying helplessly on the ground, and you want to kill him. Is it to protect the community or to seek revenge for what you have just witnessed? It's all over Ethan. Let's go home." Ethan lowered his gun and returned it to his waistband as he dropped down beside Krystal and took her in his arms. Together they watched as the two security agents walked out with the handcuffed assailant between them. With tears in his eyes, Abram knelt beside the couple and laid his hands on their shoulders and prayed.

Slowly helping Krystal to her feet Ethan could tell she was in a lot of pain. She put her arms around his neck as he picked her up.

"Are the children okay?" She faintly asked.

"They're okay and well taken care of, my darling. Anna has taken them to Elena's."

"Where are we going?" She whispered.

Ethan never answered her as they walked down the path towards Doctor Winston's cabin. He could see the predawn glow in the eastern sky. It had been a long night.

Chapter Forty-Six

The shockwaves of the invasion still riveted through the community. No time in its history had it experienced the intensity of such an onslaught of physical aggression. The only surviving invader was tucked safely inside the City Hall jail. Interrogators had their methods, and they worked. As expected, he squealed like a pig when pressed.

Ethan walked through the meat locker and found the cipher lock. It had been three days since the attack, and Krystal was up and walking. Physically she would recover quickly, emotionally would be a struggle. *If I had only got there sooner,* Ethan told himself time after time. The scanner accepted his thumb, and the door swung open. Security agents were all intently watching screens and did not even acknowledge his presence.

Arnold looked up as Ethan was sitting down in the only empty chair in the room. "It's nice of you to join us, Mr. Dawson. We have been patiently waiting for an hour."

Sensing the sarcasm, Ethan smiled at the security chief, "Someone had to tend the livestock, or you would be eating venison and bear meat all winter. Sorry boss."

"You can pay me back later. Okay team, we have a lot of work to do, let's get started."

Arnold leaned back in his chair and put his hands behind his head. Looking around the table and eight faces he asked the dreaded question. "What happened?"

An awkward silence prevailed. Finally, Oliver half-heartedly slightly lifted a hand. "Sir, as I'm sure you have read in our report, we never had an inkling they would come from the west. When reviewing the historical data, we discovered the motion detection system had failed on the Charlotte mountain camera array."

"So, the first alert was the barn cameras?"

"Yes, and they worked perfectly," Oliver answered.

"Did they? Then why do we have two dead agents?"

Ethan winced with the rest of the attendees. *That's a little sharp.*

The red-bearded agent wasn't about to let this one go. "We have two dead agents because our system was not designed for a full-scale invasion."

"That may be true, Keenan, but in this case, only one would have inflicted the same number of casualties. Am I to assume our agents on patrol did not have night vision capabilities?"

Keenan looked down at his tablet for a moment before answering. "They did have night vision binoculars, but we have no idea if they used them. It would have been proper protocol for them to scour the area before moving forward. I imagine they felt it was just an animal or false alarm. That would explain their lack of precaution. Some of these questions will just have to go unanswered."

"That may be true, but we're hired to protect the citizens of this community, and that is what we will do. I expect a report once the technicians find the source of the glitch. How is the investigative report coming along, Loraine?"

"I have three more interviews and then compiling my notes. It'll be ready in a couple more days. It's been a difficult report to write. While we only lost two agents, the invaders lost all but one. Some of those were not even twenty years old. I feel for their families."

"Remember, we are not responsible for their demise. It was of their choosing. Let me know when it's done. The community elders are already asking for it. Ethan, how is Krystal doing?"

"Thanks for asking," Ethan answered. "Physically she is recovering well. Emotionally, there is a lot of work to be done. Please pray for her."

"That we have been and will continue to do."

"I'm sure Loraine has already got your report from the night of the attack, but I believe we need to go over a few things. Maybe even revisit some ground rules." Looking over his tablet, he nodded his head. "It looks like you took out nine of the twenty attackers by yourself. Is that right?"

Ethan looked at the ceiling as he tried to count. Finally, he shook his head. "Actually, I don't like to put notches on my gun, but if you're counting put me down for only eight. Anna got the ninth one. He was about to execute me when she took him out."

"Eight or nine, it doesn't matter the number. What does matter is that you may still have a little personal vengeance. The reports I'm getting from the meeting house and the clothing store counter assaults, lead me to believe you know a little more about combat than we are aware. How much time did you spend with an urban assault team?"

"All my time in Afghanistan I was connected to a close combat team. While my specialty was sniper, I spent a lot of nights knocking down doors. Not an easy thing to do when the people behind the door want to kill you."

"Understand. From now on I would like for you to try and follow orders. Do you realize I have to go tell the village leaders that one of my men took out forty percent of the enemy? That's not going to look like teamwork."

"Sorry, sir, but it was only thirty-five percent. Remember Anna?"

"Of course, I remember Anna, good grief. Who could forget her? Sometimes, I think she's about as much trouble as you." Looking at his notes, Arnold continued. "What about Kearsarge Pass? Where are we there?"

Oliver still a little shell shocked from the surprise attack, at least had his update ready. "There is still a lot of activity in and around Lone Pine. All the campgrounds are filled up with what our informants are calling a mercenary army." Scrolling up through his tablet, he found what he was looking for, "It's now estimated, around two hundred in number. The good news is that the demeanor in the campgrounds does not reflect one of the battle-hardened warriors. There is a lot of drinking and fighting going on. We do have reports that they are being financed by a far-left fringe group associated with, what you could say, some of Ethan's old friends."

"I gather you're saying that with sarcasm?" Ethan interrupted Oliver.

"Of course. They are only your friend because you uncovered their corruption."

"So are your informants getting any information on movement?" Arnold asked, pulling the conversation back to the mercenaries.

"It sounds like they are waiting on their leader who has been tied up in the New York court system. He is expected to be arriving in a week or two. Supposedly he has alpine experience."

"Does anyone have anything else to add?" Arnold looked around the table and found no responders. "Okay team, go do your job. Ethan, stick around for a moment."

Once the room was cleared, Arnold shut the door and sat back down. "I think we have a mole."

"Who is it?"

"I don't know, but this group of invaders had too much knowledge to not have an inside track. They knew we were guarding the east side. They knew about the singings at the meeting house. From the interrogation, we found out that they knew where you lived, and the two guys you took out from the hillside were on their way to visit you in the crater. They know that you are heavily armed and an excellent sniper. What they didn't know was that you were also a master at urban assault."

"So, knowing that, I would imagine the group down in the valley is for a decoy only. It's almost certain the ringleader sent the hit squad, expecting them to finish the job. Now that he hasn't received a report, he will assume they did not succeed."

"I agree. That is probably why the ringleader is making his way out to join the group. They're planning to send in the second string."

"Do you have any ideas on how to lay a trap for our mole?" Ethan asked.

"The best way is to disseminate a fake plan of attack using a unique code or version for each recipient and wait for it to make it back through our informant. That can take time we may not have. I do have people I trust, and we will work on that. You keep your eyes and ears open. It's going to get tough."

Ethan was going over who was aware of his weapon cache. Well, now a lot of people know, but before the attack it was limited. Anna was the only one in his circle that knew, and he trusted her. It had to be someone on the security team. It was time to relocate his weapons.

Chapter Forty-Seven

Ethan sat on the porch as the rain splattered off the tin roof. It had started during the night and continued to worsen as the day went on. It was still a little early for winter weather but at this altitude, anything could happen. He was trying to figure out his day. He had plans of going to spend the day with Krystal and the children. That was before the storm hit. He was still contemplating doing it anyway when he noticed the riders coming over the crest. He went inside and put a pot of coffee on to percolate.

He soon recognized the riders and watched Robert and Keenan coming up the trail wrapped up in their oilskin dusters with their Stetsons pulled low over their faces. Swinging off the horses the men stepped in under the roof and pulled off their wet dusters.

"Is it any warmer inside?" Robert's sarcastic baritone echoed the thunder.

"I reckon it's just a smidgen warmer and a bit dryer as well." Ethan tried to match his boss's demeanor. "It must be serious to bring you up here in this weather. What's up?"

Stepping into the cabin the aroma of freshly brewed coffee competed with the smell of a fire burning in the cookstove. "I'll tell you over a cup of coffee. Smells like you knew we were coming. Do you really think Krystal's going to like it up here?"

"Guessing we will find out soon."

"That's why we came. We're thinking of building you folks a home closer to the village."

"What!" Ethan's raised voice showed his shock. "You know I like it up here. I don't belong in the village."

"We never said you were going to live in the village. As a matter of fact, we think it would not be wise for you to live too close to anyone."

"What do you mean by that?"

"Don't get me wrong Ethan. Almost everyone in the community loves you. It's just that as hard as you try to be like us, you're not. When it comes to teaching others to live a peaceful quiet life, you are not the teacher. We do have a proposal if you're cooled down enough to listen."

Ethan sat down in his favorite chair and took a sip of semi-cold coffee. "Go ahead but it had better be good."

Robert nodded to Keenan to go ahead. "Ethan as you know, I oversee security for the gold operation from the time it is mined until it is sold. We would like for you to join our team and relocate closer to the mines."

"I don't know. I came up here to find a peaceful, simple life, and it sounds like you want me to be a hired gun. I'm just not sure that is what I want to do. Eventually, I plan on having a family and think tending livestock might be a better fit."

"It's too late for that," Robert said. "After last week nobody sees you as a sheepherder. And we did think of Krystal and the children. The community leaders have decided we will build you a home on the shelf up above William and Claire's. It's a fairly level spot for a couple of hundred yards before cutting up into the valley. We think that would be ideal for you. It's wooded and has a stream that flows year-round. Think about it."

I bet I don't have a choice. Ethan turned to Keenan. "Tell me, what is it you want me to do?"

"We would like you to be a link between the community gold mine and City Hall. The miners know what they are doing and do not need oversight. They just don't want to be involved in City Hall. It means a lot to them that their labors provide a means by which the community can meet the needs of its people. You will, from a distance, oversee the complete operation from pick up to payment."

"As you know I should not be around gold. It has a strange effect on me."

"Like pouring it into streams? Ironically that was right outside your future front door. Maybe you could go panning."

The sarcastic humor did not go unnoticed.

Keenan continued, "Don't worry, you will not be physically involved in the process, you will only monitor and examine each phase. What you will be trying to find is the weak links in the security chain. As you are keenly aware, they pull millions of dollars each week from the mines. It doesn't show on the surface, but via City Hall, the community is extremely wealthy."

"Sounds all good and everything, but can we still live

in a simple cabin and cook with a wood stove? Can we, as much as possible, live like all our brothers and sisters we go to church with? Because if we can't do that. I want no part in it."

"Of course, you can. We highly recommend you do such. Remember City Hall stays underground. We do not discuss it in the community. Let us know as quickly as you can. We have the lumber for a cabin and are ready to start."

Stepping out onto the porch, they were happy to see the rain had let up. After they were gone, Ethan sat down on his favorite rocking chair and sobbed. *"My God, my God. What have I done? All I wanted was a quiet and peaceful life. I was so happy to be getting a family again. I trusted in you. Why are you letting me down? What am I supposed to do? Please answer me, God."*

He soon quieted enough to listen to the One he cried out to. For quite a few minutes he sat there in silence and then he heard that still small voice. *"I have not left you, nor have I let you down. I did not bring you to this mountain to spend the rest of your life at ease. Recently you had become complacent here in the crater of protection. Open your heart, and I will show you My plan for your life."*

That was all he needed to hear. Ethan went inside and pulled his Bible out from under the magazines on the table and took it back outside. When it got too dark to read he came inside and knew that he was back on track. Tomorrow was another day.

Chapter Forty-Eight

The morning sunshine soon melted the light frost as Ethan hiked down from the crater. He needed to find Robert and tell him of his decision. The sound of hammering echoed across the lake, and he could see the construction workers busy on the hillside overlooking the village. *Don't tell me they've started already. I haven't even given them my answer.* Sure enough, a big pile of timbers and lumber had already been moved to the building site and like a thousand ants, they were going about the business of building a cabin.

Walking past William and Claire's he got sidetracked as they welcomed him to the neighborhood.

"I haven't even told them I'm moving down here yet. Don't you think they jumped the gun a little?"

"I would imagine God told them to build it, and you would come," was William's smiling response. "Do you have time for a cup of coffee?"

"I believe I'll always have time for you," Ethan

answered as he slid into the chair next to William. "How long before the front porch gets shut down for the winter?"

"Oh, it's about time for that to happen. I'm just enjoying every sunny day the Lord blesses me with. How have you been since the skirmish we had the other day?"

Did I just hear him call it a skirmish? Ethan took the cup of coffee from Claire. "Thank you, Claire, you're the sweetest person I know." Claire's blushful smile reminded him of his grandmother when he was a young boy. Turning back to William, he tried to think of the correct answer. *How have I been? I just terminated eight lives. How have I been? From what I can tell, I'm responsible for bringing violence to a peaceful people. None of this would have happened if I had not come here. How have I been?* Escaping from his self-condemning thoughts, he answered William the best he could. "I've been doing fine."

"Ethan, you may fool some of the people, but I was watching your face just now and a mess load of conflict was bouncing around inside that head of yours. Tell me the truth. How are you doing?"

"Not real good. Yes, there are a lot of conflicts affecting just about every moment. I'm having trouble sleeping at night and have started hearing things. I have started questioning if I should even be here."

"Where would you be if you weren't here?"

"That's not the point. I just don't know if it's a good idea for the community to keep me around. I have brought a lot of pain and sorrow to these peace-loving people."

William interrupted. "You have brought a lot more than that. Before you arrived in the community we questioned if an outsider could assimilate to our way of living. Not only did you accept our lifestyle, but you also embraced it. You worked hard without complaining. You did come with a past life that has caused several challenges which have helped the community understand the pitfalls of the world. I found it refreshing when they were willing to forgive."

Ethan tilted his head and looked at William. "I'm having trouble understanding what you are driving at."

"Ethan, you are here only because the people of this community have invited you to stay. Even with all your shortcomings, they have found you have a heart for serving God, and they like that about you. Do you hear the sound of the hammers up on the mountain? They are not building you a home because of your past, they are doing it because they love God, and they love you. Don't let them down."

Ethan hung his head in shame. Why was he thinking about himself? Just the contemplation of William's last statement felt like one of the hammers on the mountain had just smashed into his soul. Instead of the negative thoughts that he had been having, he needed to repent and make things right with God. With a clean heart, he could go thank the men and women who worked so hard to give him, and his future family, a home.

Chapter Forty-Nine

The construction noise stopped soon after he left William's. Now the only sound he heard was the stream cascading down the mountain. Finding a shady spot, he sat down on a rock and listened. Listened not only to the sound of the water but the still small voice that would give him direction. It came in the remembrance of a scripture he had read. He could not remember where, but he was thinking in Isaiah said, *"For my thoughts are not your thoughts, neither are your ways my ways," declares the* LORD. *"As the heavens are higher than the earth, so are my ways higher than your ways, and my thoughts than your thoughts.*

"That is so true," Ethan told the cascading stream and the two squirrels that were watching him intently. "God's ways are much higher than mine. Why am I having problems with that?" And then he remembered a passage in Proverbs. *Trust in the* LORD *with all your heart, and lean not on your own understanding. In all your ways acknowledge Him, and He shall direct your paths. Do not be wise in your own eyes; fear the* LORD *and depart from evil.*

"God, you are an amazing God. You continue to open my eyes to who you are. Please remove any sin that I may have hidden in my heart. Please lead me, Lord, and I will follow." Ethan continued praying until he heard the sound of hammers echoing around the valley.

Coming up over the crest, he could see the progress was moving quickly. The exterior walls were four logs high, and more being added every few minutes. The men had the cabin surrounded and by the looks of it, they knew what they were doing. He recognized a number of the men from the church and was trying to figure out where he might help when Eli motioned for him.

"Are you looking for a job?" Eli asked.

"I'm always looking for a job. Do you know anyone that's hiring?"

"I hear the guy they're building this for is pretty finicky. You might not meet his expectations."

"I have firsthand knowledge that he is overjoyed with the love and generosity that he has witnessed."

Ethan wiped the edge of his eye to keep the tears from forming. "Seriously Eli, I would love to work alongside any of these men. Just show me the way."

"Great! If you haven't eaten, go grab a bite, and then you can work with me."

The invite reminded Ethan that he was hungry and headed over to the scrub oaks where a dozen or so ladies were busy cleaning up the tables. He instantly recognized Anna as she was wiping down the tablecloth. Her smile showed that she still hadn't forgotten him. *Why does she do that?* He still had some lasting feelings for her, but his love for Krystal was much stronger. He would need to keep up his guard.

He was certain the other ladies noticed her enthusiasm to help him, and he soon had a plate full of fried chicken and mashed potatoes. He was sitting on a shaded log watching the fast-moving progress of the cabin when Anna sat down beside him.

"You know, this could have been ours?" she said softly.

"Oh, did you and Cody have the opportunity to move up here?"

"That's not what I meant. It could have been for the two of us."

"You don't give up very easily. Are you getting cold feet with Cody?"

"Not so much cold feet as much as I'm getting some bad feelings."

"Have you talked to anyone about these bad feelings?"

"I am right now."

"Anna, you know this is not a good thing. We have been just too close to be discussing your feeling about your fiancé. When you head down this mountain, I want you to stop in and tell Claire about your feelings. She'll know what to do."

"That's true, but Cody is even more mysterious than you. I don't know what he's up to most of the time. He does strange things."

"I shouldn't ask, but I'm going to. What kind of strange things are we talking about?"

"It's hard to say. He's cordial with me and we talk about a lot of things. I really do love him. I always have, but I'm concerned."

"Concerned about what?"

"His spiritual life is in shambles. At times his actions make me think he doesn't even know the Lord. When we were growing up, he was a really sweet boy, even as a young man he respected me and always wanted to do the right thing. Since he's been home, he has displayed a bad temper. He keeps talking about a better world outside this community. He talks about things that tell me his heart isn't really here."

"Are you encouraging these conversations, or do you let him know where your heart is?"

"I try to tell him that's all silly talk, but then he just yells at me. I'm hoping it's just the stress of the invasion and our upcoming wedding."

"Where was he the night of the invasion?"

"That's another thing. He told me he was going to be working with security on the east side, but when they all came down from the ridge, he wasn't with them. I asked one of the men if they knew where he was at and…"

"And what?"

Anna was now tearing up and Ethan knew this was exactly what he wanted to avoid.

"Not only had Cody not been seen, he was not even assigned to the security team. He's been lying to me, and I don't know why. Not only that, where has he been going when he says he's going to work. All he would have to do is tell me the truth. I love him and would understand."

"Okay Anna, we weren't supposed to do this. Even

though Claire is Cody's grandmother, she is the one that needs to counsel you in these matters. Krystal and I will be praying for you two. I need to get to work."

Anna started wiping tears off her face as Ethan stood up to go. "Great," he said softly so only Anna could hear. "Now all the ladies are going to think I made you cry. That will go over well"

"If I give you a big hug and kiss, will that change their opinion?" she countered

"At least you still have a sense of humor. Here, thanks for the lunch, and please talk to Claire." He handed her his plate and utensils and walked away.

All afternoon Ethan could not get Anna's conversation off his mind. All he wanted to do was take in the whole process of building the cabin, not deal with drama. *What about Cody? What was he up to? If he even as much as lays a finger on her. Oh, why do I let her take up brain space?*

By quitting time, the carpenters had the walls up and the ridge beams hung. Tomorrow they would finish the roof and get the doors and windows in. Sitting back and admiring the cabin, Ethan was starting to understand how the community existed. Forty men came together with the common purpose of building a cabin. Each one knew the process and had the skill set to do the work. They do not quarrel, nor do they whine. All they do is praise God and work hard.

Eli, with his nail bag hanging over his shoulder, walked up to Ethan. "It has been a successful day, Ethan. Two more days and it'll be ready to move in."

"It is so much appreciated. I would be happy staying

in the crater, but I suppose this will be better for a family. Speaking of family, I should stop in and check on Krystal."

Together the two men walked down the trail to the lake where they split up, and Ethan headed around the lake to Elena's.

Chapter Fifty

Krystal was sitting on the couch with a blanket wrapped around her and Jonah as she read to him from a children's book. In the kitchen, Cathryn and Christiana were helping Elena fix supper. Krystal scooted over and motioned for Ethan to sit down.

"I'm kind of dirty, my dear. Just wanted to stop in and see how you are feeling."

"I think I am okay. It's just going to take some time and prayer." She replied as she got up still a little unsteady. "I'll walk you out."

Outside on the porch, she grabbed his hand. "Thank you for coming by, even if it is for a little bit." He felt a bit of a twinge as he wrapped his arms around her. "Are you sure you're okay?"

Ethan felt helpless as he could feel her sobbing against his shoulder. *I let her down. What could I have done?* Within his soul he was feeling the pain she was unintentionally transmitting. His search for words of comfort came up void. *What can I do?*

"I'm scared." The barely audible comment caught Ethan off guard.

"You went through a horrible ordeal, my darling. What is causing your fear?"

"Not fear, I'm scared. I could have been killed. I am just a mortal being and God could take me home at any moment. What will become of my children?"

Ethan's only response was to wrap his arms tighter around her and hold her tight. He could feel the tension flow out of her body as she relaxed in his embrace. He kissed her gently and walked her back inside.

It was dark by the time he made it to the crater. On the way across the meadow, he started noticing fresh tracks on the trail. They were going in both directions and the downhill ones were on top. At least whoever was up here is no longer here. Maybe Growler kept them at bay. Reaching the door, it was unlatched, and the apprehension grew. Reaching around his back for his Beretta his hand came back empty. "I'm going to need to start wearing that thing all the time." He told himself as he pushed the door open and stepped aside, expecting bullets to fly. The only thing that flew out the door was his old buddy Growler. He was excited and hungry.

"Did you chase them away, boy?" He asked as he roughed up the hyperactive canine. The cabin had not been ransacked as Ethan had expected but he could tell someone had been searching for something. The tablecloth over the coffee table had been moved. Going into the bedroom he could see that the mattress had been moved. Pulling out his drawers, he found crumpled clothes. He was thankful he had moved his weapons.

Locking the front door and closing the drapes, Ethan slid the coffee table to the side and rolled back the carpet. Opening the recently installed trap door, he pulled out the duffel bag and inspected the contents. To his relief, nothing had been taken.

Wrapped in a blanket to fight off the evening chill, Ethan nursed a steaming hot cup of coffee. The serenity of the surrounding mountains was being chipped away by the gnawing feeling that a storm was brewing on the horizon.

Chapter Fifty-One

From his vantage point above the Kearsarge Pass trail, Ethan was well hidden. His night vision goggles showed every detail of the rugged mountain landscape. He had not seen a soul since he had arrived just before dark. He checked his watch. If what Anna had told him was true, it was almost time. He rechecked his equipment and watched for activity from both directions on the trail.

Right on queue he watched the light from a headlamp making its way down from the ridge above Bullfrog Lake. Focusing in on the light, Ethan could see it was a solo hiker with a small backpack. Arriving in the clearing just twenty feet below Ethan's position, the hiker pulled off his backpack and set down on a rock. Excellent! I'll be able to hear everything they say. Ethan turned his NVG towards Charlotte Lake. He could not identify the hiker he watched coming up from the lake but was certain who it was. No one else would be out this time of night. Sure enough, as the hiker crossed the Pacific Crest Trail, the NVG focused in on the hiker revealing Cody making his way towards their position.

"Did you get it?" The unidentified hiker asked as Cody walked into the clearing.

"Yes, I did. Did they agree to my request?"

"They said they're willing to leave the place alone if you do the job."

"You know I can't. It would just be too dangerous. My girlfriend already is getting suspicious."

"Forget about her. She's not in your future."

"It's not that easy. Anyhow, I have your picture, take it and get out of here. Tell your boss that I will not do the job, and if they're smart, they will stay away from this place." Ethan silently gasped as he watched Cody hand over a small, framed picture.

That's my picture of Kendra. Why are they wanting it? Every part of his conscious was screaming for a reason. The desire to get back what was rightfully his was what came to the surface. He could not let the guy get off the mountain with his picture.

"If you don't do the job, you know the boss will not be happy." The hiker said as he pulled on his pack. "I'm getting out of here. This place gives me the creeps."

"You tell Haidar to stay off this mountain." Cody answered. "They may seem peaceful, but they are well-armed. When it comes to Dawson, he is bad news. You will never see where the bullets are coming from. You'll just be dead."

"Sounds kind of like a threat. When we do come up here, I would suggest you disappear because Haidar will be bringing an army. We have over two hundred well-trained mercenaries in the valley just waiting for him to arrive." With that the hiker turned and headed up the trail.

Ethan hit the stop button on his NVG and waited for Cody to leave. *Why won't he leave?* Cody seemed to be lost in thought as he sat on the rock and kicked some stones around. Finally, he stood up and with a defeated look stumbled down the trail towards Charlotte Lake. As soon as he was out of sight, Ethan silently followed the trail towards Kearsarge Pass.

Ethan slowed down when he spotted the headlamp on the switchbacks above the lake. The almost full moon was rising over the ridge giving Ethan enough light to proceed without his night vision goggles. He had no clear plan on retrieving the picture. There has to be a clue in the picture that they don't want found out. Why didn't they just destroy it? The headlamp was now heading back to the east and was slowly making its way up the side of the mountain.

Through the night vision goggles, Ethan could see the now fatigued hiker dragging his feet as he approached the pass. Keeping a distance of a couple hundred yards, Ethan cautiously advanced. He had to get within striking distance without being detected. He had pulled his Beretta out and had attached the silencer. The last thing he wanted was to have a shot echo throughout the valley walls.

The words of Abram kept echoing through his head as the distance shortened between Ethan and his target. *To personally administer retribution is a sin.* Ethan quieted his conscious by making the decision to only use his weapon as an act of defense. Just in case, he would need to make sure they got to lower altitude before the confrontation took place. It would be hard to hide the evidence in this rocky barren landscape.

Ethan stopped as he watched the hiker take off his pack and set it on a boulder. Pulling a sleeping pad out of his backpack, the hiker was soon sound asleep. All this time Ethan was intently scoping the area through his NVG as he advanced towards the target. The snoring rattled against the granite walls allowing Ethan the opportunity he needed to achieve his goal.

Pulling the backpack off the boulder Ethan retreated a hundred feet before sliding open the zipper. The first thing he felt was the cold steel of a handgun. *What a novice.* Removing the gun and his picture he replaced them with a rock of about the same weight. He chuckled with the thought of discovery. It may get thrown through a window. Inching his way back to the snoring hiker he had just set the backpack down when the snoring stopped. Ethan froze, his eyes on the hiker. A couple of snorts followed by a groan, the hiker swung his arm around and grabbed his backpack. Ethan dove behind a boulder just as the hiker sat up.

Ethan sat silently against the boulder listening to what might be transpiring on the other side. He could hear the hiker moving around and shortly walk away. Pulling on his NVG, he could see the hiker now moving down the mountain on the east side of the pass. He surveyed the rest of the area before starting his trip back to the crater. The moon, now high in the sky, gave off all the light Ethan needed to make his way along the trail.

The hour trip home gave Ethan a lot to think about. What was he going to do about Cody? He felt sorry for the guy. He had literally dug himself a grave. He had returned home only to deceive those who love him. The people he was now associated with would think nothing of terminating him once he had served their purpose. The recording of Cody's meeting with the hiker was enough to convict him for life. How would Anna take it? Her love for him had deep roots. She had so graciously forgiven him. How could Cody be so hardened to deceive someone that loves him that much? How would the community at large react? Could it be enough to destroy them? Hopefully not. *I'll just keep it to myself until next week. That meeting should be interesting considering the missing picture.*

Chapter Fifty-Two

Ethan sat at the table looking at the picture of his wife. Why is this so important to them? It can't just be the fact that she was one of their victims. There had to be something more. Pulling out his knife he removed the back. Inside he found a folded piece of paper. His fingers started shaking as he read the handwritten note from Kendra. In her own unique way, she had written a love letter thanking him for taking her to Hawaii.

That's not worth killing for. Looking over the frame Ethan found a small slit in the side of the frame had been filled in with wood putty. His knife popped out the filler along with a memory stick. *Bingo! Who would have thought? It's time for a trip to City Hall.*

"Its password protected." Oliver pounded away at the keyboard trying to open the memory stick. "Are you certain it wasn't your wife's?"

"How can anyone be certain of anything anymore? I'm pretty sure it was put there by someone who has ties with the syndicate. Whoever they might be."

"It doesn't matter. We have our ways." Oliver opened another program that easily broke through the password firewall. With a couple more clicks Oliver had the files scanned and transferred to the mainframe. Pulling up a flagged file, he gasped. "The security team needs to see this. Let's go."

Arnold was the last to arrive and immediately kicked off the conversation. "As most of you have been briefed, Cody met a hiker up on the trail last night. Ethan had suspected some foul play and had from a hidden position observed Cody give the hiker a picture that Ethan recognized as one taken from his home. The picture has considerable history which we will not take the time to discuss. What is important is the memory stick Ethan found hidden in its frame. What we're about to see is its contents. Go ahead with the first file, Oliver."

The file filled the screen with a list of names, numbers and dates. Ethan looked around the room and could tell that, other than Oliver, the team had little interaction with the outside world. He scanned down through the names and recognized all but two as political figures from up and down the east coast.

Oliver already had his laser pointer out. "Along the top you can see the importance of this spreadsheet. The first column is the name of the recipient, the second is the date of the transaction, third is the amount of the bribe, and the last is a description of what the briber expected in return."

"Oliver, did you look up who these recipients are?" Arnold asked.

"Yes, I did. They are all prominent political figures. I

also cross-checked the responses to the briber's request and found a vast majority of them have been fulfilled. Bottom line, the bribes paid off."

"Thanks, Oliver. This information will be of great value to the FBI. What else did you find?"

A new spreadsheet showed up on the screen. It took a little time to read and understand the data they were looking at were the resources of the syndicate. Everything from their bank accounts to the names and numbers of their assassins. It was a treasure trove of information.

Arnold was the first to speak. "I have never seen such a complete work of conviction. This data alone could take down a lot of well-known public figures and criminals. What do we do with it?"

Then it hit Ethan. "Go back to the other list."

Oliver complied and Ethan scrolled down through the lines.

"There he is. Remember me telling you about the second individual that killed my family? That is Congressman Eduard Adams. His henchman was the shooter."

Arnold looked at him with a frown, "Do you have evidence to sustain that accusation?"

"If you call raw video footage evidence, I do."

Digging through his backpack Ethan pulled out a thumb drive. Handing it to Oliver he sat back and waited for the show.

The team sat in silence as the black and white video played out the assassination of the criminal. The periodical glance at Ethan did not go unnoticed. Once it ended, they were speechless.

"Yep, that's evidence." Arnold smiled at Ethan. "Why did I doubt you?"

"My apologies on you guys having to witness that. I have already handed this video over to a friend of mine in the FBI. Hopefully, it will play out in the proper way."

"It has to give the Department of Justice added ammunition on cleaning up this ring of corruption. Now let's talk about Cody."

Chapter Fifty-Three

The meeting between Cody and his contact was only three hours away. Ethan checked his weapons. Things had a chance to go off the rail and fire power might be needed. As the sun dropped below the mountain peaks, Ethan crossed the Pacific Crest Trail on the way to the rendezvous point. Making sure he was not being followed he made his way through the scraggy oaks, and in the deepening darkness, he nestled down within the boulder field. He checked his earpiece and could hear the rustling of the leaves sixty yards away. The hidden microphones surrounding the meeting spot allowed him a better vantage point farther up the hill.

Twenty minutes before the meeting Ethan spotted a headlamp crossing over the pass. He knew somewhere to the west Cody would be leaving the village for the rendezvous. Looking back at the pass, he saw two more headlamps appear. Just as I thought, he's bringing help. *Cody needs to be warned. But how?* He needed to stick with his plan, and if necessary, he would terminate the enemy. Just maybe Arnold was watching this unfold in the command center and would intercept Cody.

The soft hum of electric motors snapped Ethan's attention to the western sky. Total darkness. Turning on the NVG, he scanned the sky and finally found it. Only a slight variant in the darkness was moving swiftly across the sky heading in his direction. Cody must be on his way and security is engaging. *Why don't they just apprehend him before he gets here? Considering this could be considered treasonous, they must want to get more evidence.* He finished setting up his sniper rifle and calculated the sixty yards to the target.

With the drone now in a stationary position overhead, Ethan had mixed feelings. He liked working alone and with the eyes of the security team watching over him, he was now part of a team. Arnold's last order rang in his head. Shoot only if fired upon, period. Ethan knew that he would not be taking incoming fire from his position but was having misgivings about Cody's safety. *Yes, he is a traitor, but he doesn't deserve to go down like this. I can take out all three and ask for forgiveness.* Abram's admonition on revenge pushed back that idea. *Maybe I can just pray, and all of this will go away. Will it? Anyway, what is God's plan for a traitor? Is this his judgment?*

His earpiece came alive. "Spotter, this is security, do you copy?"

What the..... Ethan gave a thumbs up to an invisible drone somewhere above him. *How did they know the frequency?*

"Good. We show three bandits descending off

Kearsarge Pass. The orders are to continue on with the rendezvous. We need more information. Do not fire on the bandits. I repeat. Under no circumstance fire on the bandits. Verify you understand."

Ethan wanted to ignore the response but felt it best to keep the security team off his back. With a thumbs up, the voice in his ears went away, and he continued preparing for the show. *How in the world am I supposed to just sit here and watch?* He didn't have to wait long as the lights from the pass were approaching the clearing.

His earpiece came to life with the arrival of the three bandits. They shuffled into the clearing and tried to find a comfortable place to sit. Ethan focused in on each one and soon spotted Cody's contact. Within minutes the leader ushered the other two guys out of the clearing and into the brush. What he did next caused chills to run down Ethan's spine. He pulled out a handgun and slid a round into the chamber. *That can only mean one thing.* Turning his NVG to the west Ethan spotted Cody coming up the trail.

"What's the latest news?" Cody asked as he walked into the clearing.

"Why did you do it?"

"I told you I wasn't going to do it. So, I didn't."

"I'm not talking about knocking off Dawson. Why did you take the picture? The boss is mad."

"What are you talking about? I took the picture and gave it to you last week."

"I don't know what trick you pulled, but when I got to town the picture and my gun were missing."

"It wasn't me. Did you lose it along the trail? It could have fallen out of your pack."

With that the guy smashed Cody in the face with his fist, and Cody fell to the ground. Ethan switched to his sniper rifle and centered the crosshairs on the gangster's chest.

"Don't ever accuse me of not doing my job." The gangster was yelling now. "I don't care about the gun, but I need that picture. Where is it?"

Picking himself up off the ground, Cody looked like a whipped dog. It was starting to raise Ethan's blood pressure to think how this scum was treating a fellow veteran. Yes, Cody was in the wrong, but he did not deserve this kind of treatment.

Cody was rubbing his jaw and keeping his distance from his assailant. "You didn't need to do that. I'm just trying to help. I seriously have no idea what happened. Am I still getting paid?"

"Oh! You are getting paid. Did you bring the codes?"

"They were almost impossible to get. I'm not sure I want to give them to you after what you just did."

"Where are they?"

"They're in my pack. Did you bring my pain meds?"

"You won't be needing them." He motioned for his friends to join him, and the two guys came out of the brush.

"What are they doing here?" Cody started backing up towards the edge of the clearing.

"They do my dirty work. Give them your pack."

Cody was clutching his pack as he continued slowly backing up.

Ethan first noticed the gun in the leader's hand, and as he raised it toward Cody, he could not help himself and slipped off the safety and pulled the trigger. He was too late.

The flash from the gangster's gun appeared as a flash in his night vision scope as the explosion shattered the night sky and blanketed the muffled sound of the sniper rifle.

Ethan watched as Cody fell to the ground. From his training in the military, his mind was moving in only one direction. Neutralize the area and help his fellow soldier. Where were the words of Abram? Where was the order from the security chief? He heard nothing as the two remaining gangsters spun around in absolute confusion before they felt the sting of death.

Ethan exited his nest with his Beretta leading the way and methodically made his way to the clearing. He had gotten clean shots, and none of the gangsters were moving. It was then that voices were screaming in his ear. *Stand down! Ethan Stand down!* He knew that nothing he did now could fix this disaster. He pulled the earpieces from his ear and knelt down beside Cody. He felt a weak pulse and looked for bleeding. Finding only minor bleeding where the bullet had entered his chest, Ethan started to shake.

Cody stirred and opened his eyes. "I feel cold. What happened?"

"You have been shot; I'm going get you to the doctor."

Cody moaned as he tried to sit up. "I don't think I'm going to make it."

"Hang in there, I'll get you out of here."

"Tell Grandma and Grandpa I'm sorry."

"Stay with us, and you can tell them yourself. Let's go."

Ethan threw Cody's arm over his shoulder and slung him onto his back.

Ethan and Cody were halfway down the hill when four men from the security detail met them with a stretcher. Relieving Ethan of the heavy load he followed them to hospital located deep within City Hall.

Doctor Winston was already there, and they immediately took him into surgery. Exhausted, Ethan turned to head back to the clearing for his gear when he heard Arnold call his name. His long exhale exposed his feelings as he turned and walked into the conference room.

Chapter Fifty-Four

The atmosphere around the table was grim as Ethan slumped into his chair. He shut his eyes in hopes that it would all go away. The silence in the room was interrupted by a conversation all too familiar to Ethan. Ethan opened his eyes to the synchronized video from the drone. It was much clearer than he was able to capture with his night vision goggles. Ethan recalled every second and started to cringe when it showed Cody backing up towards the brush. He wanted to shut his eyes but could not. The instability of his emotions were spinning circles inside his conscience. Arnold froze the video.

Using a laser pointer Arnold directed the team's attention to the gun being pulled from the waistband of the gangster. "Ethan, at what point did you see the gun?

"Considering the situation, I was expecting an execution, but did not notice the gun until he raised it towards Cody. My vision was not as clear as we're seeing here."

"We haven't seen the recording from your NVG, so we have to trust what you're saying is true. Is that when you switched from the NVG to your rifle?"

"No, sir. I switched to the rifle when the guy cold cocked Cody."

"Did you consider that a life-threatening action?"

"I considered it a flat-out assault on an American soldier. I was ready to take him out."

"But you didn't. Why?"

"I had orders, so I held my fire."

"Watch the timer on the video."

Arnold rolled the video in slow motion as the gun slowly came up from the side of the gangster, and he extended his arm. Just as he reached his limit a flash emitted from the end of the barrel and the gangster's head jerked back.

"Please note from the time the gun came up into view until the bullet pierced his chest was seven-tenths of a second. Ethan, are you sure you saw the gun before pulling the trigger?"

"Yes, sir, I did. I do apologize for disobeying orders, but it was impossible for me to sit there and watch an execution take place when I had the potential to stop it. If I had only been more alert, I could have prevented him from getting a shot off."

"Yes, you did disobey orders, and that will be dealt with later. As for now we have bigger problems." Arnold motioned for Oliver to proceed.

Oliver scrolled through his tablet and linked it to the flat screen. On the left side of the screen, a dark blurry video showed a drone moving across the sky. On the right side a map showed a target moving up the mountain from the east.

"We were not the only ones with a drone out there tonight. We are not sure if it was being operated by the gang or the government. We did not pick it up until three minutes before the shooting. As soon as the shooting was over, it headed back down the mountain. We can only assume it had reached its return to base time."

Arnold drummed his fingers on the table. "Thanks Oliver. Gang or government, either way we have a problem. We don't know how advanced their drone is, but it could have conceivably witnessed everything. Have we heard any rumblings from the Independence agents?"

"None at all, boss, but it is a little soon. It's only been ninety minutes."

"What about clean up? Do we have a team up there?"

"Yes, it will be cleaned up within an hour or so."

Arnold let out a long exhale and looked around the room. "It's late people. Get your ducks in a row and get some sleep. If it was the government, we will cooperate with an investigation. If it was the gang, we may be at war." As had been common lately, he motioned for Ethan to stick around as the rest were making their way out of the room.

The grimaced look on Arnold's face told the story before he spoke. "He's gone. I got a message a few minutes ago from medical. He never made it through the surgery."

Ethan hung his head. He wanted to doubt that it was true. He had expected this outcome but had hoped for a miracle. Looking up with a defeated spirit, he asked. "I let him down. What do we do now?"

Arnold shook his head. "It was not you that led Cody down the path he chose to travel. If you wouldn't have been there tonight, he would still be gone. The only difference is that his killer would still be walking this earth. Someone needs to break the news to his grandparents and Anna. I'll go see the Lindberghs. Sorry, it may be difficult, but I'm going to let you tell Anna."

"It is the least I can do." Ethan's head was spinning with the thought of the task. He stood up to leave.

"Try not to be doing anymore shooting tonight if you don't mind. I have to meet with the community leaders in the morning, and it's going to be difficult to explain your involvement in this fiasco."

"Ouch. Sure boss. I'll try."

The night had taken on an eerie feeling as Ethan made his way around the lake. Areas of heavy fog seemed to engulf his spirit. All of a sudden, he felt extremely vulnerable. He shivered as he felt the cold moisture work its way into his soul. The sound of an owl seeking a mate, added to the tightness in his chest. He picked up the pace not wanting to get sucked into the vortex of fear. All too soon, he turned up the path leading to Anna's home. To his surprise, he saw the glow of a lantern in the window. He paused and stared at the window. *God, I do believe You are real, and You can help. Please be with Anna as I bring her the news. And God, give me the words to say, because I am broken.* He stepped up on the porch and tapped on the door.

Anna's ruffled hair and tear-stained face greeted Ethan as she opened the door. Explanation for this late-night visit was not necessary. He was not surprised when she wrapped her arms around him and sobbed on his chest. The lump in his throat continued to grow as Ethan silently asked God for help. Finally, Anna pulled back and wiped away the tears.

"Is he gone?" she asked.

Ethan nodded as he looked into her defeated eyes. "Just about an hour ago. Doctor Winston tried to save him, but he died in surgery."

"Just tell me you didn't do it."

"No, it was a gangster from the valley. Cody met him up on the mountain, and things went bad."

Anna's frown turned to tears. "I had a feeling this was going to happen. He came by here this evening, and we talked for a long time and…." Her hesitation told Ethan that the conversation was going to get difficult.

"He told me everything, Ethan. Said he was tired of living a shadowed life and wanted to make things right. He said he was going to tell the guy tonight that it was over. I told him not to go, but he said he had to, otherwise they would come looking for him."

Ethan thought of the conversation between Cody and the gangster. "Did he tell you he was selling some codes? I assume to the security here in the village."

"He told me about the deal he had with the pain medication. He said the codes weren't real. I tried to get him to go see Doctor Winston but he didn't want to. He said that this would be the last time. I wish he would have talked to you."

Ethan could tell that Anna wanted to believe Cody, so he refrained from sharing additional information. "Are you going to be alright? Would you like for me to go get Sandra?"

Anna squeezed his hand and showed a small smile on her smudged face. "Thank you for caring about me. I will be fine." She kissed him softly on his cheek and let him go.

Climbing up the trail towards the crater, Ethan exited the fog to witness the Milky Way stretched across the sky. His energy was drained as he walked along the meadow and over the new bridge.

Chapter Fifty-Five

Walking through the village, Ethan felt the icy breeze blowing down off the mountains. The recent storm had left the surrounding peaks covered with snow. A sense of pending turmoil lay heavy within the community. It had been a week since the funeral, and on the surface, things seemed to have quieted down.

Ethan had not attended the funeral, chose instead to observe from a distance. After failing to save Cody, he had become more withdrawn and battled every day with the demons that haunted him. He spent his days holed up in the crater home questioning the reason for his existence. The defeated spirit that continued to gnaw at his conscience blinded him to the truth. He needed help.

The rocking chairs were empty as he walked up the path. Ethan paused. *I really don't belong here. Will they even listen to what I have to say?* He knew that behind the wispy smoke rising out of the chimney and the light in the window, there was sadness. Their prodigal grandson had returned only to be taken from them in reckless violence. Was his empathy enough? As Ethan turned around and walked back down the path, the howl of a wolf resounded from somewhere down along Charlotte Creek.

He should go talk to Krystal. Maybe she had found it in her heart to forgive him. The last time she had seen him she told him, in no uncertain terms, that it was best if he stayed away from the children. Nevertheless, he turned up along the stream. At the top of the rise, he paused and looked at the new cabin. It looked like a home now. Flickering light from a lantern shown through the windows, and smoke billowed from the stovepipe. Walking up to the porch, Growler let out a couple barks before jumping up and meeting him at the steps.

Krystal, stepping out, closed the door behind her. "What are you doing up here?"

"I just thought maybe we could talk."

"I'm sorry, but that is not possible right now. You need to go home."

The agony of seeing the hurt running down Krystal's rose-colored cheeks was more than Ethan could bear. He had apologized, he had begged for forgiveness. There was nothing else he could do. He mouthed *I love you* as he turned and dejectedly retraced his way back down the path.

His heart was broken, his spirit crushed. He felt as if the weight of the world was coming down on him. Where could he turn? He made his way down to the lake and sat down on a log. Clouds were rolling over Mount Bago and sliding down the slope of the mountain where they settled on the lake. He watched as the clouds continued to come. Soon they made their way around the mountain and slid up from the valley to the west. Each one shoving the foggy embankment closer to his cold desperate existence. The depressive feeling of loneliness was in the process of consuming his soul. The swishing sound of the wind in the pine trees brought an added dimension to the encompassing fog coming across the lake. The fog and fear reached Ethan at the same time. His chest tightened around him as he tried to scream. Nothing but desperation came from within. Ethan shut his eyes and begged for God to help.

"Isn't God's creation beautiful?"

Ethan jumped at the sound of someone behind him. Turning around he recognized Eli standing in the haze. *Great, he's here to add to the torment.* "Good evening, Eli. What brings you down to the lake?"

"I was looking for you."

"Why?"

"I was comfortably relaxing at home when something told me to come here."

"Something or Someone?"

"Let's just say God sent me here. What is going on, Ethan?"

"Now's not a good time."

"Good time for what?"

"Whatever it is that you're trying to accomplish coming down here to torment me."

Ethan didn't see the grimace on Eli's face at the cutting response. The ensuing silence brought back the chill of the oncoming darkness. Finally what little pride Ethan had left gave way to brokenness. "It has become obvious that this place is not where I belong. I think it's time for me to leave. I'm sorry for the pain I caused the community. You were right in not trusting me. The others should have listened. I'll pack up my stuff and leave tomorrow morning."

"Where will you go?" Eli asked.

Ethan ignored Eli's question and stood up to leave. "Eli, I will leave it up to you to tell the community of my departure. I never meant for harm to follow me here. I pray that once I am gone, peace will return."

Crossing the bridge on the east end of the lake Ethan considered going down and saying goodbye to Anna. Yet, he knew that to do so at this time could only escalate the negative situation. Turning up the trail to the crater he trudged along, defeated and alone.

Chapter Fifty-Six

— • ● • —

The sound of rapid gunfire echoed through the canyons. He could not see where the shots were coming from. Just give him a target, and he would end the chaos. The flash from a muzzle pinpointed the enemy. Steadily he took his aim and squeezed the trigger. The muzzle disappeared behind the rocks, but the gunfire continued. Using his field glasses he searched the area. *Where is it coming from?* Despondency overcame him, he was ready to surrender. He left his secure position and walked out into the open area with his hands in the air. He saw the flash of the muzzle before he felt the bullet rip through his torso. Grabbing his chest, he let out a silent scream and woke up.

The banging on the door continued as Ethan struggled to gain his composure. Reaching under the mattress he retrieved his Beretta. Someone banging on the door at this time of night was not a social call. He must have upset someone.

Keeping the heavy door between him and the visitor

he swung it open and stuck his Beretta in the face of a frightened Jonathan. Lowering his weapon, Ethan invited the young lad in. "What is the emergency?"

"They're coming."

"Who's coming?"

"The mercenaries. A message arrived at the command center an hour ago that fifty armed men were climbing the trail."

Ethan's first instinct was to implement a battle plan. He could probably repel all fifty of them by himself if he set up an ambush. *Wait! It's not my fight.*

"Who sent you?"

"Grandpa. He said you would know what to do."

Why would Abram send for me? He knows my history of negotiating with terrorists. It must be bad. "This may be a dumb question, but has the community been alerted?" His greatest concern was for Krystal and the children.

"Yes, the alert went out a couple of minutes before I headed up here."

"So, I guess you wouldn't know if the women and children are on their way to the cave?"

"You can be assured they are. They are probably already on lockdown."

"Thanks Jonathan. Stay safe."

Ethan could hear more than see Jonathan running back through the meadow. How he sees in the dark gets me. Must have been born with night vision eyes. Back inside he moved the coffee table and rolled back the carpet. Ten minutes later he hoisted his loaded tactical backpack over his shoulders and headed into the night. Once again, he was at war.

With his night vision goggles turned on, he could see the layout of the land and a lot of activity in and around the village. He looked to the east and only spotted a couple of lights this side of the pass. If he hurried, he would meet the intruders at Bullfrog Lake. If he took the high ground, he would have an advantage and could eliminate a large number. *What then?* He would figure it out as he went.

Ethan felt the vibration of his radio on his chest. Trying to ignore it he moved along the upper meadow and across the rocks towards the trail. It vibrated again and so did his conscience. *I'm doing this for them. Really? Remember the team? The team has turned on me. Really? Think about it.*

Ethan kicked at a rock and turned back towards the nest. Again, his radio vibrated. Finding the knob, he exhaled as he turned it on. The sound of adrenaline was evident in chatter coming across the secure channel. Once the chatter settled down Ethan clicked the mic. "Hawkeye is on the way to his nest."

"About time Hawkeye; this is S.C., keep your eyes open, we may need you."

May need me? If fifty armed mercenaries come over Kearsarge Pass, they're going to need everyone old enough to pull a trigger. "I'll be ready. What are the rules of engagement?"

"As always Hawkeye, fire only if fired upon."

"Let me get this straight. We are a team. So, if anyone on the team gets fired upon, I can eliminate the threat?"

"I can tell a leopard never changes its spots. You are correct. May God help us."

"Do we have eyes in the sky?"

"Affirmative. Two are currently airborne and two more are on standby. You may want to take a look as soon as you can. Available on channels three and seven."

Making his way across the boulders to the nest, Ethan spotted numerous lights descending the trail from Kearsarge Pass. Looks like they are for real. Reaching the nest, he pulled out his tablet and opened camera three. It showed the position of the drone over Big Pot Hole Lake, and the camera was focused on the trail. Ethan could see a line approaching the pass. Zooming in, he could see the individual hikers were each carrying a rifle. *Do these young men realize this could be their last hiking trip? Have they been told a lie? Do they even know why they are fighting this fight? Why am I fighting this fight?*

Switching to camera seven he had a good picture of the west side of the pass from over Bull Frog Lake. A number of the terrorists were gathered at the switchbacks two hundred yards west of the pass. Either they were exhausted from the climb or they were waiting for the others to make it over the top.

"Hawkeye in the nest and watching the rodents"

"Roger Hawkeye. Standby for orders."

"Will do. Are all the chickens in the coop?" Ethan really wanted to know if all the women and children were hidden away in the cave.

"Affirmative. All civilians are secure."

Ethan settled down and surveyed the valley with his NVG. Scanning up and down the west slope of the pass. To the north he could see a line of about sixty from the security detail digging in. Focusing in on his team, he was happy to see they had the Rocket Propelled Grenade launchers.

Looking back at camera seven he could see the group at the switchbacks had grown to the point they were moving off the trail.

A movement lower on the trail caught his eye. Switching on his sniper rifle scope, he focused on the movement down by Bull Frog Lake. It was four hikers moving methodically towards the west. *Why are they down on the lower trail? It's a lot closer to take the one higher on the contour. It looks like they have a forward scouting team.*

"Hawkeye to S.C."

"Go ahead Hawkeye."

"Four hikers on the trail along Bull Frog Lake. Looks like scouts."

"Roger, Hawkeye. We're on it. Expect camera five online in three minutes."

The camouflage covering the nest started flapping causing Ethan to look to the west for signs of weather. Nothing but stars. *Come on God, you know a storm right now would be to our advantage.* Tightening the ropes he returned to his tablet and found camera five was active and moving east towards Bull Frog Lake. What was that? Something had flown underneath the drone. Ethan paused the video and reversed it a couple of seconds. Finding the frame, he froze it and zoomed in.

"Hawkeye to S.C. Come in."

"Go ahead Hawkeye."

"We have an unidentified drone just east of Charlotte Lake. Looks like we aren't the only one with eyes in the sky."

"Do you have a position?

"Not exactly, but I assume it's watching our

defenses."

"Roger that. Let me know if you locate it. We'll launch camera four to assist."

Ethan turned on the night vision scope and surveyed the sky above the defense. Unable to locate the target, he redirected his attention to the scouts now on the west side of Bull Frog Lake. Camera five was now hovering over the scouts. Zooming in, Ethan could see that they had stopped in a clearing and it appeared as if one was operating a drone. Ethan calculated the distance at six hundred and fifty yards. *I can take him and his toy out in one shot.*

"S.C. this is Hawkeye. Located drone operator. Request permission to remove threat."

"Come on Hawkeye, you know the orders. It may not even be the enemy. The media has drones too."

Ethan hadn't thought of that. He would just kill the drone.

"Attention all security personnel. Be advised the invaders are on the move. Expect conflict engagement time in forty-five minutes."

The general announcement redirected Ethan's attention towards the pass. Switching to camera three he could see a much tighter line moving west along the trail. *What are they doing?* Ethan watched as the front of the line walked right past the high trail and took the switchbacks towards Bull Frog Lake. That's going to add twenty minutes to their time.

"S.C. this is Hawkeye, it looks like they're taking the lower trail."

"We're on it, Hawkeye. Keep alert as they may be splitting up. Check out camera four."

Ethan acknowledged Arnold's warning and switched to camera four. It was hovering directly over the defense, and Ethan could see the clear image of a drone beneath it. Noting the position, he pulled up his sniper rifle and turned on the night vision scope. Locating the enemy drone, he calculated the distance at four hundred and thirty yards. He felt the breeze and made the adjustment. Should I get permission to fire? Instinct overrode doubt as he switched off the safety. A slight pull of the trigger and thunder echoed through the valley.

Chapter Fifty-Seven

Silence ensued as the valley registered the echoing gunfire. Ethan was already looking at camera four. Sliding back the recorded video just a few seconds, he watched as the unidentified drone exploded. *Splash one!* It was time to turn back to the invading force.

The radio came alive when the command center processed what had transpired. "Enemy drone is down. Be advised, enemy troops will be arriving at Bull Frog Lake within twenty minutes."

"Unauthorized shot Hawkeye. We'll discuss that later. Nevertheless, great shot."

"Sorry boss, just protecting the team."

Ethan wasn't so certain there would be a later unless the rules of engagement changed quickly. He redirected his attention to the scouting team. They were still in the clearing. He was certain they were at loss of what to do next. He doubted this group had a contingency plan.

"Hawkeye to S.C., request permission to take out the

scouts."

"Negative, Hawkeye, we still don't have confirmation on who they are."

"The media doesn't carry assault rifles. These guys have a goal to kill us before we kill them."

"You have your orders, Hawkeye. Stand down."

Ethan didn't acknowledge the last transmission but did move on the main force. They were at the bottom of the switchbacks and were stopped. The shot must have planted a seed of doubt in their leader.

"Hawkeye to S.C."

"Go ahead Hawkeye." You could hear annoyance in Arnold's tone.

"They're all taking the lower trail with no eyes in the sky. If you send some men up on the high trail, you could set up an ambush. We can take them out and minimize our losses."

"Absolutely not, Hawkeye. We are the defense, not the aggressor. We will wait until fired upon, period."

Ethan let out a disgusted sigh. *Why am I even here. The best defense is an aggressive offense. I just pray none of our guys take the first bullet.* He went about verifying his weapons were ready. His primary weapon was his sniper rifle. He had plenty of ammo ready to load quickly. Next to him in the nest was the AR-15 he acquired during the last raid. For it he had ten clips of thirty rounds each. *Probably a little overkill considering there's only fifty invaders. I suppose I ought to leave a couple for the rest of the team.* On his side was his Beretta with five fully loaded clips on his belt. An RPG up here would have been nice, but he was certain it would get him in trouble.

Ethan watched on camera four as the security team repositioned along the ridge where the trail made its way back up to the upper plateau. At only five hundred yards from the nest, the invading force would be easy picking as they navigated the switchbacks. Looking for the scouting team, he found them still on camera five. They were standing around at the base of the switchbacks apparently waiting for the rest of their party. He turned on his spotting scope and calculated the distance at just under six hundred yards. *I could improve our numbers. Better not. Already in trouble with the boss. Who cares? I'm out of here anyway.*

Switching on the sniper scope, he focused in on the now lethargic foursome. They were sitting on the ground, leaned up against their backpacks with their weapons across their lap. Three were smoking a cigarette which made them real easy targets. I guess they haven't heard about Smokey the Bear. He calculated the slight variance for the breeze and…. *No, I can't do this yet.* His hesitation shocked him. I know my faith is supposed to be in God. But is faith as real as these bullets in my gun? If God is real, why am I battling with this doubt?

"Hawkeye to S.C. Come in."

"Go ahead Hawkeye."

"The scouting team has the drone video, and as you see they are all reclined at the bottom of the switchbacks. If we could get down there and take them into custody, we would keep that information out of the invaders' hands."

"Understand, Hawkeye. Command Center, how much time do we have?"

"Main force three quarter of a mile away and is estimated to rendezvous with the scouting team thirty-five minutes."

"Roger that, Command Center. Team three, you copy?"

"Team three heard it all, we are at the top of the switchbacks and await your command."

"Execute capture plan. Do not fire unless fired upon."

"Wilco S.C., advancing now. The target is in sight."

Ethan shook his head at the rule of engagement. If he heard that statement one more time, he may just give them something to fire at. Might just be time to take one for the team. He returned to his sniper rifle and honed into the target sight. One shot from these lazy scouts, and he would do his job. He scanned up the hill to where he picked out four security force specialists moving stealthily down the mountain. Picking up his night vision goggles, he surveyed the area above the target for the drone. To his surprise, he spotted two drones.

"Hawkeye to Command Center. Verify you only have one drone over scouts."

"Affirmative, Hawkeye. You seeing something."

"Affirmative. Can you take your drone up fifty feet or so?"

"Wilco. Here goes."

"Hawkeye, this is S.C., could you put a suppressor on that pea shooter?"

"Negative S.C., don't have the time. Stand by for the kill shot."

Ethan watched as the top drone climbed to a higher altitude. The second drone was slightly below his altitude and in a direct line with the approaching force. He could conceivably take out the drone and hit an invader. Without hesitation, he put the drone in his crosshairs and squeezed the trigger. The drone disappeared, but Ethan had no idea if he hit it or not. He'd have to go back on camera five to verify. What he could see was a majority of the invaders diving for cover. *How are they going to fight a battle if they're that gun shy?* Refocusing in on the scouts, he could see they were on their feet with weapons in hand. *Well, that wasn't supposed to happen. I'd better be ready to help the team.*

"Team three, the scouts are on their feet. Proceed with caution."

Not expecting a verbal response, Ethan watched one of the security team give a thumbs up. They were within earshot of the scouts and spread out in a semicircle. Two minutes later, the scouts sat back down and laid their weapons at their side. Within seconds the team broke the clearing, and Ethan could tell by the way the hands all went in the air that these were not hardened fighters. He was starting to feel a little better about the outcome of the invasion.

"Attention all security personnel. Please be advised we have just received a report that an additional three hundred heavily armed mercenaries are approaching Kearsarge Pass."

Well, that changes the picture. Ethan pulled up camera three and could see a half mile line of invaders approaching the pass. Looking at his watch he noted it was one a.m.

"Hawkeye to S.C., come in."

"This had better be good Hawkeye, go ahead."

"We have an hour to neutralize the first wave, or

we're going to have a battle on our hands. They're not coming for me. They are after the community's natural resources. If they join forces, we're going to be in trouble. Loss of life is inevitable."

"Standby, Hawkeye. Expect rules of engagement change shortly."

Ethan could see the first invading force had come to a standstill at the bottom of the switchbacks. Up on the pass, the main force was taking the high trail. They knew all along what they were doing. They plan on using the fifty to surround our forces. *Sly dogs.*

"Attention, all security personnel. The cameras at the mine are showing a large contingent of armed individuals coming up from the west. Standby for identification."

Now we are in trouble. Do we even have the forces to hold off a three-prong attack? Ethan was ready to start reducing their numbers immediately.

"S.C., give me a green light. A few well-placed shots will scatter the first group."

"Can you do it without killing someone?"

"Only by accident, boss. That's not how I work."

"Standby, Hawkeye. You do not have permission to fire."

Great! Ethan picked up his night vision goggles and surveyed the surrounding area. He needed a close-in battle plan. One that would take him out of his nest and into the fray. What the world… Down below him just a hundred yards away he spotted someone in the rocks looking through field glasses. Was it one of the scouts we missed.

"Hawkeye to command center, come in."

"Go ahead Hawkeye."

"Do you have a recon agent in my proximity?"

"Negative, Hawkeye, you're all alone."

"Thanks CC, Hawkeye out."

Ethan removed his Beretta and quietly descended on the lone scout. At ten feet, he stopped and lifted his weapon. "Turn around real slow and keep your hands in sight or you're dead."

The scout raised his hands and slowly turned around.

Ethan's heart dropped as fast as his gun. "Anna, what are you doing up here?"

"Ethan, you scared me. I figured you would be with the security team. Did you follow me up here?"

Ethan was starting to question Anna's allegiance when he surveyed the situation. She was wearing a combat jumpsuit with her hair up in a ponytail. An AR-15 lay on the rocks beside her backpack. The night vision field glasses laying on the rock were top of the line. "I'm thinking you're the one that needs to be answering some questions, and you need to do it quickly. A war is about to start, and I need to know who's side you're on."

A hurt look fell over Anna's face. "I know this may look suspicious, but I am on your side."

"Really? Why then did the command center tell me no one else was up here?"

Anna sat down on the rock and put her head in her hands.

"Hurry it up, girl, this is no time to get emotional. You have thirty seconds to clear this up before I zip tie you to the mountain."

"I guess I have no choice. I work for Homeland Security."

"Are you serious? Prove it?"

"Okay, you're going to kill me when I tell you, but how do you think your friend Steven was able to find you. He is my contact."

Ethan's blood pressure started to mount. "So, tell me, this whole thing about love and God and trusting in Jesus, is that all a sham?"

"No, please don't say that. Everything I ever told you was true. Just like you, I didn't tell you everything."

Both their heads jerked around as gunfire erupted in the valley below. "I need to get back to my position. What's your mission up here?"

"Reinforcements are on the way, and I am painting the target."

Ethan shook his head. "How far out are they?"

"Don't know for sure, but it's going to be close."

"I still have questions for you but they can wait until later. Stay safe."

Anna jumped up and gave him an awkward hug. "You, too."

Chapter Fifty-Eight

Back in his nest Ethan had to clear his mind. Surveying the valley, he found where the skirmish was coming from. A group of security agents had positioned themselves on an outcrop next to the switchbacks, some hundred and fifty yards above the first wave. The invaders must have spotted them as they were in a defensive position and had guns pointed at the rocky outcrop. *If I only knew who fired the shots.*

"Attention, all agents. Information has just come in that the invaders on the high trail are heavily armed and well-organized. It is being led by a rogue special forces veteran. May God help us."

Ethan surveyed the local force and saw that Arnold had set up a majority of the men facing the high trail, and the rest on the ridge above the switchbacks. He questioned how long this group would hold out. And what about the contingent coming up Charlotte Creek? Feeling overwhelmed, Ethan did what he had never done before in battle. He turned his face towards heaven and asked God to intervene. When he finished praying, nothing had changed. The invaders were still there and getting closer, but what Ethan felt was a peace about the outcome. Looking at camera seven, he could get a close in on the larger of the two forces. Sure enough, they were heavily armed. About every third one was carrying RPG launchers. *It would be nice to have one up here.*

Switching to camera four, he found it was now down over Charlotte Creek monitoring the arrival of invaders from the west. From the best he could count, there were about a hundred.

Ethan keyed up his mic. "Any update on the contingent from the west?"

"Affirmative, we just received word that they are adversaries and are heavily armed as well. We are moving resources in that direction."

What other resources do we have? Ethan had come to the conclusion that they did not have enough firepower to fend off this invasion. If the reinforcements Anna had said was coming did not get there soon, it would be a blood bath.

"Attention all security personnel. Stand by detonation in five seconds."

What in the world are they talking about?

He was still watching camera four when the waves of an explosion started in the valley below the village and in slow motion moved up across Lake Charlotte and riveted off the mountains to the east. The flash on the screen lasted only a microsecond before going dark. An eerie silence followed and then Ethan heard the rumble before he felt the earth begin to shake. It only lasted a few seconds. Then once again things went silent.

Still monitoring camera four, Ethan tried to decipher what he was seeing. It looked like a big cloud of dust. He watched as the projection changed as the drone gained altitude. Once the picture focused, he could see a plume of dust covered the trail between the invading force and the west end of the village. *Thank you, God.* It would only slow the attackers down, but it did give the security team time to respond.

Ethan stiffened up as the distant sound of helicopters echoed through the valley.

"Hawkeye to Command Center, we have company. Multiple helicopters coming in from the southeast."

"Roger that Hawkeye, we're just getting word that it's Homeland Security. All agents pull back."

Ethan watched as the security agents started backing away from their positions. Turning his scope down to the first wave, he saw nothing but chaos, as the thundering vibrations of the incoming helicopters increased. For these intruders, Armageddon had arrived.

Turning to his right he spotted two AH-64 Apaches coming in fast. They climbed straight up the switchbacks before one of them spun its tail around and it dropped towards the target. Lighting up its thirty-millimeter guns, it destroyed everything in its path. The other Apache overflew the larger force, all the time taking incoming small arms fire from the invaders. Returning to the west, he was joined by his wingman. Facing the high trail, now occupied by three hundred battle-hardened criminals, they each cut loose with a pair of Hydra 70 air-to-surface rockets. The explosions rocked the valley and echoed throughout the surrounding mountains.

In unison, they turned west crossing low over Charlotte Lake before disappearing down the valley. A new sound arrived as four UH-60 Black Hawks came up through the pass. Ethan watched as troops repelled out of the sides and took up a defensive position. After dropping the troops, the Black Hawks flew right over Ethan's position and landed in the meadow behind him.

"How did you like that?"

Ethan turned to see Anna standing behind him. "I could have done that without destroying the whole side of a mountain."

Anna laughed at his comment. "I have someone that wants to talk to you."

She keyed up her mic. "Go ahead sir. He's here."

"Ethan, old buddy, this is Steven. Say position?"

Ethan shook his head, "A real soldier never gives away his position to his enemy."

"Come on, my friend. I'm not your enemy. I'm up here in your meadow. Your mission is over. Come on up, and let's fix some coffee."

Chapter Fifty-Nine

— • ● • —

"So, Anna, now that we have a moment, start at the beginning. When did you join Homeland Security?" Ethan was slowly rocking back and forth nursing a fresh brewed cup of coffee.

Anna, sitting in the other rocking chair, looked completely out of place. "Do you want me to start at the beginning or tell you when I joined the DHS?"

"I think I liked you better as sweet little Anna with a sprained ankle. That Anna was a lot cuter."

"If that is supposed to be a compliment, it's not working. Just over fifteen years ago."

"Okay, you told me you have been up here since you were six and have not been back in civilization. How does that add up?"

"I have a friend who is a forest ranger over at Rae Lakes. One day he introduced me to an agent from Homeland Security. He was a really nice guy, and I was certain I was falling in love with him, that is until he explained that he was a married man, and our relationship was strictly business. To make it short, I became a contact person for them here in the community."

"So, are the elders okay with that arrangement."

Anna grimaced. "They don't know. I never even told Cody."

"How do you communicate with the department?"

"I have a single contact on the outside, and it is done normally on a preset schedule. I use a solar-powered, encrypted SAT phone."

"And a radio?"

"Yes, but that is only for line of sight. As you know, it doesn't work well here in the mountains."

"So, have you been doing a lot of spying? Can you sleep at night knowing you are a traitor to the community?"

Anna looked like she had just been punched in the gut. "I am not a traitor. Please don't call me that. I love my home, and I would do anything to protect them. That is all I was doing."

"How much information have you shared with your boss?"

"Not much. The only thing the department is interested in is threats to the American people."

"How about the IRS? Do you think they might be interested in what's going on up here?"

"Finances are never discussed. Even though they probably know, they have not been told where our resources come from."

Anna was fidgeting and looking very uncomfortable. Ethan knew it was time to ask the hard questions. "When did you notify them about me being here?

"Do I have to tell you?"

"That or I hang you for treason?"

Steven, who had been quietly listening almost fell off the edge of the porch.

Tears were working their way down Anna's face. "It was after I found your weapons. I loved you so much that I wanted us to work out, but it scared me. I didn't want to tell the elders for fear that they would send you away. The only thing I knew to do was find out how dangerous you really were."

"What did you find out?"

"They said that while you were a wanted man, you were only dangerous to those who you found to be the enemy. They had been looking for you and thanked me for letting them know you were here."

"So, you loved me so much you betrayed me. With friends like that, who needs enemies?"

"Your words are hurting. I didn't know, and I am sorry. I should not have done it."

Steven stood up and stretched. "Ethan, it may not seem like a blessing, but you need to seriously thank Anna. If it wasn't for her, you would be knee deep in a battle for not only your life, but for the whole community. We are fortunate that the right agent intercepted the message and redirected it to my department."

Ethan understood what his friend was saying and figured it was time to give Anna a little break. "Anna, it's going to take a bit to forgive you, but I will in time. I'm sorry for being harsh with you and will try to hold my tongue." He reached his hand out as they had done in the past, and she reacted with passion as she took his hand in hers.

"What is going to happen to the community now?" Ethan asked.

Steven was looking out at the eastern sky as the first sign of day was showing forth its hues of orange and red. "We are going to get this mopped up over the next few hours and do our best to return things to normal. You will see a number of choppers flying in and out as we recover the bodies. There's only one thing."

"What's that?" Ethan knew there had to be a catch somewhere.

"We need to take you out."

"Okay. Please explain."

"We have done an excellent job of keeping the media out of this story, but we can't suppress the news from getting back to the people financing the invasion."

"They wouldn't happen to be about four dozen politicians?"

"We don't have proof, but we are investigating a large crime ring involving a lot of bribery across many levels of government. Like I told you when I was here last. You have caused a lot of pain for a lot of high-level bureaucrats. They don't take kindly to being outed."

"Would you like proof?"

"What do you have?"

Ethan thought about the video of the congressman and the files they had found on the memory stick. How much could he reveal without giving away City Hall? He would discuss that with the team. "Let's just say we have plenty. I'm sure it can be worked out depending on what this 'taking me out' entails."

Steven looked a little shocked at Ethan holding the information hostage but expected nothing less. "It's for the safety of the community, Ethan. We need to remove you, so they leave the people here alone."

"How long do I have?"

"Let me get it set up, and I'll be back for you in two days. That should give you time to say goodbye."

Ethan and Anna stood on the bridge and watched Steven and his team board the helicopter. Anna reached out and took Ethan's hand. "Is there a chance for us?"

Ethan squeezed her hand as they watched the Black Hawk lift off and disappear around the ridge. They stood there watching the impending sunrise over Kearsarge Pinnacles. "You never give up."

Chapter Sixty

The conference room was packed when Arnold and Ethan walked through the door. The private meeting in Arnold's office had not gone well as the security chief had laid into Ethan. It reminded Ethan of the days his lieutenant had done the same thing after he would unilaterally expand the rules of engagement. He took it like a true soldier and apologized for disobeying orders. He was sure it was not the last apology he would be making. *Why can't I be like these people and just live a quiet peaceful life?*

After what had just gone down, Ethan was surprised the team left a seat open for him. It was not hard to see what the topic of the meeting was about, as the screen was frozen on the battle scene. *Wonder if they have any pictures of me? Worse, I wonder if they spotted Anna? That could be bad.*

Arnold looked around the room as if he was looking for someone to blame. Fortunately for the attendees, he didn't locate a target. "We have all received a preliminary briefing package, and I'm sure you have studied it. If not, get out of here and come back when you're done. I don't have time to babysit you. One thing I haven't found out yet is who called the cops? Does anyone know?"

The awkward silence persisted as everyone looked bewildered and looked at Ethan. *Wow! They sure like to blame the new guy.* "It sure looks like you guys are expecting a confession out of me. You're not going to get it because I did not call anyone. As you can see in my statement from Homeland Security, they had been monitoring the gathering in Lone Pine and Mill Flat Campground for the last few weeks."

"Oliver, what have you found out?

"Not a whole lot. From our drone footage, we are certain that they had an operative up here prior to the attack." Oliver changed the video to camera four and the base of the switchback came into view. "This is after Ethan has taken out the enemy drone and just before the Apaches arrive. What I want to show you was taken from the on-board laser detector." Oliver paused the video and using his laser pointer circled a bright spot on the screen. "This is coming from someone painting the target. Unfortunately, we have no idea where it was coming from. Roll the tape."

The night vision camera picked up the first Apache as it flew through under the drone. Two seconds later the second entered the screen and gave an airshow performance as it pulled up towards the drone before its tail came around, and the helicopter dove towards the invaders. Ethan could see everyone in the room glued to the screen as the thirty-millimeter chain gun annihilated the armed invaders. Once it left the field of vision, Oliver switched videos.

"Next, we will take a look at the larger force on

camera three. As you can see, there is a long line of heavily armed invaders along the high trail. Now watch as the second Apache lines up almost at the same altitude of the target. You will see the same white spot." The Apache flew almost directly under the drone before the exhaust gases of the air to ground rockets lit up the screen followed by a pair of massive explosions as the warheads did their job.

The room was silent as the security team processed what they had just witnessed. It was not normal for them to see so many lives snuffed out so quickly. They knew that each one of those individuals who had come to the mountain to do them harm was some mother's child. Each one had a soul that had gone to meet his maker. Most likely without the saving knowledge of the Lord.

Finally, Arnold broke the painful silence. "Ethan has something he would like to share."

Ethan had only been part of the security team for a few weeks but felt the judgment of a lifetime coming down on him. By now everyone in the room knew that he was a whirlwind of destruction when it came to dealing with the enemy. He was certain they would breathe a sigh of relief when he was gone.

"At the request of Homeland Security, I will be leaving the community. They believe it is for your safety, and I tend to agree with them. If I willingly leave, they have agreed to set up parameter protection for the village. Parameter, meaning off the mountain and out of sight. They also agreed not to interfere with the governing body of the community. They know that we have security, but they are not certain of its capabilities. Therefore, I will be leaving on Monday morning. Thank you."

"What if we as a community asked you to stay?" Keenan asked.

"Not an option. If I don't go DHS will be all over this place and bring with it a whole mule train full of regulations. That is something you don't want."

"Would it be acceptable to you if we as a community voted on the issue? We may want you to stay."

"You are at liberty to do what you want but remember my past. Even if I refuse to go with them, it would only be a matter of time before someone from the DOJ would send a federal marshal in here looking to take me in. It's best if I go on these terms. If it's God's will, and I pray that it is, I will return some day. Then it will be to live in peace."

Arnold slightly lifted his hand. "Thank you, Ethan, you will be missed, may God go with you. For the rest of you, we still have some cleanup to do. What shape is the trail in now that DHS blew it to smithereens?"

Ethan stood at Arnold's dismissal and walked from the room. He had some amends to make with little time left.

Chapter Sixty-One

They sat together on the log overlooking the stream. She firmly gripped his arm, and her head was on his shoulder. Every now and then, Ethan could hear a soft sniffle coming from the woman he loved. Upon receiving the letter she now held crumpled in her hand, she had asked him to meet her here. He had stopped by William and Claire's for some much-needed wisdom before climbing the hill to this special spot along the stream. There was no easy solution, no magic answer, only humility and grace.

Krystal had been crying when she had arrived and opened her arms to his embrace. They held each other for a long time before either one was willing to break the silent healing. Finally, they moved to the log, and she snuggled up against him. "Can we go with you?" she had asked.

Why would she want to do such a thing? Ethan knew it was only emotions. She knew they could not go where he was going. The best she could do was pray for his return. He had questions if that was even a possibility.

As the sun started setting, the chill of the high-altitude dusk pronounced the inevitable.

"Let me walk you back up to the house, my dear."

"How about you walk me to your house?"

Again, Ethan knew that it was her emotions speaking. He helped her up and held her hand as they walked up the path to her home. Elena met them on the porch assuring Krystal that the children were down for the night.

"Thank you, Elena, be safe going home."

Ethan's conscience told him that it would be best if he left as well. It would not be proper or wise for him to be up here alone with Krystal. "I'm leaving now Elena, I'll walk you home."

The sad look in Krystal's eyes were killing him. He leaned over and kissed her on the cheek. "See you at church in the morning, my dear."

Her half smile told him she was hurting. He had done all he could. He again kissed her on the cheek and turned to walk away. She grabbed his hand and held on. He tried to get her to let go as he saw Elena already dropping below the ridge. "Come on, Krystal. I must go."

Krystal threw her arms around him and kissed him passionately. "Please come back as soon as you can. I will wait for you."

Ethan stumbled down the trail, still traumatized by Krystal's kiss, as he prayed that God would allow him to fulfill her request.

He soon caught up with Elena, and they walked together down to the trail. Ethan wasn't much for conversation as his mind was up on the mountain. Elena chit-chatted about the children and how much they loved

Ethan. She sure knows how to demoralize a guy. *I don't want to leave.* Making their way around the lake his thoughts went back to the first time he walked down this trail. He was so mesmerized by the little cabins with lanterns lighting up the windows. Rocking chairs on the porches told him of a society that had long been lost in the real world. He must come back. But who would he be if and when he returned. One thing was for certain. The God he had decided he would serve, does know, and Ethan was okay with that.

Ethan said goodbye to Elena and made his way across the stones on the west side of the lake. Walking along the south side of the lake, he passed the greenhouse and the dry goods store. Nighttime had arrived and his eyes adjusted to the darkness. He heard a door shut off to his right and few seconds later saw a figure he recognized, approaching the trail.

"I have to say, even in the dark, you look better in a dress."

"Ethan! You scared me. What are you up to tonight?"

"I walked Elena home from Krystal's. What are you doing going out this late?"

"I have unfinished business to take care of that doesn't do well in the daytime."

"Workers of evil, love darkness."

"Says the man who just scared me, walking in the dark."

"You have a few minutes?"

"For you? Sure."

They walked up the trail towards the crater and found a place overlooking the lake. Anna was happy to sit down next to Ethan and grab his arm. He thought of shrugging it off, but he had been there before. She didn't have a chance as his heart was on the other mountain.

"Anna, I have a lot of questions that only you can answer."

"I'll tell you everything if you make me Mrs. Dawson."

"Don't go there, Anna. Now seriously, I have decided I want to be a believer, and there's only one thing standing in my way."

"What's that?"

"It's you, Anna."

He could tell she was shocked at his revelation and decided to let her think about it.

She gripped his arm tighter. "I'm sorry. What can I do?"

"Anna, we spent a lot of time together, and you shared the gospel with me many times. You shared with me all the wonderful things God has done for you and how much you love Jesus. What you can do is tell me if that was real? Or were you just playing the part in order to fit in?"

Anna looked at her feet as she shuffled them in the dust. Looking at him in the darkness she answered. "My love for Jesus is real. My faith in God is real. Yes, I do live a double life in a way, but my salvation is certain.

"Why did you get a job when the community provided you with everything?"

"That is a difficult question to answer. In hindsight, I would have to say my focus was misguided. If I would have been living my life for the Lord, I may not have succumbed to the temptation. I know now that it was not the right thing to do. You are right, here in the community I don't need a paycheck. When I found all the money you were carrying in your backpack, it scared me. I have accumulated a lot of cash myself over the last fifteen years and don't know what to do with it. I just keep it hidden."

"Now I understand why you didn't spill the beans. One last concern. There is a lot of corruption in the FBI, and I don't want you to get hurt. The adversaries that attacked us gained their information via the FBI computer database. That data was put there because some young lady from Charlotte Lake inquired about my record and revealed that I was here. Do you understand?"

Anna didn't verbally respond. Ethan could feel her shaking and knew that what he told her was tearing her apart. If there was ever a chance of him returning, he needed her to be on his side. She must understand. "Yes Anna, you are partially responsible for those who lost their lives here on the mountain. Don't take it too hard as all of us have some level of responsibility that must be shouldered."

"I, I never even thought of it that way. They never would have come if it wasn't for me. I am so sorry. I never meant for anyone to get hurt."

Ethan put his arm around her and gave her a light hug. "I know that, Anna, and so does God. Come on, I'll walk you home."

Chapter Sixty-Two

Ethan could hear the singing coming from the meeting house as he made his way around the lake. He had intentionally arrived late to avoid the onslaught of questions. He would have preferred to have disappeared in the night, but Krystal had been persistent and here he was. Arriving at the church, he sat down on the bench outside and listened to the singing. It had been four months since he arrived. He had found a people who loved God and loved others. He had found a community that were generous and kind.

I guess I should go in now. He pulled his tired frame up off the bench and made his way to the door. He had come here seeking to live a peaceful life, and all he did was bring violence to these peace-loving people. He had not sought out violence; it had come to him. Yet, he was the common denominator in all the attacks. He wanted to experience the peace found on the other side of this door.

Stepping inside he was temporarily blinded until his

eyes adjusted to the dimly lit room. The singing continued but almost everyone had turned to see who had come in late. Ethan made his way to the back of the church and hunted for a seat. A small hand tugged at his pant leg. Looking down he smiled as he reached down and picked up Jonah. Jonah whispered in his ear and pointed to where his mother was sitting. Sitting down next to Krystal, Ethan kept Jonah on his lap. Looking down into Krystal's upturned face, he could not help but see the tears.

Ethan's attempt to listen to the preaching was in vain. He knew the words that Eli was sharing was from the Bible. He knew that the truth was in the message. He knew he needed to heed the warnings being shared. The knowledge was there, but where was his heart? It was evident that Anna was not misleading him in her faith. He then realized the firmness in which he was holding Krystal's hand.

After the church service was over, he walked Krystal and the children home. It was not a joyful climb up the trail. The children stirred up the dust as they drug their feet. Krystal didn't say much, just hung onto Ethan and laid her head on his shoulder. Arriving at the cabin, Krystal went inside to fix some lunch as the children helped Ethan load the wood box.

"This is how I imagined Sunday afternoons." Ethan was helping Krystal clean up the kitchen as Jonah was playing on the carpet and the girls were reading books. "If God is so great, why can't He make it happen?"

Krystal continued drying dishes and looked at him with a vacant stare.

"I know, I know. He can, but why doesn't He?"

Again, Krystal said nothing but raised her eyebrows.

"What? He knows the desires of my heart. Why doesn't He listen?"

She finished drying her hands and wrapped her arms around him. Her embrace made the questions seem of little importance. She then looked him in the eyes and asked, "Have you put your faith in Jesus?"

He stiffened as he pulled back from her. "Why do you ask?"

"You didn't answer the question. Again, have you accepted Christ as your savior?"

"I, I believe I did. I really don't know if I did it right. Last night I got some clarification on some things that had been holding me back. This morning, I was having trouble focusing on the message but believe that God was speaking to me. Finally, realization set in that I was holding on too tight. Remember how firm I was holding your hand?"

"Do I? Thought I was going to cry."

"When I released that grip is when I decided I needed to release my doubt. Right after that is when we sang that last hymn. Don't remember the name."

"It is Well. I love that song. It's got a great story behind it."

"Well, it has another one now. Like I said, I had trouble focusing all morning but for some reason when they started singing, I heard every word. The words 'Whatever my lot, Thou hast taught me to say, it is well with my soul.' That really got my attention. Then it kind of explained my whole predicament. It was the lyrics that stated my sins were nailed to the cross. Not just some of them, but all. That's when I got it. Let's just say, 'It is well with my soul.'"

Happy tears were running down Krystal's face as once again she embraced him. "Please tell the children. They have been praying for you."

Chapter Sixty-Three

Ethan shivered as a cold gust of wind swirled about him. The billowing clouds to the west were pushing over the ridges. It would not be long now before the mountains would be covered with snow. He hated that he would not be here to experience the winter. He looked out over the windswept Charlotte Lake at the smoke rising out of the chimneys of the scattered cabins. He reflected on the Sunday morning church services and the fireside chats with Abram. He longed for Anna's laughter, for Eli's reprimands. He thought of Krystal and the children. How he desired to look into her eyes and tell her everything's going to be all right. Having the knowledge that God is in control gave Ethan a peace that he had never experienced before coming to this place.

A hand rested on his shoulder. "It's time."

Ethan stood and followed Steven down the rocky slope of Mount Bago. Stopping at the stone house, he did a final walk through as his throat tightened. Shouldering his backpack and picking up his duffel bag, he crossed the bridge, stopping long enough to watch, what little water there was, trickle down the stream.

"Come on Ethan. We need to get out of here before this storm hits."

His experiences in Afghanistan flooded Ethan's memories as the Black Hawk lifted them off the meadow. At his request, the pilot made a left turn and flew down over Charlotte Lake. Looking out the window, he could see the house where he and Krystal were going to raise her children. Again, his throat tightened as he spotted Cathryn and Christiana in the clearing waving. On the porch stood Krystal holding Jonah whose face was buried in his mother's neck.

Epilogue

"Black Hawk helicopter with five on board missing after early winter storm hits central California." It had been three weeks since Ethan had left, and no one in the community had received word of his whereabouts. Now as Arnold read the headlines he understood why. Reading the article brought no real closure. The DHS spokesperson stated that the Black Hawk had taken off from a remote valley in the mountains returning to Fresno when it lost contact with air traffic control. Before the controller lost radar, the helicopter was descending rapidly and dropped below the minimum safe altitude. The aircraft's emergency locator transmitter did not activate, and the wreckage has not been found.

Folding the paper, he sat thinking about the whirlwind Ethan had brought to the community. He struggled with accepting the news of a missing helicopter. Did it really go down? Was this a cover-up to throw off the enemy? Who else was on that aircraft? Yes, that's it. Someone had the crew manifest and the key to a whole lot of questions.

Arnold picked up his phone and looked at it. *Should I? Do I really want the answers?* Ethan left on his own free will, and for all the world to believe he has been lost in an accident is probably the safest thing they could do for the community. The decision was made. He typed out a community news release with the contents of the newspaper article. Reading it over one last time he emailed it to the community editor.

With a groan, Arnold pushed back from his desk and stretched. Pulling on his parka, he picked up the paper and headed out into the cold winter night. There was only one person that needed to be told. Snow was drifting down through the pines, and he walked along softly humming the tune to "Silent Night." He stepped upon the porch, hesitated for a few seconds and knocked on the door.

Acknowledgments

First and foremost, I give thanks to God, whose guidance and grace have been the foundation of every step on this journey. Without His light, none of this would be possible. To my wife, Sharla—your unwavering love, patience, and belief in me have been my greatest source of strength. Thank you for your steadfast support and for being my partner in every adventure. A heartfelt thank you to my mentor, Colleen Coble. Your wisdom, encouragement, and generous spirit have shaped my path as a writer and inspired me to reach higher.

To our daughter, Aurora—your courage in tackling the raw manuscript without hesitation is amazing. To Cynthia Hickey of Winged Publications, your trust in my storytelling has expanded my vision. To my friends and family who have endured countless story ideas and brainstorming sessions, your patience and feedback have been invaluable. Thank you for listening, supporting, and believing in me. This book is a reflection of all of you. Thank you for being a part of this journey.

D.L. Reavis Bio

Donald L. Reavis grew up in a conservative Christian home where reading and playing games were the primary forms of entertainment. At nineteen, he earned his pilot license and aspired to become an air traffic controller. After a 24-year career controlling aircraft in Southern California, he retired and moved back to his home state of Indiana, where he now lives with his wife, Sharla.

In 2012, his passion for backpacking took him and Sharla on an adventure along the John Muir Trail in the High Sierra Mountains. This journey sparked an even greater love for the backcountry, and the following year he hiked the Pacific Crest Trail, which led him back to Charlotte Lake. Inspired by his time in the wilderness, he began writing the *Charlotte Lake* series.

Donald is a father of three married children and a grandfather of seven grandchildren. He enjoys golfing, painting, and creating memories with his wife of over 42 years.